Praise for *The Opportunist*

"Part thriller, part family story, *The Opportunist* is by turns funny and shocking—a twisty, page-turning delight."
—Lynn Coady, author of *Watching You Without Me*

"The rich are different and Elyse Friedman brings the receipts in this twisty story of familial double crossings. *The Opportunist* is a visceral joy to read and Friedman's storytelling has more levels than a superyacht. She never hides from the staggering truth that money, in fact, changes everything." —Emily Schultz, author of *Little Threats* and *The Blondes*

"*The Opportunist* is a wry and unsettling novel featuring one of the nastiest families ever committed to paper. It's a dark Highsmithian treat about love and greed and murder, and it will make your screwed-up family look like the von Trapps. I devoured it in one sitting. Highly recommended!" —Michael Redhill, author of *Bellevue Square*

"In *The Opportunist*, family brings unavoidable dangers. So does money. So does our memory of who we used to be. For her part, Elyse Friedman brings wit and pace and plenty of surprises to a novel you think you've figured out at least three or four times, but each time you'll be thrilled when proven wrong."
—Andrew Pyper, author of *The Residence* and *The Demonologist*

"It's midnight and you promise yourself you'll read just a few more pages of *The Opportunist* before turning out the light. Well, suddenly, it's 2:47 a.m. and you're completely hooked and dying to know how the story will end. Tomorrow will be a total write-off, and you can blame Elyse Friedman and this extraordinary book." —Neil Smith, author of *Jones*

THE OPPORTUNIST

ELYSE FRIEDMAN

mira

ISBN-13: 978-0-7783-8695-7

The Opportunist

Mira
22 Adelaide St. West, 41st Floor
Toronto, Ontario M5H 4E3, Canada
BookClubbish.com

Printed in U.S.A.

To my friend Gil Adamson

And, as always, to Max

THE OPPORTUNIST

1

When the calls started up again, Alana ignored them. Ditto the texts and emails, including ones with red exclamation points attached. She had a part-time job that felt full-time and a daughter who required around-the-clock care. She had neither the hours nor the inclination to delve into family drama. And she already knew why her brothers were so desperate to reach her. The younger of the two, Martin, had been messaging sporadically for months about the "skank" their father had taken up with—a nurse, hired by the eldest, Teddy, to tend to the old man's needs as he grew increasingly infirm and cranky. Nurse Kelly, a woman forty-eight years their father's junior, a gold digger, obviously, and a clever one according to Martin. *Pretty sure she had him at the first sponge bath.* Alana was more amused than disturbed. She told her brothers she couldn't care less. She had more important things to worry about. Eventually, they stopped contacting her.

Then a few weeks ago an oversize envelope had arrived in Alana's mailbox. Thick creamy paper, her name embossed in swirling gold script—an invitation to the wedding of Edward Shropshire Sr. and Kelly McNutt. Ha! Clever indeed. She felt a fizz of satisfaction, even as she braced for the onslaught from her siblings, who would be outraged at the prospect of losing any portion of their massive inheritance. Alana hated her father and felt nothing but disdain for her brothers. She had no interest in "protecting the family investments" or "presenting a united front" or "having Dad's back" or any of the increasingly urgent drivel that trickled in from her greedy siblings. She had been estranged from her father for decades and had no stake in this game. It was frankly a shock that she had been invited to the wedding. It must have been Kelly McNutt who insisted on that. The calls, texts and emails started up again with renewed fervor. When Alana finally concluded that her brothers would not leave her in peace until she responded, she composed a simple three-word text, not exactly a family joke, but something they would recognize and understand: *BEYOND OUR CONTROL*. She added a laughing-so-hard-I'm-crying emoji and sent it to Teddy and Martin.

She stopped hearing from them after that.

It was a rough night. Lily's BiPAP alarm had gone off twice. She could breathe without the machine, but not as well, and Alana was programmed to leap into action from the deepest slumber. The first time it sounded, around

1:00 a.m., it was a mask-fit alarm. A quick adjustment and back to bed. The second was more annoying: a leak alarm at 4:28 that took forever to rectify—no matter how much she fiddled, the alarm kept sounding. She finally got it fixed and Lily was able to get back to sleep, but Alana couldn't. She lay in bed, her brain churning. At 5:40 she got up, made coffee, and bolted two cinnamon buns in quick succession, an act she immediately regretted, even as she was scraping the last bits of hard white icing from the aluminum pan into her mouth.

It was a workday, so she woke Lily early, helped her dress, and did her hair in French braids. Ramona was coming for the day and Lily liked to look nice for her favorite support worker. Unlike Alana, Ramona was big into girlie stuff: hair, nails, fashion. She would give Lily mani-pedis, and they would flip through *Harper's Bazaar* and *Teen Vogue* and critique the outfits. Ramona had been with them since Lily was three years old, and Alana trusted her completely. She was hugely competent and a ton of fun. Lily was an earnest child, but when Ramona was around, she let herself be silly and boisterous. It would not be unusual for Alana to come home and find them both with teased-up hair and full-on glitter makeup, binge-watching *RuPaul's Drag Race*. Ramona was what Lily called "chill." Pretty much the opposite of Alana, who was always stressed out and exhausted.

"What time will you be home?" Lily asked.

"If all goes well, five thirty."

"When does all ever go well?"

Alana laughed. "It's rare, but it has been known to happen. I was home on time twice last week."

"True."

"And you have Ramona."

"OK. But try."

"I always try, lovey. But if someone shows up out of the blue at four thirty, I can't just leave. I have to help them."

"I know."

Alana worked part-time at the RedTree Shelter, which offered emergency housing for victims of domestic abuse. It was a foolish job for her to have: low-paying and high stress. Not what she needed in practically her only hours away from managing Lily's health. She should have taken employment that was easy on the soul, like flower arranging—some vaguely pleasant, not overly cerebral activity that would give her time to refresh and restore. She often fantasized about becoming a professional dog walker or making perfect heart shapes in foamy coffees all day, but she stayed with RedTree. It was important work that made her feel a little better about herself. She sometimes wondered if her motivations were selfish at root.

When Ramona arrived, Alana kissed Lily goodbye and left for work. On her third try she managed to get her Stone Age Honda Odyssey to start and was backing out of the drive when a Lexus pulled in behind her, blocking her way. She tapped the horn—a polite "I'm actually leaving here" signal. Nothing. The car just sat there. She honked again, harder, wondering why it always seemed to be a Lexus or a Mercedes or a BMW that cut her off in traffic, or jumped its turn at a four-way stop, or blocked her driveway when she was trying to get to work, for fuck's sake. She curbed an impulse to ram her SUV into the shiny roadster, and instead left the Honda running while she strode toward the offending vehicle, getting ready to unleash years of pent-up luxury-car-inspired fury on the entitled asshole behind the wheel. But before she could bang her fist on the tinted window, it slid down smoothly, revealing her brother Martin talking on a cell phone. He had it resting flat on an upturned palm held in front of his face. "OK," he said. "I know. I'll take care of it."

"What the hell, Martin? I have to go to work." It had been years since she had seen him, but he looked pretty much the same—a slightly higher hairline, maybe a few extra pounds. He was still conventionally handsome, fair and blue-eyed with their father's chiseled chin, but he now had the slightly puffy face of a drinker, the lightning-bolt blood vessels on the side of his nose. He smelled faintly of good cologne with a top note of leather from the luxury rental car's seats.

He gave Alana the "I'll-just-be-one-second" finger. "Listen, Damian, I gotta go. I'll call you in an hour." Martin pocketed the phone and smiled at his sister. "Sorry about that."

"What are you doing here?"

"You didn't get my texts? I need to speak to you. You have a minute?"

"Not at the moment, no."

"I flew across the country to talk to you. You can't give me two minutes of your time?"

"I have to go to work, Martin. If you want to ride with me, you're welcome to. Just let me out, then you can park in the drive and Uber back."

Martin eyed the dented Odyssey that was belching out exhaust. "Why don't I drive you and give you cash to cab home?"

"No, thanks."

He smiled tightly. "Fine."

Alana returned to the SUV to wait for her brother. When Martin climbed in, he was carrying a stiff white envelope with a button-and-string closure and an airport gift-shop bag.

"Here, I got this for…your daughter."

"Her name is Lily."

"I know that. Of course…you named her after Lillian."

A demented-looking doll with stiff blond ringlets stuck out of the tissue paper.

"Thanks," said Alana. "She's a little old for dolls though."

"Oh. How old is she now?"

"Eleven."

"Wow. Time flies. But I thought…"

"What?"

"You know… I figured she'd still be into dolls."

"She's not slow, Martin. Her brain is fine."

"Oh. So…?"

"She has a rare form of muscular dystrophy. Well, rare for girls, common for boys."

"Right."

"She's inside, by the way. You want to meet your niece?"

Her brother looked confused and pained, as if she'd asked if he wanted to donate a kidney or breastfeed a cat. "I thought you were in a hurry?"

"I am. I'm just messing with you." Alana eased the Odyssey out of the driveway. She knew Martin wouldn't want to meet Lily. And she didn't want Martin to meet Lily.

"Can you turn the AC on?" Martin fanned himself with the white envelope. "It's so freaking humid in this city."

"Sorry, it's busted." Alana opened the rear windows to let in more air but felt a perverse pleasure in depriving her brother of climate control.

"So, look, I understand you don't care about Dad's wedding—"

"I really don't and I'm not going."

"I don't give a shit if you go or don't go, but I'm here to tell you that you should care, actually."

"And why is that?"

"Because this Kelly woman is seriously messing with Dad's head."

"His head or his assets?"

"Both. She's got him wound around her finger. They're in the process of setting up a charitable foundation."

"And that's a bad thing because...?"

"Because guess who's going to run it and have access to three hundred million dollars?"

"Kelly McNutt?"

"Yes, Kelly McFucking Nutt. It's a problem. This girl is dangerous." A harp gliss sounded from Martin's pocket. He switched his phone to silent mode.

"Well, it's not *my* problem. And anyway, how do you know she won't use the funds charitably and wisely?"

"Very funny."

"I'm serious."

"The same way I know that a twenty-eight-year-old nurse doesn't fall madly in love with her seventy-six-year-old patient."

Alana shrugged. "Unlikely, but you never know. I saw his picture in *Forbes* a few weeks ago. He still looks like Charlton Heston on steroids. Maybe she has daddy issues."

"It would have to be more like granddaddy issues. I doubt she gets off on adult diapers."

"He wears diapers?"

"He's been incontinent for years."

"Hmm."

"You must have seen a pre-stroke picture in *Forbes*."

"Dad had a stroke?"

"Yes. I told you that last year, Alana."

"You did?"

"Jesus. Don't you read your emails?"

"Sometimes the family stuff slips through."

"Anyway, between that and the prostate surgery, I doubt he can even get it up for Miss McNutt."

"OK, you know what? I don't want to talk about this. I'm sorry you and Teddy are going to lose a chunk of your inheritance. But I'm sure there's more than enough to go around."

"Yeah, in a perfect world, we'd all be satisfied with our piece of the pie. He's had playthings before, right? And wasted money on them. But this is different. This one is setting off alarm bells. She isn't satisfied with having the run of the house and getting a Ferrari and—"

"He bought her a Ferrari?" Alana laughed.

"An 812 GTS. I don't even want to tell you what that costs."

"Like how much?"

"A lot."

"Like a hundred Gs?"

"Try four times that."

"Whoa."

"Yeah. You think she'd be happy with the lifestyle, right?

And some agreed-upon sum in a prenup that would effectively let her retire in high style eight years out of college. But no. Apparently, there isn't going to be a prenup because he *trusts* her."

"Really? That's surprising."

"I know. This is what I'm saying. Because she makes him exercise and eat his greens, he actually believes she has his best interests at heart. The woman is very savvy, and basically on a mission to alienate us from Dad. She's been trying to discredit us from the beginning. And she's subtle about it. She's supersmart. He's already given her power of attorney for personal care. How long before she's in charge of his property too?"

"To be honest, it's kind of fascinating. But again, not my problem."

"But it is, partially. In a worst-case scenario. Say they get hitched and she convinces him we're all undeserving ratbags and she becomes the sole heir, you can kiss your inheritance goodbye."

"I don't have an inheritance."

"You do, actually. A modest one. He left your daughter five million in a trust."

"What? No way."

"Way."

"He's never met my daughter."

Martin shrugged. "Maybe he feels guilty." He waved the white envelope. "I brought a copy of his will. Of course, this'll be void after the wedding."

"He left it to me or Lily?"

"To Lily. But until she's an adult you administer it. So as long as it's used for her care in some way… I mean, you could sell your house and buy one that's better suited to her needs."

"You think I own a house in Toronto?" Alana laughed. "It's a rental, Martin."

"Well, there you go. You could buy a place. And get a new SUV, which you obviously need. You drive her in this, right? How old is this thing?"

"It's a 2004."

"Jesus. How old is that doughnut?" Martin kicked a half-eaten fritter on the floor by his feet.

"Pretty sure that's this year's model." Alana turned down the alley that ran behind the shelter. She moved through the narrow laneway and maneuvered the SUV into her spot next to the Dumpster.

"This is where you park?"

"Yup."

"Well, you could also quit your job if you think spending more time with Lily would be beneficial."

"I like my job," said Alana, but she was eyeing the white envelope.

"Here," said Martin, taking out the will and flipping to a turquoise tab. "I marked the relevant spot."

She read the paragraph that outlined the bequest and its provisions. "And what if I don't want to take his dirty money?"

Martin laughed. "Really? You're going to get all Greenpeace-y about it? You know we've cleaned a lot of that stuff up over the past few years. He sold all the paper mills."

"Yeah? Did he sell all the refineries? All the mines? Has he paid a cent in tax over the last three decades? I could go on, but I think you know that's not what I was referring to," said Alana.

"Whatever. The money's not left to you. It's left to Lily. It'll be up to her to decide."

"I guess he knows I wouldn't take it."

"Miss Goody Two-shoes. Can you really afford to be so pure? Even now, with a kid?"

Alana shrugged.

"You still single?"

"No one's supporting me, if that's what you're getting at."

"Isn't your ex some Silicon Valley type?"

Alana laughed. "Yeah, and I'm sure he's doing fine. But I haven't seen or heard from him in seven years."

"Wow. OK. So how would you feel about taking money from me and Teddy?"

"Why? What are you talking about?"

"Let's just say we have a plan."

"A plan?"

"A proposal, actually. And we need your help."

RedTree was thankfully quiet that day. A clogged toilet had required Alana's attention—the plumbing in the shelter was abysmal, the whole building was falling apart—but there were no new intakes, which meant she could spend the afternoon focusing on fundraising, or not focusing on it, as it happened. She was supposed to be gathering donations for the shelter's annual silent auction, but her mind kept drifting to her brothers' proposal, a straightforward scenario in which she would undertake a simple task and be well compensated for it, whether or not the gambit worked. All they wanted her to do was show up before the wedding and offer Kelly McNutt a sum of money to go away. Alana would let her know that should she choose to go through with the marriage, and should Ed expire while they were hitched, Alana and her siblings would hire a team of the nation's most terrifying attorneys to ensure she received only the slightest of payouts—no matter what the will stated. She would also tell Kelly that the siblings planned to drag out litigation indefinitely, so that even if she were eventually granted the greater part of their father's estate (unlikely, given the optics of the age difference), it would take at least a decade to get there. They would tie up the money in court for as long as legally possible and portray Kelly in the media as a gold digger who preyed on a vulnerable old man. They would dig deep into her past too. Did she really need the hassle? Wouldn't she prefer to accept a handsome check, hop in her Ferrari, and bugger off without ever again having to share a bed with sagging Ed Sr.? Martin added, "And you can ask her if she really wants to go up against a single mom who works in a shelter and has a disabled daughter." *Ah*, thought Alana, *that's why they want me, I'd look good in court.* But it was more than that. If Kelly squealed to Ed about the attempted payoff, the brothers could deny any knowledge of it and simply blame Alana. She was, after all, the errant offspring who had detached from the family. Martin and Teddy were the dutiful sons and, until Kelly had come along, the rightful heirs to a multibillion-dollar empire. They couldn't risk making the offer themselves. They had too much to lose. If Alana were exposed, the worst thing to happen would be a revoked wedding invitation and the loss of Lily's bequest—and even that wasn't certain. Old Ed might not see fit to take it out on his granddaughter.

"But he would know you guys were involved," Alana had pointed out. "I mean, everyone knows I don't have the money to pay off my credit cards, let alone Kelly McNutt."

"If she runs to Ed, which I highly doubt, you could just say you were testing to see if she really loved him. And that clearly you had no intention of going through with it."

"But why would I care? He must know I'm not exactly obsessing over his welfare."

"But he also knows you'd be curious, and that you'd probably get a kick out of exploding his romantic fantasy. It's the kind of thing you might do."

"So, I'm the mean-spirited asshole?"

"No, you're Miss Morality. Exposing all the truths, going after the hypocrites, righting all the wrongs."

"Yeah, right," said Alana.

"Look, all of this is moot. The girl is going to take the cash. I'm ninety-nine percent sure of it. Why would she put up with Dad for one second longer than she has to?"

"True."

"We just need you for that tiny one-percent chance. And at the end of the day, we all know that Dad would believe you. As for Teddy and me in the same situation, no way."

"I guess," said Alana, smirking at the *Miss Morality* label.

Martin told her that if she agreed to make the offer to Kelly, he and Teddy would pay for her travel to Alfred Island and give her fifty thousand dollars. If the plan worked, if Kelly took the payout and disappeared, they would reward Alana with twenty-five million dollars—one million once the woman was gone, then twelve million each from their inheritance when Ed died ("popped off" was the term Martin used). If Kelly ratted her out and Lily's bequest was removed from Ed's will, they would each pony up two and a half million to cover the loss.

"You guys can afford that?"

"Of course," Martin sniffed.

"Will you put it in writing?"

"Do I look like an idiot?" said her brother.

Alana went over the proposal again and again, mulling the ramifications. In a way, the thought of going through with it amused her. But by the end of her shift, she had decided it didn't make sense to get involved. She didn't trust her brothers and had zero desire to ever see her father again. She left the shelter at five on the dot with the idea of stopping at Greg's Ice Cream to pick up a tub of roasted marshmallow and still arrive home ahead of schedule. But when the Odyssey refused to start and she had to sit sweltering beside the stinking Dumpster for more than an hour, waiting for CAA to show up and tell her the SUV couldn't be boosted and had to be towed to the garage, she wondered if it was a sign. And the following day, when the mechanic called her at work to tell her that, in addition to a bum starter motor, there was a crack in the Odyssey's engine block, and the exhaust system was full of holes, it sealed the deal.

If Alana did the deed, she would get fifty thousand, no matter what transpired. That was enough to buy a new vehicle—one with air-conditioning and a remote-controlled wheelchair ramp. She could breeze into a dealership and buy one tomorrow. The thought of that made her a bit giddy. She had never purchased a brand-new car.

Plus, if she were being entirely honest with herself, a little respite from her day-to-day routine wouldn't be so horrible. Apart from Lily's week at MDA summer camp each year, she had never been away from her daughter for more than one night. It might be good for both of them to have a break from each other. Just zoning out for five hours on an airplane seemed like a vacation in itself. Plus, she would be able to have a look at the clever Kelly McNutt.

Alana told the mechanic to fix the starter but hold off on the other stuff. Then she texted Ramona: What are the odds you could stay with L for a full week (sleeping over/time + half per hour)? A few minutes later she received a message back with a selfie of Lily and Ramona smiling and giving the thumbs-up sign: The odds are good.

2

Ed Shropshire owned homes in Victoria, Vancouver, New York, Montana, and Turks and Caicos, but he had chosen to remarry in the one in which Alana had spent every summer of her childhood—a six-thousand-square-foot estate on a private island off the coast of Vancouver Island. In many ways Alfred Island had been an ideal vacation spot, especially for an introspective child who was happy to spend her free time exploring the seemingly endless stretches of beach and forest on the nine-hundred-acre playground. Alana's brothers were more likely to be found in the estate's swimming pool, or on the Stanley Thompson–designed golf course, or messing around in the abandoned industrial buildings from when the island, with its dense clay soil, served as a brickworks and tile manufacturing hub in the early twentieth century. Alana wasn't sure where their sister Lillian would disappear to. She was an aloof girl, four years Alana's senior, who was always wandering off and staying away too long, requiring impromptu search parties to go find her and drag her home for lunch or dinner or whatever private lesson had been scheduled with this or that instructor. Alana could remember her childhood nanny, Patsy, complaining about this, about constantly having to go on wild-goose chases to track down wayward Lillian. She seemed terrified of something happening to the girl "on her watch." Lillian wasn't allowed to swim alone off the beach, but they often found her bathing in the cold waters of the strait, causing Patsy to curse and reproach.

Alana's memories of her sister were mostly indistinct— like seeing something familiar through a gossamer curtain. Lillian had seemed so much older than Alana, and often distant. But when Alana was in her orbit, Lillian was always very loving and protective. She was an athletic girl, a tomboy who wouldn't take guff from Martin and Teddy, giving them hell whenever they teased or harassed Alana. Alana, who had always been chubby and slow moving—the anomaly in the family—was an easy target. And not just for Teddy and Martin, who pushed her around and called her names (*furball/fatso*) but also for their trim and fit parents, who scolded and shamed her for eating between meals or finishing everything on her plate, a big no-no in the Shropshire household. Slender Lillian was allowed to raid the kitchen with impunity and would nab treats for Alana, or sneak her second and third helpings at the dinner table. Their mother, Kat, who regularly reminded Alana that she wanted to "grow *up*, not *out*," was generally too intoxicated to notice. And Ed was often away on business.

Now, wedged in her economy-class seat and stress-eating Pringles—so much for a relaxing flight—Alana felt a flicker of self-consciousness. The last time she had encountered her father was at her mother's funeral, sixteen years and thirty pounds ago—one of the few times in her life when she had been skinny. It was in the midst of a period of self-loathing and self-destruction, when her five food groups were Bushmills, Benzedrine, Nicorettes, espresso, and the occasional piece of toast. Ironically, her father had praised her at the time for "finally getting yourself together." No doubt he would express disgust for her current chubby state. And just like when she was a kid, he would eye everything she consumed with disapproval and make passive-aggressive remarks about how wonderful everyone else was looking or how much vigor his juice-fasting regime had given him. *Well, fuck it*, she thought. Bring it on. Her days of constant dieting were done. She brushed some chip crumbs from her chest, yanked the Air Canada Bistro menu from the seat pocket in front of her, and perused the snack selection. Then she summoned the flight attendant and ordered a KitKat and a bag of strawberry Twizzlers.

The moment the plane landed in Victoria, Alana checked in with Ramona and Lily. Then she headed to the luggage carousel, where an alarmingly young-looking pilot—acne, *Lost Boys* T-shirt—was waiting to retrieve her bags and guide her to the Cessna for the short hop to Alfred Island. Alana had expected to be driven to Saanichton and then ferried over in one of her father's boats, but the pilot informed her that Martin had changed the plan after learning of a "paddle event" in the Cordova Channel.

As they neared the island, Alana spotted dozens of canoes and kayaks encircling the property. And she discovered that the so-called paddle event was, in fact, a protest in support of the First Nations band that had claimed Alfred Island as part of their traditional territory. A similar dispute involving the Tsawout First Nation and neighboring James Island (owned by an American telecommunications entrepreneur) had inspired the band to launch their own lawsuit against the Canadian government. The litigation petitioned the government to purchase Alfred Island (assessed at seventy-one million dollars) from her father's company and return it to the band, alleging it was part of the Douglas Treaties, which guaranteed them the land. What the lawyers didn't know was that her father, as a matter of twisted principle, would never relinquish what he considered to be his, no matter how much the government offered. What her father didn't know was that Alana, though hopelessly impecunious, had contributed more than two weeks' wages to the band's GoFundMe campaign to help with their legal battle. The thought of this made her smile as she alighted from the plane and watched the pilot unload her luggage onto the airstrip.

"Darla will take care of you," he said, gesturing to an approaching golf cart.

"Thanks so much."

"No worries. Have a great stay."

He climbed back into the cockpit, flipped up his sunglasses, and started typing on his phone. The golf cart pulled to a stop, and a large woman with close-cropped gray hair jumped out and strode to Alana, proffering a calloused hand.

"Welcome," she said. "I'm Darla."

"Nice to meet you. I'm Alana."

"Yep," she said, then shouted, "Hey, Frank," to the pilot. He waved as Darla swept up the luggage and deposited it into the cart. She was a husky woman with a big head and an upside-down-triangle physique—all hefty at the top, tapering to narrow hips and legs. She reminded Alana of the Tasmanian Devil, had the Looney Tunes character been wearing a polo shirt, khaki shorts, and hiking boots with white tube socks.

"Good to be back?" asked Darla as the cart sped away from the airstrip.

"Smells the same as when I was a kid," said Alana.

Darla seemed to get the deflection and changed the subject. "Cottage 1 has been prepped for you, but Martin said the others are free, if you prefer."

"Oh," said Alana. She laughed. "For some reason I pictured myself in my old room."

"Well, if you want that, just talk to your dad or your bro."

"No, I don't. I just—I hadn't really thought about it. A cottage makes sense. That's the one nearest the house, right?"

"Yup," said Darla. "Best of the bunch, in my opinion."

"Great," said Alana. Cottage 1 would be fine. She tried to picture the other three but could only visualize the one nearest the beach. The guest cabins had been strictly off-limits to her and her siblings when she was a kid, and were always locked with the curtains drawn when she dared to explore them.

"So...do you live on the island?" Alana asked.

"Yup. Groundskeeper's quarters. I'm head groundskeeper."

"Oh. Nice."

"Mrs. Keith is the household manager if you need anything."

"OK, thanks."

Alana's heart accelerated as the golf cart skimmed past the main estate. Her strange task now felt very real and she was pumped with anxious energy.

"Almost there," said Darla as they turned down a path into a wooded area.

The Douglas firs were massive and towering here, not at all like the evergreens she had grown used to in Ontario. These trees felt prehistoric. Jurassic.

"Oh, look," said Alana, pointing to several deer browsing among the foliage.

"Crap," said Darla. "And me without my rifle."

"Yeah, right." Alana assumed she was joking.

"Those are fallow deer. They're pests. They eat all the native plants, and they're messing with the arbutus. I have orders from your dad to cull any I see."

"Oh," said Alana. "OK... But maybe you didn't see those?"

Darla fixed her with an amused side-eye. "You sound like your father's fiancée now."

Alana laughed. "Well, I'm looking forward to meeting her. I haven't heard much about her." She said it like a question and waited for Darla to provide some intel, but she didn't take the bait and just kept driving.

"Okey-doke," Darla said, pulling up to cottage 1, a sweet A-frame that had been painted a vibrant turquoise with white trim.

"I remember this," said Alana. "But it used to be natural wood."

"They got painted a few years ago. Keep 'em from rotting."

Alana stepped out of the cart and reached for her garment bag, but Darla's thick hand snatched it up.

"I got it," she said, also grabbing the suitcase, the carry-on bag, and even Alana's purse.

"Oh…thanks."

Darla hauled the luggage up the porch stairs, unlocked the front door, and handed the key to Alana.

"Thanks," she said with a small laugh. "I'm not used to people carrying my things."

"Now you're sounding like Miss McNutt again." Darla smiled and headed back to the golf cart. "Drinks at the pool at five o'clock. Martin said to tell you."

"Oh. Is everyone going to be there?"

"I suspect," said Darla. "I saw catering setting up earlier."

Alana had an impulse to jump in the golf cart and race back to the airstrip. If the plane was gone, she could swim across the channel and hitchhike to the airport. Instead, she took a deep breath and checked the time on her phone. She had just twenty-five minutes to get herself cleaned up and calmed down.

"S'that her?" Alana heard Ed say as she made her way across the long flagstone pool deck to the gathering. From her vantage point it looked like some kind of *Architectural Digest* centerfold. Her father, in white linen and a panama hat, was seated on a large curved sofa beneath a newly erected pergola—new to Alana, anyway; it hadn't been there when she was a kid, and neither had the freestanding sauna just beyond it. To his left, a leggy blonde, looking like an Italian movie star in a sleeveless black shift, oversize tortoiseshell sunglasses, and her hair pulled into a tight bun. Across from them, in a plush armchair beside a planter heaped with bougainvillea, sat Martin in a V-neck and white slacks. One crisply attired staff member tended to the fire in an elaborately tiled pizza oven, while another polished glasses at a makeshift bar. Alana instantly questioned her choice of ancient Gap sundress and rubber flip-flops.

"Hey," said Martin, rising to greet her.

"Hello," said Alana with a general wave to the assemblage, hoping nobody would try to hug or kiss her.

The blonde stood, smoothed her dress, and proffered a long-nailed hand for a limp shake. Up close, Alana could see that her lips had been artificially and egregiously plumped.

"This is my friend Gertrud," said Martin.

"Ah," said Alana. "Nice to meet you."

"Same," said Gertrud, smiling.

"You changed your hair," said Ed, who remained seated.

"Yeah," said Alana, touching her bobbed locks. She was shocked at how gray and diminished her father had become. All linen and bones.

"You want a drink?" said Martin.

I want five drinks, thought Alana, her heart hammering. "Yeah, thanks. I'll have a vodka martini straight up with a twist."

"That's Kelly's drink," said her father, breaking into an uneven smile. The teeth were still perfect, but there was a slackness to one side of the face, and a slight blur in the voice.

"What isn't her drink?" whispered Martin as he breezed by Alana.

"Oh, here she comes," said Ed.

Alana turned to watch Kelly approach. She was moving

quickly and did not look at all like a gold-digging trophy-wife-to-be. She was maybe five foot two and a hundred pounds soaking wet. No boobs or hips to speak of, frizzy orange hair in a ponytail and freckles all over her face, chest, and arms. She was wearing cutoff jean shorts, a tank top, and canvas sneakers. She looked like a kid.

"Sorry," she said. "The caterers brought vegan cheese, but I think ours is better." She waved the package she was holding then handed it to the young man at the pizza oven before sweeping over to Alana. "You must be Amanda," she said, enfolding her in a quick fierce hug.

"Um—"

"It's *Alana*," said Martin, failing to disguise his contempt.

"Oh god, I'm so sorry!" said Kelly.

"Sounds similar," said Ed.

"It does," said Gertrud, flashing Martin a look.

"Don't worry about it," said Alana. "It's nice to meet you."

"It's so great to meet you too, *Alana*. Sorry. It's all the wedding prep—my brain is mush."

A server handed them drinks.

"Hey, a martini buddy," she said, clinking glasses a little too hard. She had an impish smile and laughing eyes, large and blue with a thick limbal ring around each iris.

"Come," said Ed, patting the seat beside him.

Kelly dutifully parked herself next to Ed, who draped an arm over her skinny white thigh.

It struck Alana as both possessive and insecure. She settled in a chair across from them and sipped her drink, wondering if her face looked as hot and flushed as it felt.

"How's your daughter?" said Ed.

Alana bristled. "She's fine. She's with her caregiver."

Then, changing the subject, she gestured to the array of pizzas on the table and said, "These look amazing."

"Try the rosemary and potato," said Kelly. "They're all vegan except the one with the shrimp."

"Dad's a vegan now," said Martin.

"Why do you say it like that?" said Ed.

"Like what? I was just telling her."

"You should give it a go. You're getting a belly, kid." He said this to Martin, but he was watching Alana as she selected a variety of pizza slices.

"I like my meat," said Martin.

"We could try it," said Gertrud. "It's much better for the planet."

"You try it," said Martin, draining his drink on the way back to the bar.

"Dinner is at eight," said Ed, eyeing Alana's plate.

"Oh, OK." A familiar feeling of shame crept through her. Was she the only one eating? Apparently, she was.

"So," said Kelly, "we were looking forward to seeing you and your daughter at the wedding, but we weren't expecting this visit."

"Yeah, I, um, had some business out here, so I thought I'd swing by now, since I may not be able to make it to the wedding."

"Oh no. I'm really sorry to hear that."

"Why not?" said Ed, clocking Kelly's disappointment.

"It's just—it's difficult to travel with Lily."

"Use the jet. It'll be easier."

"Thanks, but it would still be tricky."

"We'll work it out," said Ed.

Alana didn't respond.

"Well, I hope you can stay until Friday," said Kelly. "We're going out on the boat to audition some of the wedding elements."

"Oh…maybe. I'm not sure yet."

"Are you an omnivore?" she asked, heading to the bar with her already empty glass.

"Um, yeah. I mean, I don't eat a lot of meat, but I do eat it."

"Great. You can let us know what you think of the food."

"If I'm still here, sure."

Martin shot Alana a look that seemed to say, *You mean if she's still here.*

"What's your business?" said Ed.

"Oh, just a meeting…with a donor. Hey, where's Teddy?" she said, shifting topics.

"Young Edward is watching the tennis," said Ed.

"Yes," said Martin. "He flew away on a whim."

"A Wimbledon whim?" said Kelly, returning with two fresh martinis.

"A *Whim*bledon," said Ed, emphasizing the *h*.

Gertrud laughed loud; Martin managed a smile.

"Well, hopefully, he'll be back before you have to leave," said Kelly. "Cheers."

Alana accepted the second drink, though she was only halfway through her first and already tipsy. Martin was right about one thing: Kelly McNutt could drink. Surprising, given her size.

"We should go to Wimbledon," said Gertrud to Martin. "Best strawberries and cream I ever had."

Martin laughed. "Go for the berries—who cares about the tennis?"

An unsettling image of Gertrud trying to spoon clotted cream past those lips flashed through Alana's brain. Then she thought about her brother, casually jetting five thousand miles to watch a few tennis matches.

A server set a fresh pizza on the table.

"Thanks, Des," said Kelly, exchanging a smile with the server as he moved back to his station at the oven. "OK, guys, you have to try this one. This is the good vegan cheese."

Alana watched with astonishment as Kelly plated a slice, carved it into tiny bite-size pieces, and handed it to Ed along with a fork. He dutifully stabbed a piece and guided it with some effort toward his mouth.

"Try it, Alana. It's just like real cheese," said Kelly.

Alana took a piece to be polite. "Mmm," she said. "Good." It wasn't, particularly, and Alana had to look away from her father, who was chewing loosely and methodically. She felt sickened by the whole scene. She set down her food and took a bracing swallow of cold martini.

"Are you a yoga person, by any chance?" said Kelly.

"Um, I've tried it a couple times," said Alana. "I'm more of a swimmer really."

"Oh, I wish I were. Especially with this gorgeous pool."

"I told you, get lessons," said Ed, a bit of food escaping from his mouth and clinging to his chin.

"I know," said Kelly. "I just—I guess I still have a block about it."

"Because of your brother," said Gertrud, her face contorting to an approximation of compassion.

"I had an older brother who drowned when I was a baby," Kelly confided to Alana. "My mom was so traumatized, she kept me away from water my entire childhood."

"Oh, I'm sorry."

"It's OK. I mean, I never knew him. I just—I don't know… Anyway, if you happen to be an early riser, you could join me on the beach for yoga in the morning. I start at six. Just follow the trail down past cottage 4."

Martin shot Alana an insistent look.

"That sounds good. Thanks."

"Then we go for our walk after," said Ed to Kelly.

"Yes, dear, we go for our walk when I get back." She plucked the fragment of food from his chin and patted his arm.

Alana set down her drink and stood. "Guys, I think I'm going to go lie down for a bit before dinner. But thanks for this, it was great."

As she made her way back to the cottage, she thought about her father, who used to look like the Marlboro Man (minus hat, horse, and cigarette). When she was little, she was enthralled by him. His size and strength. His confidence. He was always striding around issuing orders. And everyone came to him for approval. He seemed to decide everything, control everything. She learned early on that the greatest thing in the world was to please him. That was the goal. The only goal. To satisfy and please him. And she tried. Oh, how she tried. For a while, she did everything she thought he wanted. Everyone did. But he was not a benevolent god. He was exacting and forever on edge. He had a habit of dashing things to the floor when he got annoyed: pens, plates, coffee cups, lamps, whatever was at hand. How many times had she seen staff members stooping to sweep or retrieve after an outburst?

She thought about Kelly patiently carving up the pizza, picking food from his chin, patting his arm—*Yes, dear, we go for our walk when I get back*. It was stunning, really. Almost unthinkable. A stroke and a twenty-eight-year-old dynamo had somehow managed to extinguish the dragon's fire.

Or so it seemed.

Alana was awakened by the sound of distant gunshots. Disoriented, she checked her phone: 9:18. She had slept through dinner. Conked by vodka and pizza. She found a sweet good-night text from Lily and Ramona—too late now with the time difference to respond—and two texts from Martin. The first, summoning her to dinner, the next, inviting her for a nightcap in the games room. The underlying tone of both: *Get your ass over here.*

It was growing dark when she finally headed up to the house. As she neared the main road to the estate, she heard a motor approaching and paused in the shadows to watch Darla and an unknown staff member drive by in a golf cart. There was a low metal trailer attached to the back of it now, with several deer carcasses piled inside, their stiff legs jutting haphazardly over the edges and shaking with the movement of cart on concrete.

That explained the gunshots.

She waited until the cart had passed before crossing the road and mounting the gentle slope of the deep lawn. She made her way into the open-air dining area, through the empty living room toward the games room—a massive rectangular structure with a pitched beamed ceiling and wide plank floors. As a kid, she would ride her bike around the room's perimeter when it was raining outside. Teddy, Martin, and Lillian used to play soccer and hockey in there. Now the floors were crisscrossed with a network of vast Persian rugs. A home gymnasium was set up on one side of the room and a games area on the other, with a pool table, foosball, Ping-Pong and a card table designed specifically for Texas Hold'em. Kelly and Gertrud were playing eight ball—stripes was getting their ass kicked—and Martin was seated in a leather club chair, eating pistachio nuts, a pile of cracked beige shells on the side table next to him.

"She rises from the dead," said Martin as Alana entered.

"Yeah, sorry. I lay down for five minutes and crashed."

"I figured as much," said Martin.

"I'm sure there are leftovers," said Kelly, chalking her cue. "Feel free to raid the kitchen if you're hungry."

Martin laughed. "Yes, feel free in your own family's home," he said, obviously commenting on how Kelly, the outsider, had taken over the host role.

Alana smiled. "I'm OK, thanks. I had a lot of pizza."

With a sharp crack, Kelly sank the eight ball in the side pocket.

"Well, that's that," said Gertrud, hanging up her cue. "She's too good for me."

"Want to take me on?" Kelly asked Martin with an innocent smile.

"Oh, I will," said Martin. "But not tonight. Tonight, I will leave you to my lovely sister." He stood and brushed pistachio tidbits from his shirt and pants with a tad too much vigor. "You want to play, right?" He shot Alana a look that said she most certainly did want to play.

"Yeah, sure," she said. "But I'm not very good."

"Doesn't matter," said Kelly. "It's just something to do while we chat. I want to hear all about the shelter you work at. What's it called again?"

"Um, RedTree," said Alana, searching for a cue of the right length. "It's mostly a women's shelter, but we offer services for refugees as well… We sponsored some families from Syria and Honduras."

"Wow. Good for you."

"So amazing," said Gertrud.

"We should drink to the honest work Alana's doing. Who wants to join me?" said Kelly, moving to the bar with her empty glass.

"We're going to hit the hay," said Martin.

"So early?" said Gertrud.

"Yup, get your shoes on."

"Traveler?" said Kelly, holding up a bottle as Gertrud struggled back into her stilettos.

"She's good," said Martin.

"Is she?" said Kelly. "How can you be sure? Maybe we could let her answer for herself?"

Oh boy, thought Alana. Here we go.

"She's good," Martin repeated evenly, smiling at Kelly. "I think the aperitifs followed by the wine with dinner and then the tumbler of Scotch was probably enough for one night."

"I'm actually pretty tipsy, but thanks anyway," said Gertrud.

Martin cast one last meaningful glance at Alana, then left the room with Gertrud high-heeling in his wake.

"Your brother doesn't like me very much," said Kelly, pouring two generous shots of Scotch.

"Apparently not," said Alana. She started fishing balls out of the pool table pockets.

"You have to try this, it's incredible," said Kelly, handing her a glass.

"Thanks."

"Aberlour A'Bunadh. It's not the most expensive, but I think it's the most delicious."

"Mmm, it's really good."

"Take a bottle with you when you head home," said Kelly. "I just ordered half a dozen." She set her drink down, grabbed the heavy wooden triangle from under the table and started racking up the balls. "So, when's your meeting? Is it in Victoria or Vancouver?"

"Well, to be honest," said Alana, "it's neither. I'm not really here to meet with a donor. I've actually been summoned here on a mission."

"A mission," said Kelly. "That's intriguing. And what would your mission be?"

"Well, as it turns out, my family has a proposal for you, and my mission is to deliver it."

"Oh." Kelly slid the triangle into place on the felt and removed the rack. "A proposal. How fascinating. And what exactly is it?"

"It's an offer, essentially, an offer of a large sum of money that would be deposited directly into your bank account."

"Really?" Kelly laughed.

"Yup. And all you'd have to do to receive it is pack up and leave."

"Just pack up and leave. That's it?"

"Before the wedding, obviously."

"Obviously," said Kelly, smiling. She took a sip of her drink, then set it down and rechalked her cue, thinking it over. "And what do *you* think about that?"

Alana hesitated. "I don't know." She wasn't sure what she thought about it at this point. "If you leave, you never have to deal with my father or brothers again."

"Right." Kelly met her gaze and held it, perfectly serious now. "And am I to say goodbye, or am I supposed to just vanish into thin air?"

"I think a note was the general idea. You know, something about the age gap, you've realized that marrying someone that old is maybe not the best idea for your future. But I don't think it matters."

"I see." Kelly smirked. "Well, this is both surprising and not at all surprising. And what exactly is the large sum being offered?"

"Twenty million dollars."

"That's a lot of money."

"It is."

"But not for your brothers, particularly."

"They'll deposit a million into your account on the day you leave and the rest at the three-month mark, provided you've stayed away with no contact. And I'm also supposed to tell you that if you go through with the marriage, they will fight you tooth and nail for the estate—when that becomes an issue."

"Oh, I already expected that," said Kelly, lining up the cue ball. "That's hardly news. What's interesting is that they enlisted you for the cause."

Alana shrugged.

"Well," said Kelly, leaning over to line up her shot, "lots to think about." She smacked the cue ball hard, pocketed an orange and yellow off the break, then proceeded to sink every solid on the table.

It was past midnight and drizzling when Alana made her way back to the cottage. She was exhausted and more than a little tipsy. The path through the trees wasn't lighted and she felt vulnerable in the darkness. She wondered if there were any cougars on the island—there weren't when she was a kid, but maybe they had swum over like the deer? Could cougars even swim? She was too drunk to reason it out. She hurried to her cottage and mounted the wooden stairs breathlessly, feeling a tingle on her upper back and neck as if she were being pursued. As she let herself in, she spied a face half in shadow and screamed.

"Shhh," whispered Martin. "It's me."

"Jesus Christ, you scared the shit out of me."

"Shh. Lower your voice."

"Why are you in here?"

"We need to talk, and I didn't feel like standing in the rain for hours. I thought you'd be back a long time ago. What took you so long?"

"Fuck." Alana pressed her fingers to her throat to monitor her racing pulse.

"You left the door unlocked, so…"

"Then turn a light on. Or text me a heads-up. You scared the crap out of me."

"I'm sorry. I didn't want anyone to see me. And I don't want to put anything in writing. Calm down."

"I'm calm. But you almost gave me a heart attack."

"So, how did it go?" Martin was all business.

"Can I turn a light on? I can close the drapes."

"I'm going in two seconds, just leave it for now."

Alana kicked off her shoes and sank into a wicker armchair in the corner. The cushions smelled musty, but she was too tired to change places.

"So?"

"I think it went OK."

"What did she say?"

"She said she had to think about it. She wants to sleep on it. She's going to tell me at yoga tomorrow morning."

"So she didn't act all shocked and offended?"

"Nope."

"You see, I told you. She's playing him. She's playing all of us. Fucking cunt. There was never any doubt in my mind. You know, Teddy thought she was maybe for real, but I knew. I knew from the start."

"Fine. Whatever. I did the deed, now I have to get up for yoga in five hours to get her answer, so—"

"God, what a bitch," said Martin. "And I'm pissed at Teddy. Why do you think he took off to England?"

"To eat strawberries and cream?"

"No. So he wouldn't be around when all this went down. Just in case she ran crying to Dad."

"Well, that's pretty crappy."

"Damn right. Fucking coward. Always kissing Dad's ass and covering his own."

"Wow. I thought you guys were a 'united front.'"

"When it comes to this matter we are. But as far as the business goes, I'm sure he'd love me to screw up so he could take my place."

"Aren't you both vice presidents?"

"I'm executive VP, he's senior VP. Technically, I'm above him now, which burns his ass because I'm younger and because he's always been Dad's golden boy."

"How did that happen?"

"He messed up a deal last year—something that was in play right after Dad had the stroke. It's complicated, but basically, he went against Dad's wishes and did what he wanted instead. Maybe he thought Dad wasn't going to recover, or maybe he just wanted to assert his authority, or maybe he was afraid Dad would be pissed if he let the deal slip away. I don't know, I was busy with other stuff."

"But what was it exactly?"

"Dad was interested in some hotels but only at a very specific price. Teddy took over the negotiation and bought at way over value. They claimed there was another offer on the table, but there fucking wasn't. He really overpaid." Martin laughed as if it were a cherished memory. "In any event, it was the wrong decision, and when Dad found out, he was livid enough to swap our roles. And Teddy's been a little bitch about it ever since. Anyway, don't tell him I said that. And don't forget, if Kelly says anything to Dad, you were just testing her loyalties and neither of us knew shit about it."

"Yes, I know. We've been through it ten times. And honestly, I don't think it will be an issue. My impression is she'll either go for it or not. I don't think she's going to say anything."

"Well, we'll find out soon enough. But I guess it's a good sign she didn't act all surprised and affronted. Fucking bitch."

"Anyway," said Alana, rising from the chair. "I need to sleep."

"OK. Don't text me anything. Just come and find me after yoga. Or I'll find you."

"Fine. But if you're going to come in here again, I need a heads-up. Hang something on the doorknob or put some pebbles on the step so I don't have heart failure when I walk in."

"All right, I can do that. I'll put stones on the step. But hopefully, I won't have to. Fingers crossed she'll take the money and run."

3

Even though she had set her iPhone alarm to the relatively gentle "By the Seaside" music at low volume, Alana was jolted instantly awake at five thirty when it began to play. She swiped it off after only a few notes and lay in bed with her heart hammering. There was a fist of pressure behind her left eye, and her neck and shoulder muscles were seized and sore. It was a full ten minutes before she was able to sit up and drag her hangover out of bed. She shuffled to the kitchenette, grabbed a bottle of water and took a big swallow. Then she brewed a Keurig coffee and popped an extra-strength Advil.

It was chilly on the walk down to the beach so she pulled up the hood of her sweatshirt and tugged the drawstrings tight. She passed cottages 2 and 3, which had also been updated with coats of paint in vivid colors, but paused when she got to cottage 4. It was set back farther into the woods and had not been painted. It looked the same as when she was a kid—just a little more worn and with taller foliage around the porch. As she stood staring at the familiar bark-cloth curtains pulled tight across the windows, she felt her gut flip. She only had time to turn and step off the main path before the contents of her stomach erupted in one urgent blast.

"Oh god…" She wiped her mouth, then swiped away the film of strangely sticky sweat that had sprung up on her forehead. She took a swig of Evian, swished it around in her mouth, spat it out, then did it again. She used the remainder of the bottle to try to wash away the puke, kicking some soil over the spot before walking away.

As she neared the clearing that led to the strait, she spotted Kelly in warrior pose on the beach, her hair blazing orange in the early morning sun. It caught the light in a way that made it seem illuminated from within. When she noticed Alana, she waved and called out brightly, seemingly unaffected by the gallons of alcohol she had consumed the previous night.

"Good morning. You made it!"

"Morning," said Alana with considerably less pep and amplification.

"How are you doing?"

"I've been better," she admitted. "I just vomited on a fern."

"Oh no. Poor you."

"Poor fern."

Kelly laughed. "I'm so sorry," she said. "I guess I kept pouring that Scotch."

"Well, I kept drinking it," said Alana. "I have only myself to blame." She parked herself on a log that had washed up on the beach.

"Do you want to try some yoga? It might make you feel better."

"I think a downward dog would pretty much kill me at this point. But go ahead. I'll just sit here breathing deeply."

"OK. We can talk after."

Alana watched as Kelly proceeded to stretch, lunge, and balance her way through a series of graceful contortions—some elaborate, several gravity defying. The movements were controlled, fluid, and elastic. Pretty to watch. When the routine was done, Kelly pressed her palms together for a ritual bow, took a long drink from her thermos, and then came to sit beside Alana on the log.

"Very impressive."

Kelly laughed. "Thanks."

She hadn't even broken a sweat, but her face was flushed deep pink from exertion. She looked the proverbial picture of health.

"So, here's the deal," she said. "I've thought it over carefully and I have a message for you to take to your brothers."

"OK."

"I want you to tell them that I'm going to accept their offer."

"You are?" Alana was genuinely surprised.

"I am." Kelly dug in her pocket and retrieved a folded-up piece of paper. "This is the account to transfer the deposit to." She handed it to Alana. "I'm going back to the house to have coffee with your dad. That usually takes about half an hour. Then we're going for our morning walk, which takes about an hour or so. I'm going to head out after that. Tell them that if the first million dollars isn't in my account by the time I get back from my walk with Ed, it's a no-go. OK?" She squeezed Alana's arm and smiled. "Have a great day."

Before Alana could respond, Kelly sprang up and headed for the path to the house. Alana watched her go, then pulled out her phone to go online and check her own bank account. $3,047.96. Her brothers hadn't yet deposited the initial fifty thousand as promised. But maybe they were waiting for Kelly's answer?

All right then. She hauled herself up to go deliver the news.

"Cappuccino, espresso, latte, or flat white?" said Martin, fiddling with the most beautiful espresso machine Alana had ever laid eyes on; it looked like a 1950s Cadillac—all chrome and fins and sleekly designed lines.

"What, no cortados?"

"Very funny," said Martin.

"I'll take a latte."

"Latte it is." Martin got busy with the coffee and milk, a small smile on his face. He had received Alana's report and was uncharacteristically jolly.

"Shall I do that for you?" said a tall gray-haired woman, sailing into the kitchen like the *Queen Mary*.

"I got it. I finally figured this thing out. But maybe Alana wants breakfast?"

"You're Alana. Very nice to meet you," she said. "I'm Mrs. Keith, your father's housekeeper."

Of course you are, thought Alana, shaking Mrs. Keith's long, broad-boned hand. Never in her life had she met someone who more accurately fit the description of a "handsome woman." She could have passed for John Cleese in drag, and it was impossible to imagine her being anything but a housekeeper named Mrs. Keith. Not only did she look the part, she smelled faintly of Lemon Pledge. "Nice to meet you too."

"Would you like some breakfast? We have oatmeal, fresh fruit, homemade muffins, granola—"

"We don't do bacon and eggs anymore," said Martin.

"No, we don't," said Mrs. Keith without a trace of judgment.

"I think I'll stick with coffee for now, thanks. I imbibed last night and my stomach isn't quite there yet."

Mrs. Keith smiled. "Please let me know if you need anything at all."

"Thanks."

Martin handed Alana her latte and slopped some sugar into his cappuccino. "C'mon," he said, tossing the spoon on the counter, leaving the mess for Mrs. Keith to clean up.

They went outside to the patio, where Martin pushed his chair up close to Alana's so they could confer quietly.

"Cheers," he said, raising his cup. "Well, that was easy." He sipped his coffee then wiped some foam off his lip. "But I knew she'd go for it. Maybe we didn't even need you."

"Maybe. But you got me, so if you could transfer those funds into my account, I would appreciate it. I thought it was already in there."

"No problem. I'll do it right now. Just let me get McSlut's done." Martin worked his phone while Alana drank her coffee.

She felt calm now, but oddly deflated.

"OK, I just need to quickly find your info. You're sure the account number you sent me is correct?"

"Yup." Alana watched as Martin completed the transfer.

"All right, done and done." Martin exhaled deeply.

"Great. Thank you." Alana pulled out her phone. "I just want to make sure it went in." She checked her account balance, which now stood at $53,047.96. It was strange and thrilling to see such a hefty amount. "It's wonderful to have the fifty, but you said you guys would pay me the first million up front if she agreed."

"Yup. We'll settle as soon as Teddy gets back." He smiled wryly. "Don't worry, we're good for it. In the meantime, do me a favor and buy yourself a new car."

"I intend to. Maybe even a new doughnut."

"Ha. When are you heading home?"

"Thursday night."

"I'm sure Teddy will be back before then."

"OK."

"In fact, I'm sure he'll fly home as soon as he hears she's cleared out." Martin sipped his coffee. "Speaking of which, you might want to brace yourself for the aftermath. It's going to be brutal around here for a few days."

"You think?"

"Dad's a lot more even-keeled since he's been on the hormone treatments, but he's not going to be happy. He's going to be wondering what the fuck happened, and he'll be pissed off and maybe suspicious. Prepare for tantrums."

"What kind of hormones is he on?"

"They're basically female hormones. For the prostate cancer. They block the testosterone."

"Oh. That explains a lot. He seems so much more docile now."

"Yeah, it's made him a lot easier to deal with. But I've noticed he's getting man boobs. Not a good look."

Alana sipped her latte. "So, the more female you are, the easier you are to deal with?"

"OK, if you're going to get all feminist on me…" Martin stood up.

"Seriously? Are you trying to prove my hypothesis?"

"Yeah, Mom was really easy to deal with, wasn't she? My girlfriend is so easy to deal with."

"Gertrud seems nice. Is she living with you?"

"No. God, no. She has a condo in Vancouver. She's just visiting."

"What does she do, anyway?"

Martin laughed. "Mostly she marries well."

"She doesn't work?"

"I guess she does interior design," said Martin, dismissively. "She thinks I'm going to be hubby number three, but it's not going to happen."

Alana didn't respond.

"Anyway, I have to go to work now, Alana. I need to make money so I can give millions of dollars to you and another female."

"Wow. You know, you're the one who came begging for my help."

"And I appreciate it. I do. I just hope Dad doesn't blow a gasket when he realizes his gal pal has flown the coop."

"Do you think he'll try to find her?"

"He might. But it's unlikely. He's never been the groveling type. I'm guessing he'll just be mad as hell, especially if she leaves a note saying she didn't want to waste her life with a desiccated old fart. You told her to say that, right?"

"Not in those exact words."

Martin laughed and drained his coffee. "Well, I'm glad this is sorted. Never mind the estate, I'd pay millions to never have to look at that freckly fucking smirk ever again. My only regret is that I won't get to kick her ass at pool." Martin set his cup down. "All right, I'll see you back here at one for lunch. Except for breakfast, we have meals together whenever there are guests, so don't be late."

"OK."

"Tomorrow we'll get some bacon in this fucking house." He walked off, leaving his cup for Alana to clear.

Lily, as it turned out, was having a blast without Alana around. "We had brownie cereal for breakfast," she said proudly.

Alana had gone for a swim and was now FaceTiming with her daughter by the pool. "I'm afraid to ask what that is."

"You break brownies into little pieces then pour milk over it."

"OK, do not call that cereal. There is literally no cereal involved in that."

Lily laughed. "And we're having pizza for dinner. And we stayed up until eleven last night."

Alana couldn't help but enjoy her daughter's glee at flouting the rules.

"I'll make salad with it," Ramona called out in the background.

"No salad," said Lily, reveling in her dietary liberation.

"Just one salad. OK? I need you to stay healthy for me."

"Yeah, good luck with that," said Lily.

"You know what I mean. Are you drinking lots of water? It's important."

"I know. I am. Ramona makes me."

"OK, good. I guess I'm not going to ask if you miss me," said Alana.

"I miss you," said Lily.

"I miss you too. A lot. You feel OK?"

"Yup."

"Did you have physio today?"

"Yeah."

"Any pain?"

"Just while I was doing it."

"I'm sorry, hon. I'll be home in a few days and we'll have a big bowl of brownie cereal together."

"Yeah, right."

"Seriously."

"So, are you having fun out there?" said Lily.

"Um...I went for a swim and that was fun."

"I wish we had a pool."

"I know. Me too. Listen, tell Ramona to call or text if she needs anything. Day or night. And same for you, OK?"

"OK. Love you."

"Love you more. I'll call you before bed."

"OK, bye."

"Eat some salad."

"Bye, Mom."

"Bye, lovey."

Only when she pocketed her phone and stood to leave did she notice Darla about six feet behind her lounge chair, on the other side of the hedgerow. She and a couple of her landscaping team were moving along its length, misting the foliage with something in large plastic bottles.

"Oh, hi."

"Morning. Sorry, not eavesdropping. Just passing by."

"No worries." Alana gestured to the bottle. "That's not toxic, is it?" How much insecticide had she inhaled just lying there?

"Nope, not a bit. This is neem oil. Made out of seeds. Miss McNutt had us switch to all-natural pesticides and fungicides."

"Oh." Miss McNutt had certainly altered the way Ed's household was run. Alana was curious to know how the staff felt about it. Mrs. Keith had been a cipher, but she figured she could get the scoop from Darla. "And has that made your job more difficult?"

"Not really. Bit of a learning curve, but I like it. This won't hurt a bird, a bee, or me."

"That's good then." Alana smiled and gathered up her stuff. "I'll see you later."

"Enjoy the day," said Darla, continuing to spritz her way down the hedge.

As Alana approached the main road toward the wooded path, she saw Ed coming toward her. He was moving at a decent clip but using one of those rolling walkers, which surprised her.

"Hey," he called out. "You seen Kelly?"

"Um, at yoga this morning."

"Not since then?"

"No."

"You were at the pool?"

"Yeah, she's not there. Have you tried calling her?"

"Of course I've tried calling. She's not answering for some reason."

"I don't know. Sorry."

"All right," he huffed. "See you at lunch."

As her father trundled on with his usual impatient scowl, she noticed something new in his countenance: a trace of anguish. Ed looked a little panicked, and Alana had to work the muscles of her face hard to keep a smile from spreading across it.

Lunch was uncomfortable. Alana needed to act all mystified and placate her father while simultaneously tending to her serious swimmer's hunger. What was it about immersing herself in water that made her so ravenous? She had done only a few dozen leisurely lengths across the pool, but felt like there wasn't enough gazpacho, freshly baked bread, and grilled veggies in the world to satisfy her hunger. It was probably the hangover-and-swimming combo that had her digging in for thirds while her father, who had barely touched his food, ranted incessantly about Kelly's absence.

"It just doesn't follow," said Ed, checking his phone for the umpteenth time.

"It's probably some wedding-related appointment," offered Gertrud.

"That makes sense," said Martin. "Maybe she has a dress fitting or something?"

"Her dress is upstairs."

"Well, maybe she went to play golf," said Martin.

"She would have told me," said Ed, impatiently. "She

tells me where she's going. And I can always reach her by phone. Something's not right."

Alana glanced at Martin, who looked quickly away.

"Are you sure she didn't text or email you?" said Martin. "Or maybe she left a note? Did you check your office?"

"Bloody hell," said Ed, flinging his napkin into his soup. "Do you people think I'm senile? I had a mild stroke, not a fucking lobotomy."

Nobody responded. Alana, who had just taken a big bite of crusty baguette, stopped chewing and let the bread dissolve quietly in her mouth.

"I don't know what medications I'm supposed to have or when. She does all that."

"Well, we can figure it out, I'm sure. But that's a good point. A very good point. You shouldn't be relying on her for that now that you're…together. We'll get you a new nurse who knows exactly what her professional duties are," said Martin.

"I don't need a new nurse," said Ed evenly and murderously. As he struggled to his feet, Gertrud leaped from her chair and extended her arms vaguely toward him. "Do not!" he admonished, and she sank back into her seat.

They all watched in silence as he left the room.

"Oh boy," said Gertrud. "Where do you think she went?"

"No idea," said Martin. "But if this is what he's like after four hours…" He shot Alana a look.

"Let's hope she gets back soon," said Gertrud.

Mrs. Keith entered then and offered dessert and coffee. Alana said yes to both.

Martin, on the other hand, requested a bottle of very good champagne.

★ ★ ★

After lunch, Alana made a beeline for her cottage. She wanted to avoid running into Ed until she had to face him again at dinner. Gertrud had invited her to hang out—play tennis or maybe go for another swim, but Alana begged off, using her hangover as an excuse. She was seldom alone with nothing to do and was looking forward to a few hours of solitude. She had big plans to spend the entire afternoon in bed with a book, something she hadn't done since before Lily was born. She stripped off her dress, unhooked her bra, and snuggled up under the quilt with *Americanah*. Heaven.

The delicious feeling didn't last long though—within the hour she was receiving frantic texts from work about a mishap in the shelter's second-floor laundry room. Apparently, someone had draped a forgotten sweat sock over the edge of the laundry sink, and it had tumbled in, blocking the drain. When the washing machine emptied, the plugged sink overflowed, sending water cascading through the main-floor ceiling, flooding several light fixtures and blowing out the power. Also, "Mr. Thompson was back in town," which was code for another rat sighting in the shelter (no matter what they tried, Mr. Thompson and his ilk always managed to find their way back). There were several electricians and exterminators in the shelter's contact list, and did Alana know which ones they were currently using?

She did. She knew all too well, and texted the relevant information, after which she found herself unable to ease back into her literary reverie. She refastened her bra, slipped her dress on, and headed up to the house with a sudden impulse to go look at her old bedroom.

With a few strategic pauses, Alana was able to make her way to the estate's second floor without encountering anyone. At the top of the stairs, to the left was the main bedroom with its vaulted ceiling, numerous skylights and en suite bathroom. Except for what appeared to be a much bigger bed and headboard, it looked the same as she remembered, at least from her vantage point in the hall— she didn't dare venture in. The rug was the same. The only thing missing was her mom, lumped under the covers, sleeping it off.

Straight ahead was Teddy's old room, which had been turned into a home office with two large desks. To the right of that was Martin's old room, which had lost every boyhood trapping and now looked like a generic guest room—all beiges and creams—except for two impressive Norval Morrisseau paintings above the bed. Across the hall from Martin's room was the bathroom, which had been extensively renovated. Gone was the long wooden vanity in which Alana had once tried to keep a ladybug as a pet—she had managed to coax the creature into one of the drawers and was surprised and saddened to find it gone in the morning. The old cabinet had been ripped out and replaced with two curvy pedestal sinks that looked like porcelain calla lilies.

Next to the bathroom, at the end of the hall, was Lillian's room, and across from that, Alana's, both with their doors shut. She listened carefully for any sound from within, then opened hers first. It was a decent-sized room, but smaller than she remembered and, like Martin's, had been turned into a tasteful but bland guest room. From the looks of things, Teddy was staying here. There was an Adidas jacket hung over a chair, an array of high-end athletic shoes lined up along the wall, a tennis racket, a bike helmet, and a book on the bedside table (*The 48 Laws of Power* by Robert Greene). No women's clothing, so Martin and Gertrud were either staying in Lillian's room or in one of the cottages. Oddly, when Alana crossed the room and looked at the familiar view out the window, an invisible hand gripped her heart, and a sob rose from her chest. The stab of emotion passed as quickly as it came and confused her. What had caused it? Was it some unconscious nostalgia stirred up by looking at something she hadn't seen since she was a child? In a way, yes. But she intuited that it was more than that. She had momentarily relived a time before sadness, when looking out her bedroom window at the trees and the cottages nestled within meant nothing but a pretty view.

Alana moved away from the window. In the center of the room stood a king-size bed, but when she was little, she had a single bed pushed up against the wall. She remembered how she used to lie on her back and walk her feet up the cool plaster, how she always had to align the slats on the louvered closet doors before she could go to sleep, and how she would see things in the swirling wood grain of her pine dresser—the moose, the snail, the Spanish lady with the flamenco headdress.

As Alana turned to leave, she thought of something else from that time—being woken by the sound of her sister, and lying awake to see if the moans or calling out would quickly subside. If not, Alana would creep across the hall to Lillian's room to see if she was OK. Lillian had frequent nightmares and was a sleep talker—or, more accurately, a sleep shouter. Alana would sometimes find her sister slick with sweat but sleeping peacefully again after an outburst; sometimes Lillian would be thrashing and yelling, and Alana, terrified, would try to rouse her and show her that everything was all right, that she was just having a bad dream. Lillian, still half in the world of her night terror, would stare at her with wild, angry eyes and send her away. But on rare occasions, Lillian would be awake, quietly recovering, and she would throw back the blankets and let Alana crawl in beside her. She loved falling asleep this way, tucked up against her sister, Lillian's bony arms holding her tight, her sharp chin resting atop Alana's head.

Alana didn't understand any of it at the time. She was only six years old. And then seven years old. And then eight years old. And then nine years old.

And then...

Alana pulled her bedroom door shut behind her. She tried to enter Lillian's room, but for some reason that door was locked. And now she could hear someone on the stairs. She ducked into the bathroom and closed the door as far as possible without shutting it and making a noise. As Alana stood there, her heart bouncing, she heard the clattering sounds of a slow ascent and concluded it must be her father, struggling up the stairs with his walker. She waited for what felt like an hour for him to reach the top and listened as he entered his bedroom and then his office. She willed him to close the door so she could make her escape, but he didn't. However, a couple minutes later, he left the office and moved down the hall past the bathroom. She heard him unlock the door to Lillian's room and enter. The door closed, and she heard what sounded like a bolt being slid into place. He must have stopped in his bedroom or office only to retrieve the key. Alana thought about pressing her ear against the shared wall to try to figure out what was going on in there, but realized this might be her only opportunity to slip away undetected. She also had a sudden and overpowering urge to call her daughter and make sure everything was OK. She took off her flip-flops and held them in her hand. As she tiptoed down the hall and hurried down the stairs, Alana resolved to sneak back at some point and find the key to Lillian's room.

Dinner was called for 7:00 p.m.

At 7:26, after an excruciating interval in which the assemblage quaffed ice water and waited in vain and near silence for Kelly to show up, Ed angrily assented to the wine and first course being served. At 7:33, Martin deposited a forkful of vegan Caesar salad into his mouth and simultaneously gasped hard, sucking air, lettuce, and roasted chickpeas deep into his trachea. Kelly, who, moments before, had breezed into the room with a cheery "Sorry I'm late, I had the craziest day!" dropped the innumerable shopping bags she was carrying and ran to perform the Heimlich maneuver on Martin, who was choking to death at the table.

She wrapped her arms around him and said, "One, two, three..." before pulling in sharply on his midsection. Martin continued to choke while Gertrud shrieked, "Oh my god, oh my god, oh my god."

"One, two, three." Another short sharp pull, and this time a slimy hunk of lettuce flew out of Martin's mouth onto the floor. "There we go," said Kelly brightly, patting his back as he panted and recovered his breath. "Don't say I never did nothing for ya." She used a serviette to scoop the offending piece of vegetation from the floor before handing the crumpled linen to Mrs. Keith, who had swept in after hearing the commotion.

"Well done," said Mrs. Keith to Kelly. And then to Martin: "Can I get you anything? Some tea or honey for your throat?"

"I'm fine," he snapped before leaving the room.

Gertrud followed him out, and Mrs. Keith returned to the kitchen.

"Where the hell have you been?" said Ed as Kelly bent to kiss his cheek.

"I'm sorry—you know how scatterbrained I am. I somehow left without my phone and didn't even realize it until late in the day. I called you from Holt Renfrew a couple of hours ago, but you didn't pick up." She took her seat next to his at the table.

"I thought that was telemarketing. You went to Vancouver?"

"Yeah, sorry. I should have told you."

"Yes, you should have. If you're leaving the island, you tell me."

"I'm sorry. I wasn't planning on being gone this long." She grabbed his hand and kissed it with an exaggerated *mwah* sound.

"Well, I guess I can't be too mad since you just saved my son's life."

Kelly laughed. "All in a day's work." She let go of his hand and poured herself an ample glass of wine.

"She's something, isn't she?" said Ed to Alana.

"Yes, she is," said Alana, glancing at Kelly, who was smiling at her with highly amused eyes.

Now Martin and Gertrud returned. Gertrud paused at Kelly's chair. "Thank you," she said solemnly.

"Just doing my job," said Kelly. "You know that quote, right? 'Save one life, you're a hero, save a hundred, you're a nurse.'"

"Oh wow. That's so true," said Gertrud. "Thank god you were here."

"Thank god my insane shopping frenzy finally subsided." She turned to Ed. "I mean, you know me, I am *not* a shopper. But today, for some reason, I had the craziest urge to buy everything in sight. I got gifts for everyone. You too, Alana." Kelly smiled sweetly in her direction.

"You didn't have to do that."

"I wanted to. I was feeling generous." Kelly laughed. "I got you an Akoya pearl bracelet, Gertrud."

"Thank you! That's so sweet of you."

"I hope you got something for yourself," said Ed.

"I did. I got yoga pants."

He laughed. "That's it?"

"That's all I needed. Ooh, I got *you* a very cool pink cashmere sweater."

"Pink?"

"More like a deep fuchsia. I think it will look awesome with jeans and a white T-shirt underneath. Will you wear it?"

"I'll wear it," said Ed.

"And, Martin, I got you the best gift—a professional pool cue. A Predator. It has all these gorgeous inlays. It's like a work of art."

"Wow," said Martin, dryly.

"Of course, it'll give you an advantage when we finally

play that match, but that's all right. I'm pretty sure I can still take you."

Martin managed a tight smile in response.

"You're not going to thank her?" said Ed. "She just saved your life."

"That's true," said Martin. "I guess I'm still in shock. You know what? I am. I'm in shock. And thanking isn't enough, if you think about it." He got up and moved toward Kelly. He put a big hand on her tiny shoulder, close to her neck, almost pressing on the jugular. He smiled down at her. "I'm going to have to figure out a way to really pay you back."

"Don't be silly," said Kelly, smiling up at Martin, but Alana saw something flit across her face—like when a cloud momentarily skims a shadow over the lawn on a bright day. And Alana felt it too, radiating out from her solar plexus into her arms and up the back of her neck.

Fear.

4

There were stones on the steps of the cottage when Alana made her way back for the night, and she was unsurprised to find Martin inside, stretched out on the musty couch in the dark, drinking from a bottle of bourbon.

"Where were you? Why am I always waiting for you?" He sat up and held the bottle on his thigh.

"I was having dessert on the patio," she said.

"With *her*?"

"And Dad. I was there for the pie, not the company."

"Can you believe the nerve of that bitch?"

"Well, I guess we should have considered that possibility."

"I assumed she'd be dying to get away from the old man."

"I thought so too."

"Twenty mil and a Ferrari should have been enough."

"Five bucks and a subway token should have been enough."

"I wonder if fifty would have done it?" said Martin, not really listening. He took a swig from the bottle. "No. She's going after it all. And now she has something over me. And me alone. There's a trail going from my account to hers."

"Not Teddy's?"

"I couldn't reach him in time for her little deadline, so I had to send the full amount. He'll send me his half when he gets home. Speaking of which, I told him what happened and he's on his way."

Alana sighed. "I have to admit I was looking forward to that million."

"Yeah, well, you lost what you never had. You didn't flush five hundred Gs down the toilet."

"True."

"I should have known when she didn't try to negotiate."

"Maybe she actually loves him."

Martin laughed. "Don't be daft. She's playing us."

"And winning."

"Not for long," said Martin. "A battle is not the war, Alana." He took a swig of bourbon. "Teddy's back tomorrow and we'll figure out how to dispatch Miss McNutt."

"Dispatch?"

"Who knows, maybe there's a way for you to still get your million. One thing's for sure, she's messing with the wrong family."

Alana swallowed hard.

"You know what I'd really like to do? I'd like to take that Predator pool cue and shove it straight up her ass," said Martin, slurring his words. He took another swig.

"You should probably go," said Alana.

"Yeah, I should." Martin rose unsteadily and weaved toward the door. "Hey, what'd she get you? Or should I say, what did Teddy and I get you?"

"Good question. She said she got me something but then never mentioned it again."

"What, no hideous pearl bracelet?"

"Gertrud seemed to like it."

Martin laughed bitterly. "The million-dollar bracelet and pool cue."

"And pink sweater."

"I think I'll actually puke if I see him in that," said Martin, pushing his way drunkenly out the door. "Nighty night."

Alana closed the door and locked it. She turned on the light and fished out her phone. It had vibrated several times before dinner, but she'd quickly determined that none of the messages were from Lily or Ramona; they all were from her associates at RedTree. Alana figured they could sort out whatever issue they were having without her for the next couple of hours and had ignored them. But now, reading the missives, she discovered they had nothing to do with plumbers or exterminators or electricians. In fact, they were brimming with excitement over some pretty staggering news. An anonymous benefactor had made a hefty online donation, one that exceeded their combined fundraising efforts for the previous fiscal year and would provide nearly half of the shelter's annual operating budget.

The size of the contribution: a million dollars.

Teddy had changed. Of course he had. But much more so than Martin, Alana thought. His formerly thick and wavy hair—that used to remind her of swirling soft-serve ice cream—had thinned substantially and lost its strawberry-blond luster. It was now a wispy, washed-out beige. The eyelids had grown hooded over the keen green eyes, and his forehead had a smattering of pale brown age spots. He was still fit and chiseled and would widely be considered handsome, if you could get past the resting-sneer-face. To Alana, he always looked like a fairer, more effete version of their father. Ed-Lite.

The siblings had gathered on the beach for a confab. Teddy was jet-lagged and Martin was ferociously hungover, but they wanted to meet as soon as possible to discuss the situation.

After exchanging greetings and "catching up"—a sixty-second prelude in which Teddy feigned interest in Alana's daughter, Alana pretended to care about the standings at Wimbledon, and both politely aped filial affection with the semblance of a hug (stiff/awkward)—they got down to business. Teddy had them turn off their phones and leave them twenty feet away on a boulder. He wasn't taking any chances.

"So, Miss McNutt is having some fun with us," said Teddy.

"I've been thinking about it," said Martin. "Maybe we just expose her. Tell Dad we wanted to test her loyalties, and show that she banked the money offshore without telling him."

"That just makes us look stupid," said Teddy.

"And her avaricious," said Martin.

"Not necessarily. She could say she was teaching us a lesson. And Dad would admire her for putting one over on us."

Martin chewed a hangnail. "Maybe."

"Anyway," said Alana. "She covered that base. You can't go to Dad."

"What do you mean?"

"You know the shelter I work at?"

"Yeah."

"We got an anonymous donation yesterday. For a million dollars."

"So?" said Martin.

"So, that doesn't happen every day. In fact, it never happens. Pretty sure it was her. Remember she said she got me something but then never actually gave me anything?"

"Oh fuck. You're right."

"Hmm," said Teddy. "Maybe not so avaricious after all."

"Are you serious? This just proves how calculating she is. God. How can you not see that?" said Martin.

"Look," said Teddy. "You may be right. It's likely you are. But you have to understand that there *is* a scintilla of possibility you're wrong, and we need to consider that before we act. Maybe she has some kind of savior complex and truly cares about Dad. Maybe she's toying with us because we can't comprehend or even imagine that. She could have been genuinely insulted by our offer of filthy lucre."

Martin scoffed. "No, she loves the lucre. The filthier the better—I can tell."

"Maybe. But don't forget, I checked her out before we hired her. This is no serial black widow. This is a nurse from a lower-middle-class background in Winnipeg, who worked nights at a steak house to put herself through school. She's never even been married."

"Well, maybe an opportunity never presented itself before. I'm not saying it's a pattern, I'm just saying she's messing with us now."

"I hear you. And, yes, maybe she's the Bond-villain mastermind you envision, but what if she's not? She could have kept the money, after all. A million bucks is a lot to a pleb."

"Not if you're marrying a multibillionaire in a few weeks.

She's going to personally be overseeing a three-hundred-million-dollar foundation. A mil is nothing to have something over us and show that she's Miss Charitable. It's a very savvy investment, actually. She has that in her pocket now to pull out anytime she likes. I'm guessing, once they're hitched."

"Possibly," said Teddy.

"Definitely," said Martin.

"So, what are you suggesting?"

"Duh."

"OK, please don't say *duh*. You know I hate that," said Teddy.

Martin lowered his voice. "I'm suggesting that they never get married."

"You want to offer a larger sum?" said Teddy with a small smile, but Alana could see he knew very well what Martin was proposing.

Martin laughed. "Yeah, no thanks. Fool me once and all that."

"So, what then?" said Alana. She wanted to force him to say the thing out loud.

"Look, it's not like we'd have to do anything. We know people who do things."

"Yes, but the people we know don't need our money," said Teddy. "Far from it."

"True. But we know things about some of the people we know." Teddy and Martin exchanged a glance. Alana felt her gut clench.

"That would be extremely foolish," said Teddy. "For many reasons." A dark look simmered between the brothers. Martin broke eye contact first.

"Are you talking about the people who used to come to the island?" said Alana.

Neither brother responded.

"I always wondered, did Ed go visit their homes and vacation spots? I assume he did."

"You know what, it doesn't matter," said Teddy, flashing Martin a warning look. "We're not going down that road."

Martin nodded. "OK, forget it. You're right. Not the best idea."

"Pretty much the worst," said Teddy.

"But we don't have to involve others. We could deal with things ourselves. I mean, accidents happen."

"What kind of accidents?" said Alana.

"I don't know, the woman can't swim, and we're literally surrounded by water. Not to mention we're going to be out on the yacht Friday."

"Are you staying for that?" Teddy asked Alana.

"I don't know. I was supposed to fly home Thursday."

The siblings stood in silence for several moments, each one lost in private thoughts.

"She drinks like a fish every night," said Martin. "And always stays up later than Dad. If she happened to lose her footing, tumble over the side…"

"And who's going to help her lose her footing?" said Teddy.

"Who cares? We'll flip a coin. Alana can help with logistics, bring her fresh drinks, get her to the right spot…"

"You don't think it looks highly suspicious if something happens right before the wedding?" said Teddy.

"So what if it looks suspicious? When Natalie Wood

drowned it looked plenty suspicious, but Robert Wagner's still banging Jill St. John."

"Oh my god," said Alana.

"Do you have to be so coarse?" said Teddy.

"Whatever, Mr. Manners. I'm just saying suspicious is meaningless without proof. I could pick her up like a six-pack and toss her over the rail, and so could you. Hell, Alana could probably do it."

"And you think she'll go quietly over the rail and sink silently like an anvil? How many people will be on the boat that night to hear her screaming for help? The captain and crew, that's at least fourteen people, not to mention the wedding planner and her assistants, the designer, the ten-piece band…"

"Yes, exactly. The band. We do it when the big-ass band is playing."

"There's a ten-piece band at a rehearsal dinner?" said Alana.

"This isn't the rehearsal dinner—that's the night before the wedding. This is just a run-through of the food, music, atmosphere, etcetera, to make sure everything is to Dad's liking, you know, in case he wants to adjust things."

"Wow."

"So, no guests," said Martin. "Which makes our task easier."

"We don't have a task," said Alana.

"Oh, come off it. You were just whining about losing out on your million. You help us with this, you'll be sitting pretty for the rest of your life. Right, Teddy? How about a hundred times that."

"Personally, I think we should just cool our jets. I think

it looks awfully dodgy if something happens before the wedding," said Teddy.

Martin groaned. "No. We need to act before the will is voided. Look, if you want me to be the point person on this, I can do it. I just need to know we're all working together."

"I don't know. I have to think about it," said Teddy. "And I'm too tired to think right now. I didn't sleep on the plane."

"Fair enough," said Martin. "Let's talk tomorrow. But I'm telling you, I can't take it much longer. If an opportunity presents itself…"

Teddy fixed his razor gaze on Alana. "And you're OK with this?"

She was not OK with it, but felt instinctively that it would be dangerous to say so. "Maybe. I mean—possibly. But what about that scintilla of uncertainty you were talking about? What if she is just a hardworking nurse, and you guys…you know."

"Precisely," said Teddy. "We need to consider all facets very carefully. And right now I'm too exhausted and famished to think about anything but food and bed."

"All right," said Martin. "But trust me, that woman means to take everything that is rightfully Dad's and rightfully ours." He looked at his brother. "We've worked our whole lives for Dad. Like, right out of school."

"I'm aware," said Teddy.

"Are we just going to let her breeze in and take it all away? Is that fair? After all the time we've devoted, after all the shit we've eaten?"

"I hear you," said Teddy.

"If she made that donation, it was made in self-interest, I guarantee it." Martin put his hand on Alana's shoulder.

"Look, I know we've had our issues over the years, and I know we haven't been a family for a long time, but at the end of the day, you are one of us, Alana, whether you acknowledge it or not."

Alana nodded.

"And there's a lot at stake for all of us."

"I know."

"So, of course, you're not going to say anything about any of this?" said Teddy, more order than question.

"Obviously," said Alana.

"She's good," said Martin, smiling at his sister. "She's helping us and we're going to help her. And her daughter."

"OK," said Teddy. "Lots to think about. I suggest we all sleep on it and meet back here tomorrow at three, with clear heads and full bellies."

"Speaking of which, it must be getting close to one," said Alana. "We should probably head back for lunch."

"Fine," said Martin. "I just can't believe you guys don't know malevolence when you see it."

Oh, I see it, thought Alana, following her brothers across the beach to retrieve their phones, *and I know it too.*

One of Alana's earliest memories was a sensuous one. Sweet cakes, ruby-red cordial, a white marble table, and a three-tiered serving tray dotted with the prettiest confections. She was with her mom and Lillian at a café in Paris. Their mother was drinking café crème, not wine, and she gave them sips, and they were delicious, like warm coffee kisses. It was just the girls out for the day, just Kat, Lillian, and Alana. A dazzling day in bright September.

After the café, they went shopping along Avenue Montaigne and ended up in a children's boutique where the clothes were displayed like pieces of art on white wooden plinths. There were velvet couches to rest on and plush gray carpets. Alana sat quietly while her mom and a chic saleslady with red lipstick persuaded Lillian to try on outfit after outfit. She didn't want to—Lillian didn't care at all about clothes—but her mother was determined to put together a new wardrobe for school (Lillian would be entering grade six in less than a week). The fine garments looked wonderful on her sister, and Alana wished she were the one being fussed over and dressed up like a doll.

There was one item in particular that Alana had coveted: a white cashmere coat with a thick fox-fur collar and cuffs that had been dyed the palest shade of ballet-slipper pink—as soft and luxurious as a cream puff. It must have been ridiculously expensive because when their mother discreetly turned the tag to see how much it cost, she flinched, and she never did that. (Kat liked to hide the fact that she came from a place where price had ever been a consideration.) But the coat looked perfect on Lillian, so Kat had the saleslady wrap it up with a dozen other items. As they waited at the counter for everything to be rung up, her mother glanced down at her and seemed to see her for the first time since they entered the shop. She smiled and said, "You've been *so* quiet the whole time we've been shopping." Alana shrugged. "Do you have one of those in her size?" her mother asked the saleslady, who was wrapping the cashmere coat in tissue paper. Why yes, they did have one. And Alana left the shop a very happy girl (somewhere, there was a photograph of the sisters, back at the hotel, modeling their matching coats—Alana beaming with pleasure and pride, Lillian looking constricted and sullen).

After, they stopped at another café, where Kat drank pastis after pastis. "Don't tell your father," she said, winking and ordering another round. She handed the girls a menu and encouraged them to have whatever they liked, and never once frowned at Alana's choices, or surveyed her plate, or disparaged her for eating too much.

Alana had always remembered that afternoon as one of the sunniest of her childhood. But at a certain point, it dawned on her that that was the day she'd learned a powerful and dangerous lesson.

Silence=Reward.

When Alana thought about her brothers, she thought about two entitled, obsequious men who would do almost anything for money. *Almost* being the compensatory word. She knew they were sycophants who had given up their freedom and integrity—their very souls—to their father and his fortune, but she'd never thought of them as potential killers.

Until now.

During lunch, she watched them eat, drink, and carry on as if they hadn't just been discussing the murder of the woman with whom they were now chatting faux amiably.

She had to say something.

She had to get Kelly alone and warn her. But when and how to do it without alerting her brothers to her treachery?

After lunch, the men headed upstairs—Teddy to sleep away his jet lag, Martin and Ed to deal with business issues—while Gertrud and Kelly went off to play tennis.

Alana checked in with Ramona and Lily and then made

her way to the tennis courts, ostensibly to watch the women play. She was, in reality, oblivious to the action on the court as she sat on the sidelines, turning things over in her mind, waiting for the women to finish so she could arrange a private word with Kelly.

"Want to try a game?" Gertrud called to her after about twenty minutes.

"No thanks. I haven't played since I was a kid," said Alana. "Also…" She held up a flip-flopped foot.

"Yeah, that wouldn't work," said Gertrud. And then to Kelly: "Finish the set?"

"Sure. Finish me off," said Kelly, laughing.

"Don't feel bad," said Gertrud. "I took lessons my whole childhood, even won a Challenger in my twenties."

"Wow."

"Plus, I'm about a foot taller than you, which means my reach is way longer."

"It's OK. I'm just joking. It's fun to play with someone so good."

"I'm actually surprised at how hard you're returning it. You're doing really well, especially for someone who never took lessons," said Gertrud, bouncing the ball, readying herself for a serve.

Alana watched now as Gertrud, with strength and grace, handily won the next two games. It was nice to see her in tennis shoes, moving as she was meant to, instead of teetering on stilettos, her usual self-inflicted hobbling. She felt bad for the woman, who'd thought she had to surgically alter herself—the puffy lips, the giant boobs, and who knows what else—to make herself more pleasing to men like Martin. And at the same time, Alana reflected, she had made herself a joke to men who weren't like Martin. A dirty game that Gertrud couldn't win.

When the match was over, Kelly and Gertrud high-fived each other over the net.

"Well done," said Kelly. "That was fun."

"We'll do it again," said Gertrud.

When they came to the bench to pack up their gear, Alana proposed a postgame drink by the pool.

"I wouldn't say no to a drink." Kelly smiled.

"I'll just grab a quick shower and meet you guys," said Gertrud.

"Perfect," said Alana.

But just then Ed pulled up in a golf cart and summoned his bride-to-be. After exchanging a few hushed words— *You'll see them at dinner*, Alana heard her father hiss—Kelly hopped in beside him, waved to Alana and Gertrud, and called out, "Later, guys!" before the cart sped off.

"Still want to have that drink?" said Gertrud.

Not in the least, thought Alana. But she smiled and said, "Of course."

The evening was a bust. There was zero opportunity for Alana to get Kelly alone, either before or after dinner, and she felt nervous and self-conscious the whole time—as if her brothers were watching her, although she may have been imagining that. After dessert was cleared, the family quickly dispersed. Ed corralled Kelly to go watch a show they had been bingeing on Netflix, Teddy, still jet-lagged, went to bed, while Martin and Gertrud hit the games room to play Ping-Pong. And so, it was plan B for Alana. She decided to set her alarm and go to the beach for yoga first thing in the morning. She headed back to her cottage, took a hot shower, and went to bed early. Again, she had trouble sleeping, her brain roiling with what-ifs as she ran through various scenarios in her mind. But she managed to drift into a restless sleep just after midnight.

A disturbing dream awakened her well before her alarm was set to go off. She figured there was no point in trying to get back to sleep, so she put on her sweats and made coffee. She drank two cups while surfing the internet and answering emails. Then she left the cottage early, hoping that Kelly might show up before her six o'clock start time. The sooner Alana got to the beach and back, the better, she figured. Or maybe she should stay and do yoga so that nobody would suspect if they happened to see her? Yes, she would do yoga, even though she had no idea how to do yoga and pretty much hated the idea of doing yoga.

The sun was just on the cusp of rising as Alana walked briskly to the beach, mentally rehearsing what she was going to say. But as she approached the clearing, she saw something that made her freeze in place.

Teddy was seated on the sand, facing away from her, leaning against a large felled log. At first he appeared to be just sitting there gazing out at the water. But then his head tipped back and he let out a low growl.

He stood and pulled his pants up over his bare ass, revealing Kelly, who had been kneeling in front of him, out of sight. She got up, wiped her mouth with the back of her hand, and smiled at him.

Then they kissed.

5

Alana heard someone whisper *What the fuck?* She turned and saw Martin, who had come up behind her and was now staring past her to the beach.

Teddy disengaged from Kelly, scooped his jacket up off the ground, and slipped it on.

Alana gestured for Martin to quickly follow her back down the path to her cottage. He took off in a sprint ahead of her and kept turning and hissing at her to hurry so Teddy wouldn't see them. But Alana was built for comfort, not speed. She jogged for as long as she could, then walked quickly while catching her breath, then jogged a bit more, looking over her shoulder sporadically to see if Teddy was coming up behind them. She never spotted him and was pretty sure they had made it back inside her cottage without being seen.

"What the fuck?" said Martin. *"What the actual fuck?"* He paced back and forth across the living room. "This is crazy! Like, what is going on?"

Alana collapsed on the sofa, panting and wiping sweat from her face.

"Wait, did you know about this?" said Martin.

"No! Of course not. Jesus."

"What were you doing out there?"

"I woke up early, so I thought I'd try yoga. All these formal meals—I've basically just been sitting and eating since I got here."

Martin studied her face as if deciding whether or not to believe her.

"What were *you* doing there?" said Alana, crossing her arms over her chest.

"Well, to be honest, I was following you," said Martin. "I had a feeling you weren't a hundred percent behind the plan. And I wanted to make sure you weren't going to say something and mess it up."

"Wow," said Alana. "Thanks for trusting me. You know, even if I didn't want to be part of the plan, I wouldn't run to the beach and rat you out."

He stared hard at her.

She returned his gaze, unblinking. "When have I ever ratted anybody out, Martin?"

He thought about it, then after a few moments exhaled deeply and sank into a chair. "I just can't believe this," he said. "How can I trust anything right now?" He stood and resumed pacing. "Do you think this is something recent or...?"

Alana shrugged. "No idea. But *I* just got here. You haven't seen any sign of this before today?"

"Not really." Martin started chewing a hangnail on his thumb. "Although he was always on the fence about her motives. I mean, you heard him talking about that scintilla of doubt, right?"

"Yeah."

"Well, now we know why he didn't want to do anything before the wedding. He *wants* them to get married."

"It would seem so."

"OK, so what does this mean exactly?" The hangnail was bleeding now. Martin sucked the blood away.

"Well," said Alana, "off the top of my head, it either means they've recently become involved and they're going to hide it from Dad forever, you know, until he dies, at which point they'll wait a respectable amount of time before they openly 'fall in love.' And then Teddy will essentially be the new king of the castle. Or else they've become involved, and they're maybe planning something bad for Dad at some point after the wedding—"

"Wow," said Martin.

"Or...they were romantically involved before she ever met Dad. And that's why Teddy hired her. Maybe that's why he started going out with her in the first place. Maybe he was looking for a nurse, someone to seduce Dad, so that she and Teddy could someday become the heirs to the business and fortune, cutting off *your* access so that Teddy could run the business without you. Maybe he was really angry about being demoted."

"Jesus Christ."

"I mean, it's possible."

"Would he do that to me?"

"I don't know. Would he? Has he paid you back for their little million-dollar prank?"

"Not yet, but he fucking well will. Prick."

Alana got up and moved toward the kitchenette. "You want a coffee?"

"A Keurig? Nah."

She made herself one, then carried it back to the couch.

"He said he vetted her. Do you think any of that working-her-way-through-school crap is true? Maybe she isn't even a nurse?"

"She's probably a real nurse," said Alana. "Teddy wouldn't be that stupid."

"She does seem to know all the meds and stuff," said Martin. "I could hire a private detective to get the dirt on her. I should have done that to begin with. I don't know why I trusted him."

"Well, probably because he's your brother. Also, it's possible he hired her legitimately, and they started messing around at a later date."

"True."

"That's the more likely scenario."

"I guess."

"Anyway, I would think twice before you hire anybody," said Alana.

"Why?"

"Depending on how things shake down, you might not want anyone to know that you know the things you know."

"You're right," said Martin. "I need to think about this."

"Yup. Very carefully."

"But actually, this might make everything easier. Maybe instead of pursuing what we talked about earlier, we could solve this just by getting some proof and showing Dad."

"Well, I would get it yourself then. If Dad sees you hired someone, he might not take kindly to that."

"True. I wish we'd photographed them this morning."

"I didn't think of it," said Alana.

"I didn't have time. When he put his jacket on, I figured he was heading back."

"Do you want me to try tomorrow morning? I could go to yoga, get there early again."

"Yeah," said Martin. "That would be good."

"Gertrud might wonder if you keep slipping out early."

"She wouldn't know," said Martin. "She sleeps like the dead until at least nine thirty."

Now they heard someone whistling outside. "Is that him?" whispered Alana.

Martin moved to the front window and peeked through the curtains. "He's alone. I guess she's still down there."

"Well, she actually does do yoga, I've seen her."

"I know. Gertrud went a couple times. You can go do it now, if you want."

Alana thought about it. "Nah, I don't really feel like it anymore."

Martin smiled. "That's the one good thing about this horrifying development. Now that you know she's not Miss Innocent, I don't have to worry about you tipping her off."

"You never had to worry."

"Come on, Alana, tell me honestly, I swear I won't be pissed—especially since Teddy kept suggesting she was this purehearted Florence Nightingale. When you went down to the beach this morning, were you going there to warn her?"

"Jesus, Martin, I already told you, I was going to do yoga. How many times do I have to say it?"

"OK, fine. Sorry." Martin sighed. "And I'm sorry we

haven't been in touch more over the years. I'm sorry about a lot of things. You know…"

"Yeah. Me too."

"God, I feel like I just lost a brother. But I guess I gained a sister."

Alana smiled but noted that Martin didn't seem very satisfied with the trade-off.

"OK, so listen," said Martin. "When we meet with Teddy later, here's what we tell him. We say we think he was right—that we should wait until after the wedding to take care of Kelly. That way they won't be on guard for any…unusual behavior on our part."

"Why don't I say I think we should wait, and then you disagree but then slowly come around to it. I'll say I think we need to err on the side of caution, and that it's majority rule, me and Teddy against you."

"Good idea. I've been pretty gung ho, so that might be more believable. Then we'll figure out what we're going to do once we've had time to think."

"Fine."

"All right, I'd better get back." Martin peeked through the curtains again. "If you're trying to take pictures tomorrow, you'd better make damn sure they don't see you. You could be in trouble if they do."

"I'll be careful," she said.

After Martin left, Alana thought about Teddy—about what a snake he was and how much he sickened her. What was he whistling when he went by the cottage? The snippet was familiar, but she couldn't quite place the tune. She replayed the fragments in her head until it finally stitched together. The Stones' "Under My Thumb."

6

The night Teddy first laid eyes on Kelly McNutt was one that was both typical and atypical. As usual on a Friday evening, he had left work at the company's head office in Vancouver and gone to the Lobby Lounge at the Fairmont Pacific Rim for cocktails and oysters. On a typical night, he would settle into his spot at the side of the bar—a space held for him by bartenders who were grateful for his large tabs and generous tips—and hold court with the various business acquaintances and young ladies who would assemble around him. He was well-known for buying people drinks and snacks, and his nightly bar bill was always more than a thousand dollars.

Most Fridays, he would home in on one or another high-heeled hottie and ferry her up to his regular harbor-view suite by ten o'clock. They would have sex, and if he thought he might want her again in the morning, she would be allowed to sleep over. He would leave no later than nine with instructions for her to order herself some breakfast before clearing out (and yes, she could take the robe with her). He made sure to never have the same woman up twice— although countless tried for a repeat rendezvous. He wasn't interested in forming attachments, especially with the kind of woman who would get dolled up and go to the Lobby Lounge to meet a rich guy.

On this night, however, Teddy was not feeling convivial or horny or hungry. He did not order two dozen oysters and an extra-cold glass of Bernard Defaix Chablis. He did not stand, facing away from the bar, welcoming others to approach, converse, and partake. No, on this night, he sat upon his stool, with his back to the crowd, hunched over a double whiskey. He laid his jacket over the stool next to him and ordered a beer, which he placed on the bar in front of it, to keep anyone from even thinking about sitting there. He then proceeded to get snockered. If anyone moseyed up to say hello or tried to get his attention, he shooed them away or ignored them completely. This happened every ten minutes or so. Annoying.

"Another, Mr. S?" asked the bartender when Teddy had drained his third double.

"Another," said Teddy, pushing his empty glass forward. He checked his phone, which had been vibrating intermittently in his pocket. More texts from Martin. Pretending to be all sympathetic and supportive. As if he hadn't popped a boner when Ed freaked out about the Singapore hotels. As if he hadn't put the bug in their dad's ear about taking over as executive VP. Weren't they both responsible for the business while Ed was incapacitated? But who had been doing the lion's share of the work? Maybe if Martin had been pulling his weight instead of goofing off or chasing after Gertrud, Teddy wouldn't have had to make every important decision. To hell with his brother's fake sympathy. And to hell with his father too. He'd worked his butt off for Ed since he was eighteen years old. Taking his abuse. Kowtowing. Never once did he mess up. Until now. And big deal, he overpaid a bit. So what? It's not like they couldn't afford it. It's not like they wouldn't earn it back. One tiny slip and he instantly gets demoted? And now his kid brother, who does maybe a third of what he does, is technically above him? Very nice. Especially now, with Ed poststroke and his prostate cancer numbers on the rise. He's going to die and leave Martin in charge? How humiliating would that be?

As Teddy pondered the injustice of it all, a frizzy-haired interloper sidled up beside him and leaned against the bar, trying to get the bartender's attention. She was a tiny thing, wearing a stretched out fisherman's sweater and olive green cargo pants. She had a giant canvas book bag slung over her shoulder and an armful of brochures, documents, and binders. She looked very out of place, like some high school freshman who'd wandered into the wrong room for her exam.

The girl was unable to catch either bartender's eye, and Teddy heard her sigh a few times and even emit an impatient "Excuse me" as she watched them repeatedly fail to notice her and serve others. Eventually, a bartender came to check on Teddy. He ordered another and then directed the young man's attention to the irritant at his side.

"Yes?"

"A pint of Guinness, please."

"May I see your ID?"

The girl laughed. "I'm twenty-eight," she said.

"Sorry, you don't look it," said the bartender. "I need to see ID, please."

"Fine." She plonked her armload of papers down on the marble bar and started rooting through her giant bag. Unable to find her wallet, she began pulling out items and placing them on the bar. Books, makeup, mints, phone, a long silky scarf, tissues, lip balm, GlaxoSmithKline lanyard with a zillion keys, notebook, a half-eaten sandwich wrapped in saran—Teddy was reminded of the scene in *Mary Poppins* where the nanny keeps pulling objects, including a four-foot potted plant, from her small carpet bag.

"I'll be back," said the exasperated bartender, who went to fill Teddy's order.

When he returned with Teddy's whiskey, the girl said, "I must have left my wallet in my carry-on, but I have cash, and I'm here with the NMA conference. I'm a registered nurse, not a teenager."

"I understand, but I can't serve you without seeing your ID."

"Look, here's my conference pass with my name on it." She held up her badge. "Do you know of any eighteen-year-old nurses?"

"I'm really sorry," said the bartender. "Can't you just grab it from your room?"

"No, I can't. The conference is here, but I'm not staying here. My hotel's a half hour walk from here."

"I'm really sorry, miss," said the bartender before moving off.

"For fuck's sake," said the woman.

Teddy stole a glance and noted that she was wearing sensible white sneakers—very nurse-like. As he watched her sweep everything back into the black hole that was her book bag, he noticed something else too. One perfect pink nipple almost poking through the loose knit of her ivory sweater. Sexually speaking, she wasn't his type at all; he favored trashy-looking blondes with tramp stamps and big boobs and fake tans. But something about that exposed nipple stirred him. That and the fact that she had no interest in him. And when she audaciously picked up the pint he had ordered as a placeholder and chugged a third of it, it sealed the deal. He would take her up to his suite and try to screw away his misery.

"Stella," she said, wrinkling her nose and placing the beer glass back on the bar. She burped into her hand.

"I can order all the Guinness you'd like via room service," he said. She surveyed him, taking in the finely tailored suit, the heavy watch, the shiny shoes.

"I promise I'm neither a rapist nor axe murderer." He gestured to the bartenders. "They can vouch for me, I'm a regular."

She didn't reply. She just reached over and squeezed his bicep a few times.

"What was that for?" he asked.

"I was just seeing if I could take you."

Teddy smiled. "And what have you concluded?"

"That there's a Guinness upstairs with my name on it."

Teddy was supremely hammered when they got to the suite. He kicked off his shoes and flopped onto the sofa.

Kelly dropped her bag and papers and took a wide-eyed wander through the sumptuous rooms.

"Quite the digs," she said. "Those bathrooms are nuts. And look at this view."

"It's a good view," said Teddy.

"Now I'm thinking champagne instead of beer," she joked.

"On any other day, I would agree," said Teddy. "But no champagne today."

"And why is that?"

"Because today is the day my insufferable boss demoted me."

"Damn. Sorry to hear that." She opened the minibar, pulled out two tiny bottles of Grey Goose, and tossed one to Teddy. "Maybe you should tell him or her to go fuck themselves."

Teddy laughed. "I wish." He cracked open the bottle and drank.

"Let me guess—you have a family to support."

"Wrong. I am entirely untethered."

"Mortgage? Crushing debt?"

"Neither."

"So, why then?"

Teddy hesitated. Normally, he wouldn't share personal information, but because he was exceedingly well-oiled and his companion was from out of town and entirely out of his realm, his reluctance slid away. "Because my boss also happens to be my father."

"Yikes. And he demoted you? That's fucked, psychologically speaking."

"He also promoted my little brother, who is borderline

incompetent and now technically above me." Teddy drained his drink and tossed the little bottle across the room.

"You know what I think we should do?" said Kelly.

"No, what should we do?" said Teddy.

"We should take a bath."

"What?"

"That tub in there was clearly designed for two."

Teddy sighed. "To be honest, I think I may be too wasted to have sex."

"Who said anything about sex? Let's take a hot bath. I can massage your feet."

Teddy laughed. "You're an odd bird, aren't you?"

She smiled and headed for the bathroom. A few moments later he heard water gushing into the tub. A strangely comforting sound. When was the last time someone ran a bath for him? He must have been a child. It must have been Patsy, his nanny.

Kelly returned and hit the minibar again, but this time she got glasses and cracked the ice cube tray and made proper drinks. "C'mon," she said, leading him to the bedroom.

He watched her strip down and carry their drinks into the bathroom.

Her body surprised him. She looked so young and tiny and pale. He took off his clothes and laid them on the bed.

"Go ahead," she said, dimming the bathroom lights. "I put in some of that lemongrass body wash."

Teddy eased himself into the tub with a deep sigh. The water was hot and fragrant.

Kelly handed him his drink, climbed in and turned off the taps, which were cleverly mounted in the center of the tub, allowing each of them to recline comfortably at opposite ends.

"Mmm," he said, taking an icy sip of vodka.

She took his right foot in her hands and started massaging it, pressing firmly into the arch with her thumbs.

"Oh, that's good," he said, taking his first deep breath in two weeks. "This was a good idea."

"I'm full of them," said Kelly, smirking.

She had a pretty face. Like a pixie, with big blue pixie eyes. But her chest was so flat she looked almost prepubescent. He didn't like that. He didn't get why anyone would. "Are you really twenty-eight?" he asked.

"I really am," she said.

"Where are you from?"

"Brandon, Manitoba."

"That's near Winnipeg, right?"

"Not too far."

He was faking. He'd never even heard of Brandon, which filled him with a kind of relief. A nobody from nowhere.

"So," she said with a wry smile, taking up his left foot and squeezing hard in just the right spot, "what are we going to do about that father of yours?"

7

Once again, Alana woke early and headed down to the beach. She had been charged with catching her brother and Kelly in flagrante delicto, but Teddy didn't make an appearance, so she just stayed for the yoga (which in her case meant forty minutes of awkward labored stretching). Afterward, she walked with Kelly back to the house, where Mrs. Keith prepared coffee for them. Kelly took hers and Ed's up to their room. Alana enjoyed her cappuccino and a warm banana muffin on the patio. The sun was starting to yellow through the haze, and it would have been a very pleasant experience if not for intermittent cracks of gunfire and the thought of deer crumpling nearby.

Alana was scheduled to fly home that evening, and while she couldn't wait to kiss and hug Lily—feeling her absence so keenly it was almost a physical pain (a kind of gnawing between gut and heart)—she also felt deeply unsettled by the thought of leaving. It was as if a thousand invisible hooks were gently tugging at her, telling her to stay—an intuition that something bad was going to happen at the party and she needed to be there to mitigate or prevent it.

She checked the time and then scraped her chair across the flagstones to the outer edge of the patio so she could see when Kelly and her dad left for their morning walk. She wanted to try to get into Lillian's room before she left for the airport. Ever since she'd discovered the locked door, it had been playing on her mind. Why was it the only room in the house that was secured? Ed left his office and bedroom wide-open. What was in Lillian's room that needed to be protected or hidden? And what exactly had he been doing in there the other day that required the door to be bolted? She was determined to find out. Of course, she'd have to be more careful now that Teddy was up there sleeping in her old room. How convenient that it was so close to Ed and Kelly's bedroom. No wonder he hadn't chosen to stay in one of the cottages. She wondered how many late-night or early morning rendezvous they'd risked while Ed slumbered.

It was just after eight when she finally spotted the duo heading down the path to the main road—her dad leaning on his rolling walker and sporting his new pink sweater, Kelly in a wide-brimmed hat and yellow sundress. Alana took her coffee cup into the kitchen, where Mrs. Keith was making dough in what looked like an industrial stand mixer.

"Thank you, dear, just leave it," said Mrs. Keith.

"You're making bread?" said Alana, placing her cup in the white enamel sink.

"Baguettes for lunch."

"Mmm, nice. I'll see you later." *Good*, thought Alana, that'll keep her in the kitchen for a while. She hurried through the dining room and darted up the stairs to the second floor. Her father's bedroom door was closed but unlocked. She slipped inside and shut the door quietly behind her. Now, where would her father hide a key? She rummaged quickly through his drawers, making sure to squeeze the rolled-up socks carefully—at home she had tucked her safe-deposit box key in a pair of wool socks. No luck. She felt along the underside of every drawer, where keys were always taped and hidden in movies and TV shows (but apparently not in real life). The bedside tables were full of prescription bottles, GUM Soft-Picks, reading glasses, squashed tubes of A535 and a rusted tin of something called Bag Balm. Yuck. In the walk-in closet, she searched through every pocket, shook every shoe and rifled through a heavy wooden jewelry box that contained more than a dozen men's watches— all tossed in haphazardly, all smelling of stale cologne. And this in his summerhouse, thought Alana. How many Patek Philippes and 18-karat gold Rolexes did he store at his home in Victoria? Ridiculous. She could probably sell any one of these and live comfortably for a year. On impulse, she reached into the jumble, pulled out a gold Montblanc with a snake coiled around the face, and slipped it into her pocket. She closed the box and headed for the home office. If she couldn't find the key there, she'd return to the master bedroom and go through the en suite bathroom.

She started with the two imposing oak desks that faced away from each other on opposite sides of the room, methodically scouring each drawer. She found a couple of old keys, but they were far too small for the lock on the bedroom door. She went through the filing cabinets, being as thorough as possible, given how quickly she needed to act. She peeled back the corners of the rug, took pictures off the wall and scanned their backings, pushed a chair over to the door and stood on it to see if he had placed the key on the doorframe. Nope (it was remarkably dust-free, though, so kudos to Mrs. Keith and the cleaning staff, thought Alana). She had just returned the chair to its proper place when she heard Teddy emerge from her old room and go into the bathroom. Alana ducked behind the office door, which she'd left slightly ajar, and stood perfectly still. She heard her brother take a ridiculously long piss—just when it seemed like it couldn't go on any longer, it did. Then it stopped. And started again.

As Alana waited it out, an item on the windowsill, half obscured by a gauzy curtain, caught her eye. It was an antique set of matryoshka dolls that had brought her much delight when she was a child. There were twelve nesting dolls altogether, each one painted with the finest detail, even the teensiest one at the center, which was only a few millimeters tall. Alana instantly recalled an Easter egg hunt from when she was around eight years old. The family always vacationed somewhere hot during March break but then spent Easter weekend on Alfred Island. On Easter Sunday her father would hide a specified number of candy eggs around the house, and she and her siblings would be charged with finding as many as they could (typical that her father would turn everything into a competition, she thought now). Whoever found the most eggs would get the grand prize: a custom-made chocolate Easter bunny that stood three feet tall. Teddy or Martin almost always won, and she would be frustrated by how long it took them to eat the thing. She never won, but Lillian did once, and she gave the bunny to Alana, who finished it in record time, much to the dismay of their parents.

On this particular year, her father hid precisely 150 eggs. These were not merely tucked behind couch pillows or atop bookshelves as in most homes. No, these eggs were secreted inside vitamin bottles, or poked into the fingers of gloves, or slipped into an egg carton at the very back of the fridge. Teddy and Martin had managed to tie in first place with forty eggs each. She couldn't remember how many she and Lillian had found, only that the overall total added up to 149, and none of the children could find the last egg. Martin and Teddy searched the longest, each determined to claim the grand prize—more for the bragging rights than the chocolate—but they never found it. And their father refused to divulge the location. He also refused, on principle, to reward any of the children with the bunny since there was no clear victor. He gave it instead to a staff member to take home. (Teddy, bitter about that, bragged that he'd rubbed snot and spit all over it before it left the house, which made Alana cry and Lillian tell on him. He denied it, of course.) It was more than four months later that Alana inadvertently came across the missing egg, hidden deep inside the matry- oshka set where the last few dolls usually nested. Beneath the gold wrapping, the chocolate had gone white with age, but she ate it anyway and never told anyone.

Alana heard the toilet flush and the taps run. A few mo- ments later, she heard Teddy leave the bathroom and thud down the stairs. She waited a couple seconds and then made for the windowsill. She carried the nesting dolls into the bathroom, locking the door behind her. She opened the first doll, the second doll, the third, the fourth, the fifth, the sixth—damn it, this was time-consuming (but even under these fraught circumstances, a little delightful). She got to the ninth doll, which, to her satisfaction, did not contain dolls ten to twelve but rather one silver key.

She had to hurry. Alana estimated she had roughly fifteen minutes before her dad and Kelly returned from their walk. In that time, she would have to reassemble the matryoshka set, put it back in the office and get the hell out of there. She'd placed the split-apart dolls in the tub and closed the shower curtain to hide them, lest anyone use the bathroom in the interim. With shaking fingers, she brought the key to the lock. It slid in and turned smoothly. She pushed the door open and ducked inside, closing it quickly behind her, finding herself in total darkness. She groped for the light switch and flicked it on, managing one quick sweep of the room before her eyes filled with tears.

With two glaring exceptions—a large black safe squatting smack-dab in the middle of the room and what appeared to be black garbage bags duct-taped across the window—the space looked exactly as it had when Lillian last slept there nearly thirty years ago. Everything was perfectly preserved and eerily intact, right down to the fuzzy ponytail holders scattered across the bedside table, one of which, Alana observed with a pang, had a tiny tangle of her sister's hair still caught in it.

Alana remembered many things about this room: the intricate iron headboard painted white; the baby-blue-and-pale-green tobacco leaf quilt; the framed posters of sports stars, Steffi Graf, Silken Laumann, Mary Lou Retton; the lamp with the rearing ceramic horse at its base (and the tiny chip in its tail). But she had forgotten so many other familiar elements: the antique jewelry box crowned with a silver cherub riding a swan, the *My Little Pony* collection, displayed on its own lighted glass shelf, the giant stuffed koala that sat on a white wicker chair in the corner with Lillian's ukulele propped between its paws. Seeing these remnants of her sister's childhood tore Alana's heart wide-open. And there was that framed photo of Kat when she was pregnant with Lillian (as a child, Alana would gaze at this relic and marvel at how fresh and serene her mother looked. She didn't realize at the time that it was because Kat hadn't yet met Ed).

And, oh, all of Lillian's clothes were still here too—the impossibly narrow blue jeans and shorts, the pastel baby doll pajamas, the faded Vancouver Canucks sweatshirt that Lillian lived in (and her mother despised), the tiny cotton underwear and sockettes patterned with hearts and polka dots and teddy bears and stars—folded neatly in dresser drawers.

It was all too much for Alana. And she had no time to process.

She turned her attention to the black rectangular safe, which sat so incongruously in the middle of the room. It reminded her of the obelisk in *2001: A Space Odyssey*. What the hell was it doing here? What treasure could it possibly contain if her father was fine with leaving a million dollars' worth of watches in an unlocked box down the hall?

It was time to skedaddle. It really was. But Alana couldn't resist trying a combination on the safe's digital keypad before fleeing. With an odd feeling of certainty, she typed in Lillian's birthdate: 06/01/1979. Nothing. Damn it. She'd thought for sure that would work. She typed in the date of

Lillian's death: 01/13/1992. No. She would have to come back. Alana moved to the door and opened it an inch, listening. She was about to make her escape when she heard someone jogging up the stairs, probably Teddy.

Whoever it was went into the bathroom and closed the door. As Alana shrank back into the room, a blast of anxiety surged through her. What if her brother decided to take a morning shower? She pictured him turning on the taps and soaking the matryoshka dolls before stepping in and discovering them. She pressed her ear against the mutual wall and heard nothing, which meant, she hoped, that he was on the toilet. While she waited, she thought about possible combinations on the digital lock. Maybe her father used his own birthdate. Or Kelly's. Of course, he may not have used a birthdate at all. If he were clever, the combination would be something entirely random. She decided to try his birthday. What was it again? April 13. But what year? She had to do the math to figure it out: 1943. She was about to key in 04/13/1943 when it occurred to her that she had been typing month/day/year, when perhaps she should have been typing day/month/year or even year/month/day. If this safe was like the one they had at the shelter, she had only three failed attempts before it shut down for an hour as a safety precaution.

Alana heard the toilet flush and then the taps run. She listened at the door as the person left the bathroom and moved heavy-footed down the hallway and stairs. It was past time to get those dolls back together and flee, but Alana wanted to try one more combination on the keypad. She took a deep breath and again entered Lillian's birthday but this time in a different order: 01/06/1979.

The safe made a faint *szuszing* sound and clicked open.

8

Kateryna "Kat" Kowalchuk was more than ready to become Mrs. Ed Shropshire. She was only twenty-four years old but she was tired. Very tired. One child, and another on the way. Two jobs. Zero help from anyone, anywhere. Her mother, Liliya, had died of pancreatic cancer four years ago—a fleeting yet somehow also interminable six months from diagnosis to death. Liliya's dying wish had been for Kat to leave her Food Science and Technology program at the University of Alberta and travel back to Calgary to have the baby that her Applied Swine Science professor had knocked her up with.

"Forget school," Liliya said. "Come home and have the child. It's not like you're losing money." Kat had received an athletic scholarship in volleyball. Liliya said, "This baby wasn't an accident. It was fate. Your father is going to need you."

Liliya seemed unconcerned about dying but profoundly worried about how her husband was going to manage when she was gone. Who would take care of him? Who would cook and clean and shop and do all the things that needed to be done? The man couldn't boil water, let alone plan and cook a meal for himself. He had never operated the washing machine or dryer. She feared he would be totally lost. Bereft and adrift. He already drank too much. What would happen when he was alone and heartbroken, when Liliya was no longer there to water down his vodka and make sure he had some food in his belly to absorb the drink?

"You're the end of the line for this family," Liliya told Kat. "If you don't have this child, our family is done."

"I could finish school and have kids later," Kat pointed out.

"Maybe," said her mother. "Maybe not. What if something goes wrong? What if something grows? This could be our last chance."

Liliya's sister, Kat's aunt, had wanted children more than anything, but a combination of endometriosis and uterine fibroids had spoiled that dream. Her husband left when he realized procreation was an impossibility, and she ended up moving to Chicago to start her life over. Liliya's brother didn't have kids either. He was a "confirmed bachelor" who didn't want to play it straight with a wife and family.

And so, feeling confused and sad and more than a little burdened with her family's genetic endurance, Kat took the money her prof had given her for the abortion and bought a train ticket home to Calgary. She moved back into the family home to prepare for the birth of her child and the death of her mother.

Three months later, Liliya was gone.

Six weeks after the funeral, Kat's father handed her a check for thirty-eight hundred dollars and asked her to please vacate the family home. He had started a romance with the bartender at his favorite watering hole and she would be moving in with her teenaged son and two German shepherd pups.

So much for bereft and adrift.

Kat's mother was right about one thing though. Her pregnancy wasn't an accident. She later learned through the grapevine that her prof was known for a particular slippery trick: making a show of putting on a condom but then palming it off before getting down to business with whichever female student he'd made sure was too drunk to notice (not difficult in Kat's case, since she truly loved to drink). Of course, most of those young women were on the pill. Kat was not. She'd been on it for a while but went off after gaining five pounds.

For Kat, not drinking was the worst thing about being pregnant. Even worse than having to find an apartment and a job six weeks before she was supposed to give birth. Nobody wanted to hire a pregnant woman and nobody wanted to rent to an unemployed about-to-be single mom. She was lucky to eventually find a basement apartment in the home of an old lady who lived with three Yorkshire terriers, and confessed she didn't really need the income but was interested in having someone "nice" living in the flat below her. Someone to talk to every day, Kat feared (and she wasn't wrong about that), but without options, she settled into the furnished basement.

On a cold dark night soon after, Kat's water broke. She

took a taxi to the hospital through drizzle and fog and wet snow plopping from the tree branches onto the streets. The driver thought she was crying because of contractions, not because she'd never felt more alone in her entire life.

Seventeen hours later, her daughter was in her arms. She named her Lillian, after her mother. Kat took her home to what felt more like a burrow than an apartment and spent the next several months in a hallucinatory blur. The baby was not a good sleeper. She cried and cried. And for some inexplicable reason, would only latch on to the left breast. This meant Kat had to constantly pump out the right one, which would swell to the point of pain. The more Lillian grew, the more she resembled Kat's Applied Swine Science professor—those same hazel eyes staring back at her. Three months to the day after Lillian was born, Kat switched to formula and started drinking again. When the money from her father ran out, Kat began providing aftercare for working parents who sent their kids to the elementary school across the street from where she lived. Between that, babysitting in the evening (the local parents came to trust her with their offspring), and doing various chores for her elderly landlady, she was able to survive the first two years of her daughter's life.

Then came Niko—one of the parents who picked up his son each weekday at five thirty. Unlike the other parents who ferried their offspring away as quickly as possible, Niko lingered long and flirted brazenly with Kat. And why not? She was an attractive woman who had always received a lot of male attention. And she'd made sure that within months of birthing Lillian, her body had returned to its formerly lithe and muscled state. Even her belly flattened, thanks to a regimen of six hundred sit-ups per day. She couldn't say she was surprised when Niko showed up at her door one night with a bottle of wine.

Soon, Niko was visiting regularly (and had learned to bring two bottles), his wife thinking he was either working or at the gym. Sometimes, when he was ostensibly out for an after-dinner jog, he'd stop by for a quick grope session at her door, pressing her hand to his crotch, saying, "Look what you do to me." But most of his visits were more substantial and Kat could feel their connection growing.

Niko was more cute than handsome. Dark curly hair, long lashes. He was a tad hirsute for her liking, and would surely go to fat in middle age, but he suited her in bed, and he was funny and tender. His son, Thom, was always kind to Lillian, and Kat started thinking about the four of them as a future family. Niko did too. He talked a lot about leaving his wife, who he said was driving him nuts with her jealousy and mood swings. "She asks about you all the time," said Niko. "She's crazy suspicious."

With good reason, thought Kat, but she let him go on about it. Kat had encountered Niko's wife on a few occasions when she came in his stead to pick up Thom. There was a palpable tension during their exchanges, a kind of sharpened awareness as the woman took Kat's measure, but she was always polite and friendly. She didn't read as unstable.

But Niko claimed she was a paranoid harpy and disgustingly clingy. "That's another thing I love about you," he told Kat. "You're not needy, like she is." This pointed praise worked for a time, and Kat prided herself on making no demands of Niko, but as they approached the first year anniversary of the affair, she found it increasingly difficult to tamp down her feelings. She was sick of being the subterranean sidepiece, and started pressuring him to leave his wife.

"I'm going to tell her," he'd say every time they met up. And then, when she threatened to break it off, he adopted a new mantra: "I'm going to tell her this weekend."

But each Monday, Niko returned with an excuse. His wife had just been laid off from her job; it wasn't a good time to tell her. Thom was going through something difficult at school; he couldn't tell her now. "I know this sucks," he'd say. "Thank you for being so patient with me."

But she wasn't patient. She was fed up. And after he missed seeing her on her birthday because he had to attend a family dinner at his in-laws', she realized she would have to be the one to move things along.

That was the night Kat drank a mickey of vodka and took the gift he'd surreptitiously slipped her the previous afternoon when he was picking up Thom—a gold brooch in the shape of a cat (with emeralds for eyes)—and used it to make sieves of all the condoms in her bedside table.

Kat was seventeen weeks pregnant when she told Niko the news. She didn't expect him to be instantly thrilled—didn't think they'd be off house hunting that afternoon—but she also didn't expect him to groan and pull his hair and cry, "No, no, no, no, no," while pacing back and forth across her apartment. This outburst was followed by a cascade of fury. How could she do this to him? Didn't she know he already had a family to support? Why didn't she tell him earlier when they could've easily taken care of it?

He told her she would have to have an abortion immediately. She told him to get the hell out of her apartment.

He returned the following evening, all contrite and lovey-dovey, saying he wanted to be with her but didn't think they should start their lives together with a squalling infant. He swore that as soon as she ended the pregnancy, he would leave his wife. "My hand to God," he said. "And we'll start a family someday, I promise, Kitty-Kat." Then he kissed her and tried to make her laugh by nuzzling her neck and singing the Meow Mix jingle in her ear, which had always worked in the past.

She pulled away. "And what if I don't want to end the pregnancy?"

"Well...I don't know, Kat. I guess I'd have to give you some money every month. But you know...you and I would be toast."

"Toast?" she said flatly.

"You know what I mean. And just so you're aware, according to family law rules, the money would come out to less than ten percent of my annual income. You couldn't live on it."

"You've checked already, have you?"

"Come on, Kat. What do you expect?" Niko rubbed the back of his neck. "I hate to ask this, but...are you a hundred percent sure it's mine?"

A sharp exhalation through flared nostrils. "I'm a hundred percent sure it's *mine*."

Niko sighed and checked the time. "I have to get going. I hope you'll choose the smart route, Kat."

In the end, she decided the smart route was to take 20 percent of Niko's yearly income in exchange for her silence. She wouldn't blab to his wife and wouldn't raise the child in Calgary.

Kat relocated to Banff. She could still camouflage her

pregnancy, which enabled her to quickly find employment. She got a part-time job at the Banff Springs Hotel and picked up a regular waitressing shift at Melissa's Restaurant. When she started to show a few weeks later, her employers weren't thrilled about it, but she pledged to work until the day she gave birth—as she had with Lillian.

It was a little over a month after she arrived in Banff that Kat met her future husband on the slopes of the Lake Louise Ski Resort. Kat was teaching Lillian how to ski, and people all around were marveling at how adroit the little girl was.

"There's an Olympian in the making," said a handsome man who was teaching his two young sons on the same hill. "How old is she?"

"Three," said Kat. "Well, almost four."

"Wow. And how long has she been skiing?"

"This is her first time out."

"No," said the man.

"I swear," said Kat with a proud smile.

"You must be quite the teacher."

"No." Kat laughed. "She's a natural."

"She really is." The man watched the girl ski nimbly over to her mother's side. "What's your name, dear?"

"Lillian," she said.

"Well, Lillian, you're a very good skier." The man smiled down at her.

"What do you say?" Kat prompted.

"Thank you," said Lillian, wiping her nose with a sopping mitten.

"Teddy, Martin, come over here," called the man to his sons. "This little girl is going to show you how it's done."

The boys, who were flinging handfuls of snow at one

another, tromped over to their father and stared dubiously at Lillian.

"Hi," said Kat. "This is Lillian. She's just learning too." She noticed that the boys and their father were all outfitted in shiny, high-end gear.

"These guys have had lessons, but they still want to stick to the bunny hill," said the man.

"Well, they're young," said Kat, guessing that the boys were no more than a year or two older than Lillian. They were beautiful children, especially the older one, who looked like an angel with his pink cheeks and strawberry-blond curls.

"Got any tips for them?" the man asked Lillian.

"Don't be scared to fall," she said.

The man laughed. He had big white teeth. Movie-star teeth. "That's excellent advice."

"Can we go?" said the older boy.

"Don't be rude, Teddy," said the man.

"That's OK," said Kat. "We should go too."

"Well, it was nice meeting you, Lillian and…?"

"Kat."

"Edward Shropshire," said the man, as if it would mean something to her. Maybe he was an actor. He was certainly handsome enough. He extended his hand for a shake.

"Nice to meet you," Kat said, shaking his gloved hand.

"No offense," he said, eyeing Kat's six-months-pregnant belly. "But shouldn't your husband be giving the lessons at this point?"

"What husband?" said Kat with a wry smile.

"Ah, I see."

"Yeah," said Kat.

"Well, in that case, you and Lillian should have dinner with me and the boys."

"That would be nice, but we have to catch the shuttle back to Banff. And the last one leaves at five thirty."

"Are you staying at the Banff Springs? You can come in our car and we could have dinner at the hotel."

Kat worked as a spa concierge at the hotel. The thought of being wined and dined there by this handsome man amused her. "We actually live in Banff," she said.

"Then it's settled. And now you have time for another run."

On the lift, the man pressed his leg firmly against Kat's. She couldn't decide if he was oblivious, confident or a little too aggressive. He was very good-looking—square-jawed, lean, tall. And he smelled nice; his cedar-scented cologne mingled perfectly with the crisp, cold air.

The kids were chattering among themselves, which gave her an opportunity to ask him in a low voice, "Maybe I'm off base here, but you're not actually trying to pick up a pregnant lady, are you?"

He smiled. "Would that be a problem?"

"No. It's just...surprising."

"It's also just skiing and dinner."

"I know. Sorry." She blushed and turned away, feeling stupid. Chastised.

But then he leaned in and whispered, his breath hot in her ear, "And possibly dessert."

She felt a spasm of desire. Followed by relief. Maybe she wasn't being presumptuous. Maybe he was trying to start something. Or maybe he was just a weirdo with a fetish for pregnant women. She was about to crack a joke about it, but the man had turned his attention to the children.

Dinner that night was sublime. Kat felt like she had stepped into an alternate reality, one that was free of stress and full of delights. Everyone treated Ed Shropshire with deference, and she soon learned why. He wasn't an actor; he was a big mucky-muck who owned businesses all over the world: distilleries, a shipping company, oil refineries, pulp and paper mills, a chain of luxury hotels across Europe and Asia. They took their meal in a private dining room with a stunning view of the mountain. When Kat couldn't decide what to order—secretly agonizing over this rare chance at a fancy meal—Ed took control and ordered food for the entire table: almost every entrée and appetizer on the menu, so Kat could sample widely. He engaged the kids in conversation and was patient with his boys and sweet with Lillian. And he treated Kat as if she were his partner, not some bimbo he'd picked up on the ski hill, not someone he had to hide or be embarrassed about. For the first time in her life, she could imagine what it felt like to be someone's wife. She liked it.

After dinner, a nanny who traveled with the family came to collect the boys and take them up to the suite she shared with the children.

"Lillian can go along, if you'd like to continue the evening," Ed told Kat.

"You don't mind?" Kat asked the nanny.

"Not at all. We're just going to read some stories and maybe watch a movie," she said. The woman looked to be in her early fifties and seemed cheerful and trustworthy.

"Do you want to go with the boys to watch a movie?" Kat asked Lillian.

"OK."

Ed and Kat moved to a corner nook in the lounge, where they spent hours talking. She told him about why she'd left school, about Niko, and her two jobs. They bonded over their not-so-distant losses, Kat's mom and Ed's wife, who had died of postpartum preeclampsia just hours after giving birth to Martin.

"Oh my god, that's tragic," said Kat. "I can't imagine how hard that must have been for you."

"It was especially hard on Teddy," he said. "For a while anyway. Thank god he was so young when it happened."

"That's a blessing," said Kat. "Kids are resilient."

"Have you had any issues with your pregnancy?"

"No. Not even morning sickness. Just some fatigue."

"Well, that makes sense, working two jobs and taking care of a toddler. How far along are you?"

"Six months."

"And do you know what you're having?"

"Another girl," said Kat.

"Very nice," said Ed.

"To be honest, I was kind of hoping for a boy this time." Kat whispered it, as if the baby might hear and feel wounded. "But that's OK."

"Maybe in the future," said Ed. He smiled warmly.

Kat grew quiet and stared at the candle on the table, watching the smooth wobble of the amber flame. Fat snowflakes drifted languidly outside the window, eddying like drunk insects around the lamps on the grounds of the hotel. She did not want the night to end but she was beyond tired and still had to collect Lillian and get a taxi back to their apartment. When Ed suggested booking a room for her and Lillian, she gratefully accepted. She felt so warm and full and sleepy, and couldn't bear the thought of stepping out into the cold night.

When they got to the nanny's suite, they found the boys somehow still awake at midnight, but Lillian was asleep, curled up with her thumb in her mouth.

"Do you want to wake her? Or shall I carry her for you?" asked Ed.

"That would be amazing, thanks. It might be hard to get her up." In truth, Kat could easily carry Lillian herself, but she wanted Ed to accompany her.

They moved through a labyrinth of corridors to get to the room. Kat went in first and peeled back the bedding so Ed could lay the sleeping child inside the sheets.

"Thank you," Kat said. "Thank you for everything— dinner, the room... I feel very spoiled."

"It was my pleasure. That was the most relaxing evening I've had in a long time."

"Me too," said Kat.

"Well...I should let you sleep." He moved toward the door. Kat followed.

"Are you guys skiing tomorrow?" she asked.

"No, I have to get back to work. We're leaving early."

"Ah."

A slight pause before he smiled, told her to charge break-fast to the room, and bid her good-night.

Kat felt deflated. She'd been floating all day, but now her chest was instantly filled with lead. The perfect man had just walked out of her life. She could tell there was a moment when he'd thought about kissing her and opted not to, which, of course, made sense. He hadn't talked about a girlfriend, but it would be hard to believe he didn't have one. Or several. Plus, she was pregnant. And already had a kid. If only Kat had met him when she was childless. They'd be having sex right now; she was sure of it. God, she was craving a drink. She'd watched Ed imbibe all night, while she swallowed pot after pot of disgusting chamomile tea. She thought about ordering a glass of wine to the room but was so exhausted she decided to just go to bed. Sleep, however, did not come easily. Kat felt strangely unsettled, as if the order of things had been disturbed, as if fate had somehow been derailed, and now the universe was out of whack.

Eventually, she crashed and slept hard. When Kat woke in the morning, she had one moment of drowsy pleasure before the uneasy feeling crowded her chest. She couldn't shake it that day, or the next. Only when she arrived at the spa for her shift, and a coworker handed her a FedEx package from Elpida Canada Corp. in Vancouver, did the feeling begin to relax. Inside the oversize cardboard envelope was a note from Ed:

Horribly cliché, but I can't stop thinking about you. I'd love for you and your daughter to join me and the boys for Easter at our holiday home on Alfred Island. Tickets enclosed. Call my secretary for details. Ed.

P.S. It seems I am trying to pick up a pregnant lady.

P.P.S. "Don't be scared to fall."

The uneasy feeling instantly lifted. Everything was righted. Aligned and effervescent. The world was full of light and happiness.

Kat and Lillian traveled to the island and, when Easter weekend was over, to Ed's home in Oak Bay, Victoria. They never returned to the apartment in Banff (goodbye moldy bathroom, goodbye peeling paint, goodbye fetid carpet that smelled like cream of mushroom soup). Ed and Kat were wed in a private ceremony with only their children, the pastor, and Ed's father in attendance. Ed wanted to marry before the birth of Kat's second child. "That way she'll feel more like mine," he said.

In the weeks following the wedding, Kat basked in leisure and luxury. It was wonderful to sleep as much as she liked, shop for the baby, and go for mani-pedis and aromatherapy pregnancy massages while the nanny or Ed took care of Lillian, and the housekeeper took care of everything else. But she couldn't wait to give birth. She wanted her body back so she could really make the most of her new lifestyle. She was going to go to fancy stores and buy new clothes, she was going to travel, and play tennis, and sample the glorious wines in Ed's cellar, and blow his mind in bed. She was ready to start living her dream life with her dream husband. Ed was so caring and solicitous of her wellbeing, so excited about the impending birth of her child. *Their* child. She would be called Alana after Ed's late mom, and everything was going to be brilliant once she was born.

Kat truly believed her life was on a splendid upward trajectory.

And when she went into labor a full eight days before her longed-for due date—and her husband accompanied her to the hospital to be by her side during the delivery—she was certain of it. But things didn't go quite as expected. Even though the baby wasn't full-term, she was big. Very big. Just under ten pounds. And she seemed quite resolved to remain where she was. After ten and a half hours of labor, the obstetrician recommended a C-section, but Kat resisted. She didn't want the scar or the ugly pooch she'd seen on women at the gym and beach—that unavoidable lip of fat curling over the bikini line. She was not going to present her new husband with that, thank you very much. An epidural was administered and Kat struggled on with labor for another two hours. There was excitement when the baby finally crowned, followed by alarm when the head disappeared back inside, like a turtle retreating into its shell. The obstetrician determined that the baby's shoulder was lodged behind Kat's pelvic bone, which, judging by the reactions of the medical team, was a very bad thing. An extra nurse was hurriedly summoned. While the two original nurses (who looked remarkably like Cagney and Lacey) pushed Kat's thighs onto her chest, the new nurse—a stout little thing with round glasses—stood on a chair and pressed repeatedly above the pubic bone in an attempt to dislodge the baby.

No go.

The doctor told Kat and Ed that in order to maneuver the child into a deliverable position, he would have to do an episiotomy. In tears, Kat begged him not to, said she would have the C-section instead, but it was too late for that now.

"I'm sorry," said the doctor. "We're doing this."

Ed intervened. "Is it absolutely necessary?"

"If you care about the health of your daughter."

"Go ahead," said Ed. But the doctor was already making

the incision. And though she could feel nothing but vague movement and pressure below her rib cage, Kat wept as ten pounds of baby was yanked from her body. Even with the extra surgical opening, Kat suffered a third-degree tear from vagina to anus.

Good riddance, she thought as she heard Alana's first scream.

"Oh, she's a furry one," said the stout nurse with a laugh. The child's head and torso were covered in tufts of thick black hair.

"Don't worry," said Cagney, clamping the cord. "It's just lanugo." She offered the surgical scissors to Ed (who folded his arms across his chest). "She'll lose it in a few weeks."

Lacey cleaned, weighed, and swaddled the child. She was laid on Kat's chest for a few seconds before being lifted away so that Kat could be taken to an operating room to have her ravaged perineum sewn back together.

The doctor, dazzled by the presence of a billionaire in his midst, leaned over to Ed and said, "Don't worry, I'll throw in an extra stitch for Dad." Kat heard this as her bed was being wheeled out of the room, but it didn't register at the time.

Lacey tried to hand Alana to her father, but Ed was so repelled by the giant baby that he recoiled and fled.

Ed never took to the girl. It didn't help that for the first three months of her life Alana looked like a fat old man. Her back and shoulders were especially hairy. She also had a bad case of baby acne. Kat was in so much postpartum agony that she refused to breastfeed the child. "Between icing my wound and taking sitz baths, I don't have time to feed *my-*

self, let alone the baby." She was in too much pain to pump milk from her breasts, and needed meds stronger than the over-the-counter array that were safe for breastfeeding. The nanny, who had never cared for an infant before, took over the feeding duties. Whenever Alana cried, even when she was crying to be held (a lot), or was in some kind of distress (often), the nanny would jam a bottle in her mouth. The pacifier rarely worked, but the bottle would usually quiet her.

"She looks like fat Elvis," Ed would say.

Kat would remonstrate, but laugh and laugh.

A pediatrician who visited at the three-month mark was shocked at how overfed the infant was. Nobody, it seemed, was paying attention. Feeling guilty and indignant after being upbraided by the doctor, Kat fired the nanny in a flurry of pique. She was replaced with Patsy, a woman who had raised five of her own babies. Patsy knew what to do. For his part, Ed had no interest in Alana and felt no fondness for the creature. She was embarrassingly ugly—he didn't want people to think she was his offspring—and was the cause of his new wife's ruin. Kat was turning out to be quite the wreck: pilled up, boozy, and bedridden.

Kat felt like she was being punished, as if daring to dream of an easy life had cursed her. Even six months after the birth, she couldn't sit comfortably in a chair, let alone enjoy any of the activities she envisioned herself doing at this point. She would leak urine with every sneeze or cough, and sometimes spray feces when she passed gas (which she could no longer reliably control). It was humiliating. Depressing. Fucking was out of the question. The pain was unbearable. She tried to make it up to Ed in other ways, sexually, but he rebuffed her advances, and she could see he was put off by her. He hated her immobility, her drinking, her reliance on pain medication. He viewed her as weak. A disappointment who had birthed a disappointing child.

Kat had failed her husband in every way.

She went to her doctor at least three times, complaining that something was wrong. He told her to do Kegel exercises and let time work its magic. Only when she insisted on seeing a gynecologist, a woman at Victoria General, did she learn that she had a prolapsed bladder, and that her obstetrician's "husband stitch," the "extra one for Dad" promised to Ed with a wink on the way out of the delivery room, had damaged her vagina and would need to be repaired.

Two corrective surgeries were followed by months of painful recovery and physiotherapy. By the time Kat felt halfway human again, she and Ed were firmly estranged. And yet, he was not willing to cut her loose. He advised her to keep up appearances and enjoy the benefits of being his spouse. He assured her that if she tried to divorce him, he would take her children and use his considerable power to make her life a living hell.

Kat believed him.

And so, she settled reluctantly into the lap of luxury, with a cocktail in one hand and her Dilaudid and no-limit credit card in the other. She traveled the world. She bought all the things.

It took her only twenty years to drink herself to death.

9

The safe in Lillian's room contained three items: a set of wired headphones with the cord wrapped neatly around them, a MacBook Pro laptop, and a small leather notebook. Alana opened the notebook and flipped through it. The first three pages contained a list of email addresses written in her father's cramped all-caps handwriting; the rest were blank. She took out her phone and snapped pictures of the addresses before placing the notebook back in the safe. It was risky to stay any longer, but Alana wanted to know what Ed was hiding. She slid the laptop out and turned it on. The screen lit up with a demand: *Touch ID or Enter Password*. Damn. She tried Lillian's birthdate but it didn't work and she had no time to make arbitrary guesses. Alana turned off the computer and put it back in the safe. Then she slipped out of the room and locked the door behind her. She quickly reassembled the matryoshka dolls with the key inside and returned them to the windowsill in Ed's office.

Alana made her escape without encountering anyone. As she approached her cottage, she was startled by a strange and terrible noise—like a kazoo being tortured. She followed the sound, which was coming from the woods behind the cottage. She walked deeper into the trees until she spotted movement out of the corner of her eye. A fawn in the distance, bleating in distress, standing beside a much larger deer that was lying on its side. Thirty or so yards beyond that, she saw Martin striding toward the animals, holding a rifle. As he got closer, the fawn sprang away and zigzagged toward the beach. Martin lifted the gun and aimed at the fleeing creature.

"No!" Alana yelled.

Martin laughed and lowered the rifle. "You know, it's dangerous to be walking around out here."

"Only if idiots are shooting toward the cottages!" said Alana.

"Really? You're insulting a man with a gun? Anyway, it's not that dangerous, I'm a pretty good marksman."

"Oh my god," said Alana, who had reached the felled doe. It had been shot once in the head. The sorrowful brown eyes were half-open.

"See," said Martin.

"Are you actually doing this for pleasure? Isn't this Darla's job?"

"No, I'm not doing this *for pleasure*," he said, imitating her tone. Then he lowered his voice. "Just getting the lay of the land. It occurred to me that a stray bullet might happen to find its way into a yoga enthusiast one morning."

"You're not serious."

Martin shrugged. "I'd rather resolve things on the boat. But that might be tough to handle on my own, given Teddy's... affiliation."

"You think Dad would forgive you if you shot his fiancée?"

"Forgive me? No. At least, not immediately. He wouldn't forgive me if I spat in her granola. Darla, on the other hand... Darla has no motive. She'd be investigated and fired, but she wouldn't go to prison for a hunting mishap. It would be deemed an accident."

"Are you crazy? You can't do that, Martin."

"It's not a bad plan, if you think about it. Darla sends her staff to hunt in the evening. She's the one who's out early morning. As soon as I see her anywhere in the vicinity, I do the deed and sneak back to bed. We're in cottage 3— nobody's going to see me at that time of the day. And Gertrud's my alibi. We wake up together. Later, when they find Kelly, they'll assume Darla accidentally strafed her."

"But she doesn't hunt in that vicinity. I've heard the shots. They're deeper in the woods."

"Even so, what other explanation would make sense? I may have a motive, but I'm in bed with my girlfriend. And by the way, Darla is a lousy shot. Her kills look like Swiss fucking cheese. It's totally plausible that she misses as much as she hits."

"OK. But even if she doesn't go to jail, she's going to feel like a killer for the rest of her life. Not to mention that Dad would destroy her with some kind of wrongful death civil suit. You're OK with that?"

"I didn't say I was in love with the idea."

"Good. Because it's not happening. I'm not going to let you do that to an innocent woman."

"Really? Aren't you getting on a plane tonight?"

Alana met Martin's insolent gaze and held it. "No," she said. "Change of plans. I've decided to stay for the party."

"Good," said Martin. "I can use your help. And hey, if we can implement plan A, there'll be no need for plan B." Martin hoisted the rifle in his grasp. "See you at lunch. We'll talk logistics later."

"Yup." Alana watched him go. She would now have to change her flight and beseech Ramona to watch Lily for a couple more days. She was longing to see her daughter but also determined to manage her brother, who was turning out to be far more dangerous and unpredictable than she ever imagined.

Oh well, thought Alana, *two extra days*. She could probably have another crack at the computer in her father's safe. She pulled out her phone and studied the list of email addresses she had photographed. Not a single one contained a first or last name. And they were all from an email server she had never heard of: jazzyjazz300@posta.ro; darkeyedjunco@posta.ro; callmemister22@posta.ro; yammycat15@posta.ro... What were the odds of forty-plus emails without a single real name in any of them? She thought about emailing one to see what would happen. But then she had a much better idea.

Alana pocketed the phone and stared at the mournful eye of the felled doe. In the distance she could hear the orphaned fawn's frantic cries.

10

Alana had never been on a ship like the *Andiamo*, though she had been on plenty of yachts. Because of the Shropshires' waterfront home in Oak Bay, and all the summers spent on Alfred Island, there had been a lot of boating in her childhood. Not to mention family vacations in Belize, Turks and Caicos, Italy, France, Monaco, and Croatia. She had been on all kinds of vessels—speedboats, catamarans, sailboats—including all manner of fancy yachts with plush seating and polished wood and gleaming decks and luxurious amenities, but nothing like this. Nothing even close to approaching the multilevel *Andiamo*, which was easily four hundred feet long and boasted four decks (plus a circular glass elevator to access them if the stairs proved too arduous), a beach club with a thirty-five-foot swimming pool, several hot tubs, a gym, a hair salon, a spa, a screening room, ten guest suites, and lodging for a large crew. There was also a helipad and a garage with a speedboat, a limousine tender (for ferrying groups to and from the yacht), four Jet Skis, and a bevy of inflatable toys.

The ship was so large it couldn't even dock at Alfred Island. Ed grumbled about the Islands Trust, the conservationist body that wouldn't allow him to construct a large enough dock on his own property to accommodate his plaything. Alana and her family had to travel via limousine tender to where the *Andiamo* was anchored offshore in order to board. Even from a distance the thing looked imposing, but as they got closer the yacht's true magnitude became apparent. The limousine slipped into the drive-in garage at the ship's bow like a marlin gliding into the mouth of a whale. There was no awkward scrambling from one boat to the other. They merely stepped out into the *Andiamo*, where they were greeted by smiling crew members, all of whom were fit, attractive, dressed in white uniforms, and ready to whisk passengers and baggage to berths.

Everyone in the party went to their rooms to unpack and get settled, except for Alana, who handed her bag to a porter and then set off to explore the ship. It took a while for her to cover all the ground.

The *Andiamo* was awe-inspiring. The *Andiamo* was obscene.

The *Andiamo*, astonishingly, had been decorated with tens of thousands of fresh flowers so that her father and Kelly could see what it would look like on their actual wedding day in a few weeks' time. Everywhere Alana went she encountered exquisite displays of creamy peonies, tight white roses, and a mystery flower that looked like a magical cross between the two. There were ivory orchids with pale pink throats and lush cascades of white wisteria. She had never seen so many flowers so lavishly arranged. The air was sweet with their perfume. Alana was dazzled and appalled. Every blossom would have to be replaced for the wedding. What a shocking waste of money and energy.

To Alana, the *Andiamo* seemed like it should belong to a villain in a James Bond movie, not to her (or anyone's) dad. She was both fascinated and repulsed by the superyacht. As she wandered the decks, taking photos, she couldn't help but be impressed by the cunning use of space and the quality of the finishes on the vessel. The built-in furnishings were curvy, ultramodern, and constructed of the finest materials. The flow was excellent. Whoever had designed the thing knew what they were doing. Everything was sleek and spotless. Alana noted a number of crew members lurking discreetly in her wake, polishing fingerprint smudges off surfaces, picking lint from sofa cushions, swooping up wayward flower petals, then melting into the background again. She wanted to pull them aside and explain that she wasn't an entitled asshole like her father and brothers, that she drove a fifteen-year-old car and worked for a living, but that would be fruitless and embarrassing for everyone involved.

As disgusted as Alana was by the idea of a floating luxury hotel that essentially served the needs of one man, she found herself fantasizing about bringing Lily on board to experience the opulence. How much fun would it be to cruise around the Caribbean for an entire winter? Lily loved swimming. It was when she felt the freest in her body. They could swim, bake in the sun, drift from port to port, stare at the ocean and sky. Lily had barely traveled. Alana couldn't afford it, for one thing, and because of Lily's health, she was nervous about going anywhere remote. Typically, they would spend a week at a resort north of Toronto every summer, and every couple of years go to Florida for a week over Christmas or March break. It was fine, and fun, but it wasn't enough. Alana wanted more for Lily. She knew that unless a miracle cure was somehow discovered in her daughter's lifetime, Lily would be lucky to live into her thirties. Alana was determined to take her places and show her the world while it was still possible. Recently, Lily had become fixated on visiting Greece, probably because a 23andMe DNA test had shown that her heritage was 24 percent Greek. Alana was determined to get her there. And anywhere else Lily wanted to go. Alana would do anything for her daughter. She knew that about herself. She would take her to Greece as soon as she could. But for now, all Alana could do was walk the decks of the *Andiamo* and text pictures to Lily, who kept texting back wow emojis and exclamation marks.

The ship had left the waters off Alfred Island and cruised north through the Sansum Narrows to Burgoyne Bay at the foot of Mount Maxwell. It was this site, off Salt Spring Island, that the wedding planner had deemed appropriately scenic for the anchor to drop and the nuptials to take place. Tonight, Kelly and Ed would give it the once-over and let her know if they approved.

Alana thought it was a lovely spot. She was admiring it from the beach club at the stern of the boat, lying flat on the deck, trying to compose a photograph with the swimming pool in the foreground and the shoreline with the mountain in the background, when she heard Teddy call her name. She looked up and saw her brothers leaning over the railing on the deck above, laughing at her and gesturing for her to join them. When she got upstairs, Teddy told her to turn off her phone and leave it twenty feet away on a chair cushion. He was a lot more cautious than Martin, Alana thought. "What's up, guys?"

"Nothing," said Teddy. "I just wanted to make sure we're all on the same page about tonight."

"I am," said Martin. "And I'm sure Alana is too."

"I thought we agreed we were going to wait until after the wedding," said Alana.

"We did. I'm just checking out of an abundance of caution," said Teddy. "There are going to be way too many eyes on the boat. I don't want any of us trying something risky and fouling up our chances for the future. Right now, Dad is super focused on the wedding and Kelly. In a couple weeks they'll be hitched and he'll be back to obsessing about the business. She'll be alone more. It'll be easier."

"Fine by me," said Martin. "I was planning to relax and enjoy the evening."

"Me too," said Alana. "It's quite the boat."

"Ship," said Teddy. "Yes, it is." He patted the railing in a proprietorial way.

"What time are we supposed to be presentable?" asked Alana.

"Cocktails at the beach club at six," said Teddy. He checked his watch. "I should get going, I have a manicure."

"I should have booked a pedicure," said Martin, inspecting the toes peeking out of his sandals.

Alana noted the Givenchy logo embossed on his black

neoprene slides, and that Martin's toenails looked more tended to than her own.

"You snooze, you lose," said Teddy. "I'll see you later."

"Yeah, smell you later," said Martin.

"What are you, five?" said Alana.

Martin laughed. He waited until Teddy was all the way downstairs before pointing out how conveniently low the railings were.

"I noticed that," said Alana. "It's kind of surprising."

"So, here's the plan. We make sure both Teddy and Kelly get shit-faced. Kelly's hammered every night, so it won't be an issue, but if you can deliver a shooter or two her way, it'll help. Bring her a glass of champagne, toast her happiness, whatever it takes. I'm assuming Teddy doesn't know we're on to him, but he's such a tight-ass, he'll probably be keeping an eye on me and Kelly anyway, so the more booze we can get into him, the better."

"So, you just want me to feed them drinks?"

"Yeah. Until we start moving. I've seen the itinerary, and we're stationary until after dinner. It's cocktails until seven, then we go to the lounge, where they run through the ceremony with the justice of the peace. Dinner is at eight, and the band starts at nine. At ten, the band takes a break and there's some big-ass fireworks display in the bay."

"Why?"

"What do you mean, why? For the wedding."

"You mean, like, just for us?"

"Yeah. From the beach. The wedding planner cooked it up. Personally, I think it's tacky as hell, but Kelly wanted it, so..."

"Hmm."

"I know what you're thinking—everyone's staring at the sky, it's loud, the perfect time to toss missy in the drink. But I doubt it'll be possible. She'll be front and center, watching with Dad."

"That's not what I was thinking."

"Oh. Anyway, the band comes back for another set after the fireworks, and that's when we start moving again. That's when I need you to keep Teddy away from Kelly. By that point, I guarantee you Dad will be in bed. He's never up past ten. Though tonight he'll stay up for the fireworks, but after that there's no way he'll stick around."

"OK."

"We'll be heading back through the Narrows, which is perfect—we won't see another boat at night, and no prying eyes from the shore. So, talk to Teddy, distract him. If he goes to the bar, go up to him, ask his opinion on something. If he goes to take a piss, waylay him when he comes out of the bathroom, say you have something important to tell him. Talk shit about me, I don't care. Just keep him occupied for as long as possible. I'll do the rest."

"When the band comes on for the second set?"

"Yeah. That's our window of opportunity. Everyone will be soused, the music will be blasting, we'll be moving through the Narrows. I mean, I still may not have a chance. Lots of variables, right? But it's our best bet. And if I get the opportunity to flip Asshole of Green Gables over the railing, I'm taking it."

"Oh brother."

"I thought it was funny," said Martin. "Red hair, freckles…"

"Yeah, I get it," said Alana.

"Anyway, I appreciate your help with this. It's nice to know I have one sibling who's not a treacherous fuckhead."

"Speaking of which, what's to prevent Teddy from ratting us out? He's going to be pissed, right?"

"He might be pissed," said Martin, "but he'll still have half an empire someday. He'll get over it. And don't worry, you'll be well taken care of. You know that, right?"

Alana nodded.

"You think your daughter would like the ship?"

"Nah, too puny, she'd hate it."

Martin laughed. "You could fly her here, take it down to Catalina…"

"Hmm."

"Or even Hawaii, if you had some time."

"Maybe someday."

"All right, I'm going to go get cleaned up. Good luck tonight." He squeezed her shoulder. "Don't worry about Teddy. Even if he rats us out, it'll be his word against ours. Teddy is his blood, and Dad might love him more than you, but if it were a question of who to believe, you'd win that contest hands down."

"Miss Morality," said Alana.

"Exactly," said Martin.

It was a lavish evening, even by Ed Shropshire's standards. Alana decided to embrace it and made a bold attempt to eat her own weight in caviar by seven. The champagne on offer was delicious and difficult to resist, but she needed to stay sharp. She had one glass, then cut herself off, figuring if she paced herself, she could have a little wine with dinner. Alana noticed that Teddy seemed quite relaxed and was enjoying the Pol Roger with abandon. He didn't need any coaxing from Alana in that area. Martin, on the other hand, wasn't drinking at all. He feigned a headache to explain it to Gertrud and anyone who asked.

Joyce, the wedding planner, whirled around the *Andiamo* like a toy top, careening from staff to clients, ensuring everything was just so. She was wearing a mint green skirt suit, high-heeled white pumps, and a lot of heavy gold jewelry. She had bobbed hair, dyed jet-black, and a deeply tanned, bronzer-contoured face that had been Botoxed and filled within an inch of its life, rendering her wide mouth somewhat immobile when speaking. The combined effect reminded Alana very much of Zira from the original *Planet of the Apes*, had Zira been decked out in Chanel.

Alana first encountered Joyce during predinner cocktails at the beach club, when the woman berated her for eating a jumbo shrimp and summarily fired her. Alana was wearing black pants and a white blouse—as were the entire catering staff—and Joyce had mistaken her for a server. Alana thought it was hilarious, but Joyce looked like she had been drop-kicked in the stomach when she learned that Alana was Ed's daughter. Abundant apologies ensued and Joyce became overly attentive and chummy after that, although she bristled when Alana referred to her as the wedding planner. "Wedding *producer*," Joyce corrected with a rigid Zira smile.

The run-through of the wedding ceremony was brief but intense. Alana found it deeply uncomfortable to watch her seventy-six-year-old father (who insisted on standing, though he needed to lean on Kelly) spout lovey-dovey vows to the twenty-eight-year-old at his side. It was even worse to hear Kelly recite declarations of devotion to Ed, though she managed to do it convincingly, Alana thought. The justice of the peace, a handsome fortysomething man who looked like he had just tumbled out of an L.L.Bean catalog, acted with admirable equanimity as Ed kept revising every sentence that came out of his mouth, while Joyce watched from the sidelines with shining eyes, as if she were gazing upon the first blush of innocent love. A few glances at Teddy to see how he was taking his girlfriend's betrothal to his father revealed an entirely placid facade. Alana mused that almost everyone in the room was performing. Not Martin though. Martin, who was seated next to Alana, snort-laughed quietly throughout the half-hour service, and she had to nudge him with her knee a few times to get him to behave. After Kelly said "till death do us part," Martin dug his elbow into Alana's ribs. And when Ed leaned in to kiss the bride, and did so with a prolonged and deep tonguing, almost everyone in attendance averted their eyes. The whole thing was uncomfortable.

Ed, Kelly and the justice of the peace stayed behind to tweak the vows, while Joyce steered everyone else to the main deck for dinner. The attentive waitstaff kept the wine-glasses replenished, Alana noted, which meant she could relax and enjoy the first course—marinated wild salmon and crab on a fresh herb salad. She surreptitiously photographed the food and the gorgeous centerpiece and texted the pics to Lily before diving into the delicious offering. She thought about the usual roster of dinners she and her daughter ate night after night, month after month: pasta with jarred spaghetti sauce, stir-fried veggies with peanuts on rice, pierogies and peas, rice and beans with taco chips crumbled on top, avocado wraps and frozen French fries, pizza for a treat on the weekend sometimes. It would be hard to go back to such uninspired fare.

The moment Kelly and Ed joined them at the head table, Joyce signaled to a waiter and their appetizers were placed before them—a vegan version of the first course: green salad only. Ed refused wine, but Kelly accepted a glass. "So, what do you guys think?" she asked. "Any feedback on the evening so far?"

"Are you kidding?" said Gertrud. "Everything is gorgeous. It's going to be perfect. I can't wait."

"Me neither," said Kelly, squeezing Ed's hand.

"The food is incredible," said Gertrud.

"It is good, isn't it?" said Kelly. "I hope Ed's friends don't freak out over the dearth of beef. They're pretty old-school."

"*The Dearth of Beef*—didn't that just win the Booker Prize?" said Alana.

Kelly laughed. "Yes, an unflinching look at a young man's struggle to find burgers."

"I wonder if there are any flinching books," said Alana. "They always seem to be *un*flinching."

"True," said Kelly with a laugh.

Alana glanced at Martin, who was smiling along, but didn't seem to like that Alana and Kelly were sharing a laugh.

"What do you think of the food, Alana?" Kelly asked.

"Amazing. I pretty much went full dolphin on the shrimp during cocktails."

Kelly laughed. "Good. Well, if anyone has any issues with anything, let us know. That's what tonight is about."

"Will do," said Gertrud. "But everything's perfect."

"Yes," said Teddy. "Very nice." He drained his glass.

A server instantly refilled it. Kelly, Alana noted, hadn't touched her wine. Martin also seemed to be monitoring everyone else's intake.

"A toast," Martin said, raising his glass. "To the soon-to-be-wed couple."

Ed kept eating, but everyone else raised their glasses and sipped. Kelly took a tiny swallow and smiled at Martin, who in turn took a modest sip. Then they both left their drinks untouched for the remainder of the meal.

When the servers cleared the main course plates, Ed said, "Shouldn't I have my pill now?"

The smile vanished from Kelly's face and her mouth dropped open. "Oh my god," she said, jumping up and bolting toward the stairs.

Joyce swooped to the table. "Everything all right?"

"Everything's fine," said Ed. "Kelly just forgot something."

"Oh," said Joyce, relieved that the kerfuffle had nothing to do with her.

But everything wasn't fine. Kelly returned in a panic, her face flushed pink.

"I'm so sorry," she said. "We have to go back."

"What?" said Joyce. "Why?"

Kelly ignored her and addressed Ed. "I was in such a flap when we left for the boat, all the wedding stuff, packing different clothes... I forgot your medication. I'm so sorry. I can't believe I did that."

"Do I have to have it now?"

"Yes. You absolutely have to have your Pradaxa twice a day at the same time."

"Potentially stupid question," said Joyce. "Is there any way we could wait until after the fireworks?"

"No, that's not for another hour. And then they go on for like, what, fifteen minutes? We shouldn't wait that long."

"What if we set them off now?" said Joyce.

"It's still light out," said Kelly. "We want to be able to see them. Anyway, he has to take that medicine at the same time every day."

"Of course." Joyce nodded and smiled but looked as if she had just received a cancer diagnosis.

"Send someone in the speedboat," said Ed. "They can get them and be back here in forty minutes."

"That would work," said Kelly. "But I'll have to go with. They would never know where to find anything."

"I can take you," said Martin. "I've been itching to try out the new boat anyway."

Both Alana and Teddy saw instantly where this was leading.

"No," said Teddy. "I'll go." He threw his serviette on the table and stood. "I know the route like the back of my hand."

"So do I, and I'm sober. You've been drinking." Martin stood up.

"I thought you had a headache," said Teddy.

"It's gone," said Martin.

"But you've never driven the new boat."

"A boat is a boat."

"Don't worry about it," said Teddy. "I've got it."

"Oh, for god's sake, stop nattering and get going," said Ed.

"Come on," Teddy said to Kelly.

"He's in no condition to pilot," Martin said to Ed.

"Are you drunk?" Ed asked Teddy.

"Not at all. I've had a couple glasses of wine—with food, I might add. I've been driving that way my entire life, as you know."

"Still safer to send me," said Martin.

"Who do you want to take you?" Ed said to Kelly.

"It doesn't really matter, but maybe Martin should stay with Gertrud. The band's about to start."

Gertrud gave Kelly an appreciative smile.

"All right, get going," said Ed to Teddy. "Be back in time for the fireworks."

Teddy patted Martin on the shoulder. "Enjoy yourself. I got this." He flashed Martin a pointed look: *I will take care of Kelly McNutt, don't you worry.*

Martin, in turn, shot Alana a look: *Yeah, right.*

A few minutes later, the couple roared off in the speedboat as the band began its first set.

Martin sought out Alana, who was watching her father stare blankly at the empty dance floor as one of the two lead singers crooned "The Way You Look Tonight." He sang it smooth like Sinatra. Ed drummed his fingers out of rhythm on the table.

"Well, that was a missed opportunity," said Martin.

"There's no way Teddy was going to let her out on the boat with you," said Alana.

"Yeah. Did you notice the lush was suddenly on the wagon tonight?"

"I did notice that. I'm guessing he told her to keep her wits about her, just in case."

"He definitely tipped her off. I've literally never seen her not pissed at night. Still, how long can an alky hold out? We may get an opportunity yet."

"If she's on to you, I wouldn't try anything tonight."

"I'll be careful," he said.

Gertrud approached and grabbed Martin's hand. "Come and dance. The wedding planner's getting all antsy."

"Who gives a shit? That woman is annoying."

"Oh, come on…" She swayed tipsily to the tune. "Dance with me…" She tugged his arm and pouted her lips—a disturbing sight given the filler and red lipstick. Alana was reminded of the ass-end of a baboon.

Martin shrugged helplessly at Alana as he allowed Gertrud to pull him onto the dance floor.

She watched them for a bit and then turned her eyes to the water. She felt uneasy. Restless. She went to the bar, ordered a martini and allowed herself a few calming swallows. When she saw Joyce beelining her way, she set the drink down and hurried to join Gertrud and Martin on the dance floor. The band had launched into a rousing version of "We Are Family" by Sister Sledge. Alana moved self-consciously at first but loosened up as the heat of the drink seeped through her limbs. Gertrud, energized by a new presence on the floor, danced harder and faster, beaming and flailing in Alana's direction. Relieved, Martin took the opportunity to shimmy away and go sit with Ed. Alana felt an opposite relief. She didn't have to speak to anyone; she could close her eyes and move her body for as long as the band played. And the band was pretty good—she had to give Joyce her due in that department—tight horns and superb vocals, particularly the female lead singer, who flung it like a cross between Gladys Knight and Amy Winehouse.

Alana kicked off her shoes and danced and danced, stopping only when a slow song began. "If I Ain't Got You." She slipped away for a bathroom break, wiped the sweat from her face and the back of her neck with one of the fat monogrammed washcloths that served as hand towels.

When she emerged from the bathroom, the song was ending, and the singer announced that the band was going to take a break. Had it really been an hour since Teddy and Kelly left?

They should have been back by now.

Alana found Ed and Joyce conferring. They had both called and texted repeatedly, but neither Kelly nor Teddy had responded. Ed called the house staff, who confirmed that the duo had returned to pick up the medication but had left the island more than half an hour ago. Alana couldn't tell who looked more anxious, Ed or Joyce.

Martin sidled up to Alana and whispered, "They're only about twenty minutes late. If I know Teddy, he stopped for a quickie on the way back."

"Maybe," said Alana, but she had an ominous feeling. Her heart was a timpani, her gut a fist.

"Stupid of them," said Martin. "How are they going to explain not answering their phones?"

Alana didn't respond. She peered out at the water, scanning for a sign of the speedboat.

Nothing.

When Ed's phone rang, everyone went quiet. "It's Teddy," he announced, jabbing the display to take the call. "Hello? What? Slow down..." Ed sprang to his feet with uncharacteristic strength. "Are you all right? Where are you?"

Martin shot Alana a confused look. Had Teddy actually done the deed?

"Did you call 911?"

"Oh my god," said Joyce.

"OK, good. They'll call the RCC. Hold on." Now Ed shouted to Martin, "Tell the captain to head back the way we came. And use the thermal imaging! And radio the Coast Guard just in case."

Martin took off in a sprint for the bridge.

"Hello? You there?" Ed shouted into the phone. "Hello? Hello? *Fuck!*" He stabbed at the display, trying to call back Teddy's number.

"What happened?" said Alana, holding her throat, every cell in her body tensed.

"Accident," said Ed, collapsing into his chair.

11

All the fancy food and drink that Alana had consumed on the *Andiamo* exploded from her guts into the toilet. She'd barely made it to the bathroom in time. With shaking hands, she wadded up some toilet paper and wiped her mouth. She stood there for a couple minutes, trying to compose herself, trying to breathe. She didn't want to leave the stall in case someone came into the bathroom. She couldn't face anyone. Not yet.

After several minutes of deep breathing, Alana steeled herself and went to wash up, rinsing out her mouth and splashing hot water on her face. She felt sick and dazed. She wanted to go back in time and not be a part of any of this madness. How was she supposed to go out there now? She wasn't a fucking actor. She would have to go hide in her cabin. Yes.

But when she left the bathroom, Martin was waiting for her.

"Can you believe this?" he hissed in a low voice. "I swear to god, Alana, I'm going to strangle that bitch."

"What? Who?"

"Kelly. I think she did something to Teddy."

"What are you talking about? Dad was just on the phone with him."

"No, that was *Kelly* on the phone. She called from Teddy's phone. She left her phone here. Teddy is somewhere in the water."

"What?" It took a long moment for the words to register. Finally, a sob escaped from deep in Alana's chest, followed by a spasm of tears.

Martin put a tentative, clumsy arm around her quaking shoulders. "I know," he said. "It's fucked."

When the torrent subsided, Alana exhaled deeply. "I need a Kleenex." She ducked back into the bathroom and blew her nose loudly before returning. "Oh my god, I can't handle this," she said.

"I know. It's nuts. I knew she was corrupt, but I didn't think she was a psycho. Do you think we should say something?"

"I don't know," said Alana.

"Well, we need to figure it out."

Alana took a deep breath. "I don't fucking know, Martin."

"Well, let's think about it because we'll be there in a few minutes and we have to figure it out. I mean, do we say they were together and plotting? I mean, maybe she planned this whole thing—leaving the drugs behind so she'd have to go back. If she got rid of Teddy, it's because she wants it all to herself, right? Maybe we can get her arrested."

"Arrested for what? You said Teddy was in the water. He might be out by now for all we know. Dad said they had an accident. What if they did? I mean, Teddy was driving."

"Yeah."

"We have no idea what happened."

"I guess," said Martin.

"If we rat them out or spout some crazy conspiracy theory, and then Teddy turns up, we're screwed."

"Yeah…"

Alana sighed. "Let's just get there and see what happened. It's not like the authorities are going to disappear."

"But they might ask why we didn't say something right away."

"Because we didn't want to upset Dad. He was upset enough by the accident. And we were in shock. Jesus Christ, I'm still in shock. Teddy is possibly injured, possibly drowned—"

"Or possibly murdered."

"Maybe. But it could have been an accident. And for all we know, Teddy is fine."

"Yeah. I guess he could be OK. I really hope he's OK."

As Alana studied her brother's face, she unconsciously cocked her right eyebrow.

"Well, he did fucking betray me," said Martin, looking exposed.

They saw flares and the search and rescue helicopter long before they rounded a curve in the Narrows and spotted the speedboat and Coast Guard vessels. As they got nearer, they could see that the speedboat was empty and seemingly undamaged. Kelly was standing with several officers aboard the larger of the Coast Guard boats with a blanket wrapped around her shoulders. Powerful lights swept the water as the search for Teddy continued.

Ed was on the phone with a Coast Guard officer, trying to figure out what was going on and trying to get Kelly delivered back to the *Andiamo* once it was anchored. Alana looked on anxiously, while Martin and Gertrud moved around the perimeter of the ship, surveying the scene and scanning the water for Teddy. Joyce, her staff, and the band had retreated to a lower deck to give the family privacy. A couple crew members hovered at a respectful distance, waiting to be pressed into service.

"I understand," said Ed. "But if she says she's fine, I believe her. She's a nurse, for god's sake. She'd seek medical attention if she needed it!" Ed glanced at Alana, who was watching and listening. He turned slightly away. "You checked her out, right? Yes, I understand, but she didn't hit her head. She hit her shoulder. I get it, but I think a nurse knows her head from her fucking shoulder! Yes, I take responsibility. No, I'm fine. I don't need a medic. I need my pills and my fiancée. OK, very good. Who am I speaking with? All right, thank you, Robert. Now, what about my son?" As Ed listened, he moved slowly away from Alana. She watched as her father braced himself against a table. She could no longer make out what he was saying, but when the call was done, she saw him drop his phone, sink into a chair and put his head in his hands.

Once the *Andiamo* had anchored, a Coast Guard medic delivered Kelly and the speedboat back to the ship. The officer insisted on administering Ed's medication and checking his blood pressure—*We don't need two medical emergencies tonight, sir*—before departing with several *Andiamo* crew members. They ferried the officer back via the limousine tender and then stayed out on the water to help search for Teddy, tracking the Coast Guard's Data Marker Buoy south with the current. Alana, Gertrud and Martin looked on as Kelly fell into Ed's arms.

"I'm sorry," she said. "I'm so sorry!" She was wearing a giant Coast Guard sweatshirt that came down to her knees, one of which was bruised and bandaged.

"Shhh," said Ed. He shut his eyes and pressed his lips against the top of her head. They remained clenched together for several seconds until Kelly pulled away.

"Are you OK?" said Gertrud to Kelly. "Can I get you anything?"

"Maybe a drink," she said.

"Are you sure?" said Ed.

"Yes, I'm fine. I'm just banged up—mostly my shoulder and leg."

"Oh Jesus," said Ed, gently moving the loose sweatshirt collar and inspecting the dark purple marks on Kelly's right shoulder.

"Martini?" said Gertrud.

"Anything," said Kelly. "Thanks."

Gertrud hurried off to order the drink, happy to have purpose during the calamity. Alana and Martin just stood there, awkwardly waiting to find out what happened.

"Do you want to get showered and changed?" said Ed.

"Not until they find Teddy." She grabbed his hand and squeezed it. "This is all my fault. If I hadn't forgotten your medicine…"

"Bull," said Ed. "I shouldn't have let him go when I knew he'd been drinking. If it's anyone's fault, it's mine."

"It was an accident," said Alana. "It's nobody's fault. And Teddy might be fine."

"Oh god, I hope so," said Kelly.

"What exactly happened?" said Martin.

Kelly sighed deeply. "It was so fast..." she said, organizing her thoughts. "The way there was fine, we got the meds and headed out. It was when we were coming back up through the Narrows... Teddy was going pretty fast, I guess. Definitely faster than the way there."

"You can't do that at night!" said Ed.

"Honestly, I don't really know how fast you're supposed to be going. I know it took longer than we thought to get the pills, and he was anxious to get back as soon as possible. He was worried about you," Kelly said to Ed with tears welling in her eyes.

Martin, detecting bullshit, shot Alana a glance. Ed squeezed Kelly's hand and kissed it.

"We were going pretty fast," Kelly continued, as if piecing it together in her mind. "I remember I was kind of holding on because of it—you know that leather handle on the side? I was holding that, but I wasn't really nervous or anything. I just assumed that's how fast you were supposed to be going, and I was kind of zoned out, to be honest, when all of a sudden he screamed *log* and swerved really hard."

"Oh Christ," said Ed. "Those logs are deadly."

"Usually, you can see them from a ways off," said Martin.

"Not if they're waterlogged and below the surface," said Ed. "Not at night."

"We didn't hit it," said Kelly. "I don't *think* we hit it. But we pitched hard one way and then really hard the other—I went flying and smashed my shoulder. And waves came in the boat. I was on the floor, in the water…"

"You're lucky you didn't hit your head. Jesus Christ," said Ed.

"I know. I hurt my shoulder and leg and hip, and it took a minute for me to get up. When I finally got my bearings, I realized Teddy wasn't there. He'd been thrown from the boat."

"Oh my god," said Alana.

"And it was still going! And I didn't know what to do. I've never driven a boat in my life. I was, like, looking for the brakes, which I know sounds so stupid. I just—I don't know anything about boats. I panicked and grabbed the wheel and tried to turn back to where I thought Teddy might be. I didn't want to get too far away, you know? I didn't even know which direction I was going at that point. I couldn't really see anything, and I must have been in shock, and then… Oh my god," said Kelly, putting her face in her hands and sinking into a chair.

Gertrud returned with the drink and stood there holding it awkwardly as Kelly burst into tears.

"And then… I think I might have hit him," she said through her fingers, her face still obscured.

"You hit him with the boat?" said Martin.

"Jesus Christ!" said Ed.

"I don't know," said Kelly, lifting her face from her hands. "Maybe… I don't know. I hit something."

Martin exhaled hard through his nostrils and exchanged a quick glance with Alana.

"Maybe it was the log?" said Kelly. "Oh god, I hope so."

"Here," said Gertrud, holding out the martini.

Kelly took it, but Ed stopped her before she drank. "No," he said. "If you had your hands on the wheel, if, god forbid, you hit Teddy, you need to stay sober."

"Why?"

"Because, when the police show up, you need to prove you weren't intoxicated." He took the drink from Kelly.

"You think the police will come?" she said.

"If someone was hurt, they'll investigate." Ed handed the martini to Gertrud. "Get rid of this."

"You want a coffee or tea?" she asked Kelly.

"Get her a coffee," said Ed. "Soy milk, one stevia."

Gertrud headed back to the bar.

"Oh god, please let them find him. Please let him be OK," said Kelly.

"I'm going to check in with Robert," said Ed. He moved off to make the call to the Coast Guard.

"So, what happened after that?" said Martin. "After you hit something?"

"Um, well, I was really freaking out…and the boat just kept going. And then I finally figured out how to move that lever thingy to slow it down. I couldn't see Teddy. I called out but he didn't answer. And I couldn't find my phone. Teddy's was still in that holder thing at the front, so I called 911. And then I called Ed."

"Hmm," said Martin.

"I'm sorry you had to go through that," said Alana.

They were all quiet then, watching Ed, waiting for the update.

"Anything?" said Martin when he returned.

149

"Not yet," said Ed. "Why don't you go get showered and changed," he said to Kelly.

"Maybe I should," she said. "Will you come with me?"

"Of course."

After they moved off, Martin turned to Alana. "You buying any of that?"

"I don't know. I mean, it sounds plausible."

"Not to me," said Martin. "I thought it sounded pretty fucking cooked."

"In what way?"

"I don't know. Maybe it's more in the way she said it than the actual details."

"Hmm."

"Something about it seems off." Martin wandered over to the ship's rail and stared down into the dark water.

Alana joined him at the railing. They were silent for a bit, watching as another flare went off in the distance, bursting like a mini sun in the night sky.

"He's still my big brother," said Martin.

"I know," said Alana.

Martin turned to his sister. "I wonder what really happened."

12

Teddy drained the last sip from the Heineken he'd cracked when they'd left Alfred Island.

"Want another?" said Kelly.

"I'd better not," said Teddy. "I need to stay alert too. And I don't want to tempt you. You've been really good tonight."

Kelly shrugged. "I just watched you drink a beer—I was already tempted. Another one's not going to make a difference."

"No, I'm good," said Teddy. He glanced at Kelly, who was understandably on edge. "It's nice and dark now," he said as they made their way up through the Narrows. "Maybe we should stop for a minute?"

Kelly laughed. "Bad boy. Don't you want your daddy to get what he needs?"

"Don't you want *your* daddy to get what he needs?" He reached over and pushed the hem of her dress higher on her thighs.

"You are utterly predictable," said Kelly, batting his hand away. "Plenty of time for that after the wedding. Right now, we need to keep old Ed alive."

"Fine. We don't have to stop." Teddy squeezed his hard-on through his pants. Then he put his hand around the back of Kelly's neck and started to guide her head toward his crotch.

She squirmed away. "You expect me to fit under there?" she said, gesturing to the tiny area beneath the steering wheel.

"I can swivel." He turned his body to the side but kept his hands on the wheel and his head facing forward.

"Yeah, that doesn't seem safe," said Kelly.

"Then let's stop for a bit. We have time."

"To be honest, I'm feeling a little unsettled right now. I'm really not in the mood."

"I can fix that." He reached under her dress and wormed his fingers into her panties. "Whoa," he said. "You shaved?"

"Waxed," said Kelly, pulling his hand away.

"OK, executive decision, we're stopping," said Teddy, slowing the boat.

"Seriously? I just said I don't feel like it. Can we please just head back?"

"Oh, come on," he said, turning off the motor. "You can't tease me like that." He stuck his hand back under her dress and bit her earlobe.

Kelly stared straight ahead, her jaw tightening.

"We finally have privacy," he said, working two fingers inside her. "I promise, I'll be quick." He tried to kiss her but she turned away. "Oh, come on," he said, gripping the back of her neck and wrenching her face toward him. "You're not going to give me blue balls, are you?"

She met his eye. "Oh, we can't have that."

"Then you'd better take care of this," he said, unzipping his pants.

"You want it right now, huh?"

"Can't you tell?"

"Then turn off these lights," she said resolutely.

"Can't. If another boat happens to come through, they won't see us. Especially with no moon."

Kelly surveyed the densely treed shoreline on either side of the passage. "You think anyone will see us messing around?"

"Not here," said Teddy. "Not at this time of night."

"Will they hear us?"

"Not with this wind. But we can go below if you like."

"Nah," said Kelly, moving to the seating area behind the helm. "I don't mind a breeze."

Teddy followed and sat on the side of the horseshoe-shaped padded bench.

Kelly slid her panties off and sling-shotted them at Teddy.

"Show it to me," he said.

She lifted her dress.

"Oh," said Teddy approvingly. "Better."

"You have something against pubic hair?"

"Bush is fine, but I prefer shaved."

"Like father, like son," said Kelly. "Well, take a good look 'cause it's the last time you'll see it."

"You're going to grow it back?" he said.

Kelly smiled. She took her dress off, swung it over her

head like a stripper, and flung it at Teddy. It sailed over his head into the water. "Oh shoot!" she said. "Get it!"

"What the hell," said Teddy, scrambling to retrieve the dress.

"Get it before it sinks," said Kelly. She grabbed her panties and put them on as Teddy stood on the padded seat and leaned out over the side. He couldn't even reach the waterline, let alone the dress, which was a good two feet from the boat.

"Great!" he said. "How are we supposed to explain this?"

"I think it's floating toward the back." She pointed to the garment.

Teddy ran to the helm and pushed a button to deploy the swim platform. Then he darted back through the seating area, crawled across the polished wooden aft deck and stepped down onto the extending platform that was still in motion. He kneeled, pushed up his sleeve and stretched out his arm, willing the dress to float within reach before it lost buoyancy. When it finally came into range, he leaned out precariously, snagging the hem between index and middle finger, and pulled it close enough to fish out. "Thank Christ," he breathed.

"Don't wring it," said Kelly.

Teddy gasped. He hadn't expected her to be standing right behind him on the swim platform. He stood up. "Did you seriously just walk across the aft deck in those heels?"

"Relax, I have amazing balance."

"Are you stupid?" he said, grabbing her arm.

"Ow!"

"That is brand-new teak. With custom inlays! Do you know how much it'll cost to replace if—"

She plucked the dress from his hands and shoved him hard into the water.

"Hey!" he yelled when he resurfaced. "What the hell! Kelly! *Kelly!*"

She kitten-heeled it back across the aft deck and disappeared from view. Teddy tried to pull himself up onto the swim platform, but it was higher than on the old boat, and he was still full from dinner and also a bit drunk. His wet clothes weren't helping matters. As he reached for the hatch that contained the folding ladder, he saw the platform start to retract. *"No, wait!"* he screamed. "Kelly, I'm sorry! *Kelly!*" He heard the boat start up and instinctively reared back from propellers and engines. Then he came to his senses and lunged for the last few inches of the swim platform, but it was too late. The boat roared away.

With numb fingers Teddy searched his pockets for his phone. *Damn it.* He'd left it in the boat. Well, if she was trying to teach him a lesson, she'd better hurry—he was freezing. He listened to the sound of the engines fade as the boat retreated into the distance. He treaded water, listening for the sound to begin growing louder again, and soon enough it did. Thank god. Who knows how long she would have made him wait if Ed hadn't needed his medication? And who knew she was so bloody touchy when she wasn't boozing. For a moment he regretted getting involved with her at all. Was it really so terrible having Martin as his boss? It was humiliating, of course, but Martin hadn't been lording it over him. Was it worth all this scheming and hassle? If she was this bananas, maybe he should let Martin take care of her after all. He thought about how they were going to explain being soaking wet.

He would have to tell Ed that Kelly fell into the water and he jumped in to save her. She couldn't swim, so that added up. Then he would tell Martin and Alana that he tried to off her, but it didn't work out, or he couldn't go through with it—either way, they would think he had at least tried. So, maybe this could work in his favor, actually. Ed would be grateful, which could be useful. He just hoped she hadn't damaged the new boat. If she wrecked the teak, he was going to be very unhappy. And where was she already? He was freezing his butt off.

As the boat approached and the sound of the engines grew louder, Teddy started to feel afraid. What if she couldn't see him? But then the boat slowed in the distance, and he heard her call out: "Teddy?"

"Here," he shouted, waving. Could she even hear him over the engines and the wind?

"Oh, there you are. I see you. This boat is incredible," she said. "It handles really well."

"Can you please come get me?"

"Deck's a little slippery though," she said, ignoring his plea. "Whoops…" Kelly flung herself against the hard fiberglass side of the boat. "Ow, ow, ow, ow…" She clutched the shoulder she had just rammed against the gunwale.

"Kelly, what are you doing? I'm freezing out here!"

"So impatient tonight," said Kelly. "Well, I'm busy." She picked up a full bottle of beer and began striking herself on the leg and opposite shoulder.

He couldn't see her, but he heard her crying out in pain. "Kelly, I don't know what you're doing, but can you please come get me? It's not funny anymore!"

She appeared suddenly on the teak deck, still wearing the shoes. "You're not suffering, I hope."

"I'm freezing, Kelly. Please. Enough is enough."

"Well, *I* am not one to stand idly by while a person is needlessly suffering," said Kelly. She stepped back into the boat and disappeared from view.

Teddy heard the engines rev as she throttled forward. The boat was approaching fast. Too fast. His heart jumped when he grasped that she wasn't just mad at him, she was done with him. He had served his purpose.

He tried frantically to swim out of the boat's path, but the pointed hull of the vessel flew like a spear toward his head.

13

It was just past eleven when Ed's phone rang again. The family had moved inside to the library bar to await news of Teddy. They were picking at a reprise of dinner when the call from the Coast Guard came in.

"Hello? Yes. Oh. OK… OK, thank you. We're on our way. Yes. Thank you." Ed hung up and called the captain of the *Andiamo*.

"What's happening?" said Kelly.

He held up a finger to silence her.

Alana, Martin, and Gertrud had stopped eating and were watching Ed. Kelly sat straight and tense, digging at the corners of her thumbnails with her index finger nails.

"We need to get to Nanaimo as soon as possible. Can we dock there? Cameron Island portion? OK, let's go. And arrange for two cars to meet us there, or a minivan." Ed hung up and addressed the group. "They found Teddy," he said.

"Is he all right?" said Kelly.

"He's badly injured," said Ed. "But he's alive."

"Oh, thank god." Kelly threw her arms around Ed's neck and buried her face in his shoulder.

Martin glanced at Alana, who was watching Kelly carefully.

"They have an ambulance waiting at the Ladysmith dock," said Ed. "They'll be there in a few minutes. Then they'll take him to Nanaimo General."

"It's only twenty minutes or so from Ladysmith to Nanaimo," said Alana. "And faster in an ambulance."

"It's encouraging news," said Martin.

"Very encouraging," said Gertrud.

"Thank Christ they found him in time," said Ed. "I was afraid they wouldn't." He pat-patted Kelly's back in a subconscious signal for her to un-cling herself from his chest.

Alana noticed that when she lifted her face, it was a few shades paler than normal and her cheeks and neck were covered in strange red splotches.

When the *Andiamo* docked at the Port Authority in Nanaimo, Joyce, her crew and the band decamped. Joyce implored them to keep her informed about Teddy's status. There was no mention of the upcoming wedding, which would undoubtedly be postponed.

The family couldn't get anywhere near Teddy when they arrived at the hospital. First, two police officers waylaid them to take statements and administer a Breathalyzer to Kelly, who explained that she had only one sip of wine the entire night, and that was just during a toast (the officers seemed a lot friendlier after she aced the test). When the police departed to go inspect the speedboat at the port, a plump nurse with crispy blond hair guided the family to a "quiet room"—one of the private waiting areas in the emergency department—and explained that Teddy was in critical condition, and they were working to stabilize him.

"But he's going to be OK?" asked Ed.

"It's too soon to say," said the nurse. "His injuries are quite critical, but there's a team working with him now. I'll update you as soon as I can."

As she turned to leave, Kelly moved toward her. "I'm a nurse," she said. "Can you tell me what his injuries are?"

"Oh. Well..." She looked uncertain about how much to share but then proceeded in a low voice. "There's trauma to the left chest, underlying rib injuries, internal bleeding, contusion to the head, injuries to the pelvis and left femur, possibly a C-spine injury. We'll know more once he's stabilized. Someone will update you."

"Thank you," said Kelly. When the nurse left, she slumped into a chair.

"What does it mean?" said Ed.

"It means the boat hit him," said Kelly. "It means I hit him with the boat." She buried her face in her hands.

"Goddamn it," said Ed. "I shouldn't have let him go."

A heavy silence then, broken by Gertrud: "Well, they're stabilizing him now. I think he's going to be OK."

"How the hell would you know?" said Ed.

"Hey," snapped Martin. "This is not Gertrud's fault. How many times did I say I should go?"

Ed exhaled hard. "Not enough times, clearly."

"Seriously?" said Martin, glaring.

"Seriously," said Ed, staring back.

"It's OK," said Gertrud, squeezing Martin's arm, trying to get him to stand down. "Everyone's on edge."

He laughed bitterly but dropped his gaze.

"Based on what the nurse said, do you think he's going to be all right?" Alana asked Kelly.

"It's impossible to say. I would have to see him."

Everyone disappeared into private thoughts. And no one said a thing until the crispy-haired nurse returned forty minutes later to tell them that Teddy's blood pressure had stabilized and they were taking him into surgery.

"A doctor will come speak to you when they're done."

"Thank you," Kelly said to the departing nurse. She patted Ed's hand and did her best to look cheered, but Alana could see that the smile on her face was a rictus.

"How long do you think he'll be in surgery for?" said Martin.

"From what I could glean of his injuries, I would guess at least three hours, probably more," said Kelly.

"Oh wow," said Martin.

Gertrud jumped up. "I'm going to do a coffee run. Who would like coffee?"

"I think the cafeteria is closed at this point," said Martin.

"I'll go out," said Gertrud. "There's got to be a coffee shop around here somewhere."

Gertrud seemed uniquely energized by the drama, and Alana sensed she was almost enjoying it, though she remained outwardly solemn.

"It's late," said Ed to Martin. "Go with her."

"No, that's OK," said Gertrud, consulting her phone.

"I'll just Uber. It says there's a Tim Hortons like two minutes away."

"Are you sure?" said Martin. "I'd prefer to stay, if you don't mind."

"Of course. I'll be fine." She summoned a car, took orders and left.

Alana watched as everyone settled in for the long wait. Kelly paced the room, nervous as a cat. Ed, on the other hand, remained completely still with his hands folded in his lap. If his eyes weren't open, she would have thought he was asleep. Martin played a video game on his phone.

There was nothing to be done, so Alana pulled out her phone to check messages and look up flight schedules. She was toying with the idea of again delaying her trip home by a day or two—she didn't want to leave in the midst of the crisis—but when she read her texts and emails, she discovered she would have to fly back the following afternoon as planned. There were several messages from Lily and Ramona sent earlier in the evening. Lily was very happy that Alana would be home tomorrow. More crucially, Ramona informed her that she would like to leave Alana's place by midnight at the latest and asked her to please make backup arrangements for someone to watch Lily in case there were delays with her flight. She added that if Alana couldn't find a replacement, she could stay one last night but would definitely need to depart early the following morning (apparently, her husband couldn't handle a week alone with their twin seven-year-old boys and had pleaded for Ramona's return).

Alana checked her flight information. She had a nonstop leaving Victoria at 2:15 p.m., which, assuming no delays, would put her in Toronto at 9:45. She could collect her luggage and be home an hour later. There were no delays on the flight at this point. And the weather was fine in both cities. She decided to proceed as if all would go well. Foolish, probably. But she knew it would be impossible to find reliable backup for Ramona at this point.

"It looks like I'm going to have to fly home tomorrow," Alana said. "The woman who's watching Lily has to get back to her family."

"Fine," said Ed.

Neither Martin nor Kelly responded, but Alana felt the room grow icy.

"I'm really sorry," she said. "I've already stayed longer than I was supposed to."

"There's nothing you can do for Teddy," said Ed. "Leave now. You don't have to sit here."

"No, I want to stay. I'll leave when I have to leave. But would it be possible to get a ride back to the island tomorrow? I have to pick up my things before I head to the airport."

"That's fine. If you go back to the ship before we do, just ask any of the crew to get Terrance to take you in the limo tender."

"OK. Thanks."

Ed closed his eyes. Martin went back to his video game. Kelly resumed pacing and digging at her cuticles.

Not long after, Gertrud returned with coffees and a large box of doughnuts.

When Ed reached for one, Kelly said, "Those aren't actually vegan."

"Who gives a shit," he said.

Kelly looked like she'd been punched in the throat. Martin seemed cheered by the exchange.

"Oh, I'm sorry," said Gertrud. "I just assumed they'd be dairy-free. Just flour and water. And sugar."

"It's fine," snapped Ed.

"It really is," said Kelly. "Please don't worry. I'm not at all hungry."

"Well, I'm happy to zip back out when you are," said Gertrud.

Ed rolled his eyes, disgusted by her servility.

"Thanks," said Kelly. She moved to Gertrud and hugged her.

Gertrud, who stood a good foot taller than Kelly, returned the embrace. They looked like mother and daughter, Gertrud patting Kelly's back, comforting her. After a few moments, they broke apart.

Gertrud sat. Kelly paced.

Everyone sipped coffee.

Alana tried to stay alert. She had something she needed to do before she went to the airport, and she would have to replan the timing, given that she was now starting from Nanaimo. She Googled and found a Best Buy that was a five-minute drive from the hospital. It opened at ten in the morning. She calculated that she could do the thing she needed to do, as long as she was at the store as soon as it opened and was out of there in half an hour. She set an alarm for nine, just in case she dozed off, and then put her phone away. She was too tired to think but also couldn't sleep. She sat for hours in a jittery fog, punctuated by the occasional trip to the bathroom.

It was shortly after four when a surgeon finally came to

the quiet room. Everyone was awake except Ed, who Kelly roused so he could hear the report.

"Hi, I'm Dr. Ahuja," said the woman in scrubs. She had intense brown eyes and a small mouth with large crooked teeth.

"How is he?" said Ed.

"His injuries are quite critical."

"But he's going to be all right?"

"At this point, it's hard to make a determination on his prognosis, he has a number of serious injuries. A skull fracture, a fracture of his cervical spine. When we looked into his abdomen, there was a lot of bleeding there. Bleeding around the liver. We put some packing in, but he lost a lot of blood. He has a collapsed lung. A fractured pelvis, a shattered femur—"

"Jesus Christ," said Martin.

"He's going to be OK though?" said Ed, more command than question.

"Well, he's injured his brain, so only time will tell. There is a good chance that he may never wake up."

"Oh my god," said Gertrud.

"How much of a chance?" said Ed.

"It's hard to say. We have to give it some time to see if the brain can recover. Right now, we have him sedated and on a ventilator. In four or five days, we'll ease up on the sedation and see if there are any signs of spontaneous breathing. For now, he's in an induced coma."

"I'm a nurse," said Kelly. "Can you tell me how significant the skull fracture is?"

"Well, we did a craniectomy, but the degree of the fracture would suggest that he may never regain consciousness."

Alana saw Kelly relax a little as she nodded and exhaled deeply.

"Is there another surgeon I can speak to?" said Ed.

Dr. Ahuja's eyebrows went up. "Not at the moment, no. It's four thirty in the morning."

"There were no other doctors in there with you?" said Ed.

An uncomfortable moment when every woman in the room bristled, knowing why Ed had asked that.

"Dr. Vanderveen and the rest of my team have likely left for home," said the doctor, evenly. "But Dr. Vanderveen will be in tomorrow, if you'd prefer to speak to *her*."

Ed frowned. "You said something about Teddy's spine. When his brain recovers, he'll be able to walk, correct?"

"We don't know yet. He has a cervical spine fracture. I can't really comment on it yet. He's in a collar and immobilized. We won't know until he regains consciousness."

"Can we see him?" said Martin.

"Yes," said Dr. Ahuja. "He'll be unresponsive. But two people at a time can go in and see him."

Ed and Kelly went into the ICU first, and then Martin and Gertrud. When Gertrud came out crying and shaking, Alana told herself to prepare for a shock. But it was worse than she imagined. Teddy was unrecognizable. His face was horrifically bruised and swollen and obscured by a ventilator. His head was bandaged and there appeared to be a concave indentation on one side of his skull. His neck was being held in place by a stiff plastic collar. And there were tubes everywhere, including one running from his skull to a monitor, another poking through his ribs and draining into a bloody bag, and another that led to a bag of piss. He had multiple IVs, one leg in a splint, and his pelvis was bound in a frightening, medieval-looking apparatus. An angry incision, held together by thick staples, extended from his upper abdomen to below his navel.

Alana stared at what remained of Teddy and felt a spasm of pity. Then she remembered that he had been screwing his father's fiancée and scheming to dispossess his brother. She recalled Teddy as a kid. Beautiful. Cruel. Ed's favorite son. His most loyal and reliable sentinel. She thought of the time he scooped her up and carried her deep into the woods, yelling at her to shut the hell up and stop squirming, complaining about how fat and heavy she was, before dumping her hard on the ground and striding away. She must have been around six or seven.

Alana reached out and touched the bandage on Teddy's head. With two fingers, she pressed slowly into the concave softness until there was no more give. Then she shivered and yanked her hand away.

She took a last look at her broken brother and then made for the door.

The family returned to the *Andiamo* to rest and regroup. Ed decided they would stay docked in Nanaimo overnight so they could be near the hospital. Alana had just stepped into her berth and kicked her shoes off when she heard a faint tapping at the door. She opened it and saw Martin.

"Can I come in for a minute?"

"I'm bagged, Martin. And I have to get up in a few hours."

"Just for a sec. We need to debrief." He nudged his way past her and closed the door. "I wish you weren't leaving."

"I have to."

"I know. It would just be nice to have an ally."

"You have Gertrud."

"You know what I mean. Someone who knows what's going on. God, did you see her face when Ed told her Teddy was alive?"

"Yeah."

"I knew she was a gold digger, but I never pegged her as a psycho killer. She might be coming after us next."

"I think Dad might get a little suspicious if all his children start dropping dead."

"You think he's going to die?" said Martin.

"He looked bad. And the doctor didn't seem encouraging. Anyway, it still may have been an accident—I mean, if her goal is to marry Dad, why would she do anything that would put off the wedding?"

"I don't know. Maybe Teddy got sick of her and threatened to expose her?"

"Maybe. In that case there's a reason for her to want Teddy to be gone—he brought her in, he knows she's a fake. But she doesn't need us to be gone."

"True," said Martin. "I'm pretty sure that if he wakes up, she's fucked. Maybe I should hire security guards so he's never alone."

"Maybe. Not a bad idea if you want to protect him. Of course, if he doesn't wake up… Well, then, you're the king of the castle once Ed's gone," said Alana. "And the wedding is postponed indefinitely, so all good for you."

"That's cold, Alana."

"You said it yourself. He betrayed you. And Dad."

Martin studied his sister's face. "I guess there's no love lost between you and Teddy, huh?"

"I guess not."

"You've never really forgiven him, have you?"

"What difference does it make?"

"You know he was just a kid, right? Trying to please a dad he worshipped."

Alana shrugged.

"Do you feel that way about me too? I mean, I was even younger than Teddy."

"Yeah, but you could have spoken up when you got older. Or even now."

"What good would it do? It would be my word against his. The only result would be me getting cut off and sued. Or worse."

"I know," said Alana. "But if both you and Teddy spoke up…"

"Yeah, well, we don't have that option now, do we?"

"Not at the moment. I guess we'll have to see what happens," said Alana.

"Yeah," said Martin, "I guess we will."

Alana allowed herself three hours of sleep before rising and showering. She called a taxi, hit a bank machine, and was at the door of the local Best Buy the moment it opened. She told the driver to wait for her.

"Looking for a new computer?" asked a sales associate who had followed Alana from the entrance to the Apple display. He was a chubby man with a jovial face and a sunflower-yellow turban.

"I'll take one of these," said Alana, who had quickly inspected a MacBook Pro.

"That was easy." The man smiled. "Do you need a laptop bag?"

"No, thanks. I'm actually in a bit of a hurry."

"No problem. I'll get that for you right away." The man went off to retrieve the computer.

Once Alana had cashed out, she took her purchase to the Geek Squad counter, where repairs were done. She was greeted by a bored-looking young woman with vestiges of pink dye in her lank blond hair.

"Can I help you?"

Alana tried not to focus on the woman's acne, which had been spackled over with a thick coating of too-beige concealer. "Yes, um, this is going to sound strange, but I need to render this computer useless. So that when you turn it on, nothing happens—it's just dead."

"This is a new computer?" said the woman, eyeing the box, which was still in the bag.

"Yeah, I just bought it now. But I need it to be made unusable. And not something you can immediately detect. It shouldn't look like it was dropped or soaked, for example, although feel free to do either, as long as you can't see what killed it."

"Why would you want that?"

"Look, I just need it to be done quickly. Can you do it?" Alana rummaged in her purse, pulled out two fifty-dollar bills, and showed them to the woman.

"I mean, I can do it, but could I do it after work? I don't think I'm supposed to be doing that here."

"No, I need it now. As soon as possible." Alana slipped

the cash into the bag and pushed it across the counter. "I can pay the Geek Squad fee as well."

The woman shrugged. "It's pretty slow right now, so..." She took the bag with the cash and carried it to the back.

Alana checked the time: 10:09. She figured she had to be out of there by 10:30 at the latest if she was going to stop at Alfred Island before heading to the airport. About five minutes later, the woman came to the counter to ask Alana if she would ever need the computer to be functional again.

"No. Do what you need to do. But try to make it look like it wasn't deliberate."

"Cool." She flipped up a hinged portion of the countertop and disappeared into the bowels of the store. A few minutes later, she returned and smiled conspiratorially at Alana. "I had to microwave a few components in the break room. But don't worry, they don't look melted."

"Great," said Alana. "Is it almost ready?" She checked her phone. It was 10:21.

"Yep," said the woman. She disappeared into the back and emerged a few minutes later with the defunct laptop. "Here you go. It was kind of painful, to be honest."

The computer appeared intact and didn't look or feel like it had been messed with.

"Thank you. You're wonderful," said Alana, handing her an extra fifty. "I don't need the packaging." She slid the laptop into her purse and hustled to the waiting taxi.

Alana made it back to the *Andiamo* just before eleven o'clock. She grabbed her overnight bag from her cabin, then approached the first crew member she encountered, a young man who was polishing the chrome around the glass elevator. "Morning. I was wondering if you could help me with something?"

"Of course. And good morning to you. How may I help?" A gleaming white smile to match the immaculate white uniform. The blue-eyed boy seemed to be no more than seventeen or eighteen years old and, along with the rest of the crew, looked to Alana like he had just sprung out of a Wrigley's Spearmint Gum commercial.

"Could you put me in touch with Terrance? I need to get back to Alfred Island as soon as possible and my father said he'd be able to take me in the limousine tender."

"Of course. No problem. I'll arrange that for you right away."

"Great. Thanks."

As the young man was phoning Terrance, the glass car rose in the elevator shaft with Kelly inside.

"Morning," said Kelly, stepping out of the glass enclosure. "Are you leaving us already?"

"Yeah, sorry. I have to pick up my stuff from the island and be at the airport by one thirty. My god, your arms," said Alana, wincing at the black and purple bruises that covered Kelly's shoulders and arms. Her left shoulder was especially bad.

"My legs too," she said, gesturing to her legs, and lifting her skirt a little. "And my hip. I wouldn't usually take the elevator up one flight of stairs. I did something to the side of my knee."

"Pardon me for interrupting," said the boy. "Terrance is good to go. Whenever you're ready I can escort you to the garage."

"Thanks," said Alana. "I'll just be a minute."

The boy took Alana's overnight bag and moved a polite distance away so the women could continue their conversation without him appearing to hover.

"Maybe you should see a doctor," said Alana.

"No, I'm just banged up. *I'll* be fine."

"You must be worried about Teddy. I know I am."

"Well," said Kelly, "this week is going to be critical. But having seen him, my professional opinion is that you don't have to worry." She touched Alana's arm. "I'm sorry about what happened. But please know that I'll be at the hospital every day, making sure he gets the care he needs."

Alana nodded and thanked her but didn't feel reassured.

Kelly glanced over at the young man, who was looking off in the opposite direction, pretending not to eavesdrop. "If you want to give me your number, I can text you updates."

"Um, that's OK," said Alana. "I'm sure Martin will keep me updated."

"Well, give it to me anyway," said Kelly. "Just in case."

Alana reluctantly gave her the number.

"Thanks," said Kelly. "I'll send you a text so you'll have mine."

A silence hung between them, which Alana eventually filled with: "I'm sorry about the wedding. You must be disappointed."

"Oh, I don't care about that. Right now, all I care about is taking care of Teddy. The wedding will happen when it happens. I don't need a big wedding on a yacht. In fact, I don't want that anymore. I'm done with boats. I'm thinking city hall is the way to go. Quick and easy. No fuss, no muss."

Alana nodded. She checked the time on her phone. "Sorry," she said. "I have to get going."

"Well, safe travels," said Kelly. "It was really great meeting you." She pulled Alana into a hug and said, "Hope to see you back this way *very* soon."

As Alana walked to the garage, Kelly's words reverberated in her mind. "Hope to see you back this way soon" would have been the natural and meaningless thing to say. "Hope to see you back this way *very* soon" was a lot more pointed. Did she mean back very soon for the wedding? Or was Kelly, in her sly way, referring to another, less cheerful, event?

14

It was a relief to be home, to hold Lily in her arms, and hear her laugh, and smell the sweet scent of her—a mixture of lemongrass shampoo and that trace of fresh buttermilk that always rose from her skin. Alana held on until Lily squirmed out of her hug with animated reports of the week she had spent with Ramona. There was a lot of TV and staying up late and junk food. She had fun. But she missed her mom a lot.

Alana had managed to make it home well before midnight. She thanked Ramona and sent her off with a bonus day's pay and a cedar box full of wild smoked salmon. Lily got an airport hoodie and a giant Toblerone bar and the exciting news that tomorrow they would go shopping for a new minivan.

After Alana put Lily to bed, she took a long, hot shower. Then she cracked a black cherry soda and fished out the MacBook Pro she had stolen from the safe in her sister's bedroom when she stopped at the house, ostensibly to pick up her clothes before her flight home. If her father tried to access his files, he would find an expensive paperweight, thanks to the fuckery of Geek Squad girl.

Alana switched on the computer and got the lock screen. She spent the next few minutes typing in random passwords that she thought her father might use (including 1234 and 0000). No luck. She searched YouTube for how to crack a Mac password and found a video that provided simple steps to follow should you forget your password and wish to reset it: *Turn off the computer. Hold down Command and R. Go to the Utilities dropdown menu and hit Terminal. Type in* resetpassword. Voila!

Feeling smug and proud of herself, Alana typed in the new password: OPEN. The desktop screen appeared. It was covered in dozens of files, all with ambiguous names: CMM1 or DEJ7 or YC14, each with a little padlock icon at the top. She steeled herself and clicked on one. A pop-up window appeared. A royal-blue rectangle: *ShielderCrypt. Enter password for CMM1.* Damn it. She clicked on a few more files, but they were all password protected by ShielderCrypt. There didn't seem to be anything but these files on the computer.

She checked her father's browsing history on Safari, but it had been wiped clean. She opened his Apple email, but it appeared to have never been used. Then she noticed another mail icon: a blue bird holding an envelope. She clicked on it. It was an email program called Thunderbird. There were hundreds of emails in the in-box, and she recognized a couple addresses from the notebook in her father's safe: darkeyedjunco@posta.ro and callmemister22@posta.ro. She tried to open the most recent email, from callmemister22, but got the following pop-up: *You have received an encrypted email from callmemister22@posta.ro. To view your message, save and open the attachment and follow the instructions.*

She tried the password to her father's safe. It didn't work.

Alana again tried the YouTube tutorial route but couldn't make heads or tails of the ostensible solutions.

Clearly, her father had something to hide. And clearly, she was going to need someone beyond Geek Squad level to help her uncover it—someone she could trust with whatever sensitive information was revealed.

"Fuck," said Alana out loud. There was only one computer genius in her life. And she hadn't spoken to him in more than seven years. Her ex. Lily's absentee father.

15

Alana hadn't had many boyfriends when she met Stephen Dale. There was Jordan Butterfield in grade six, who smacked her on the head and threw her school blazer in a puddle because he "liked" her. "He's just trying to get your attention," her mother told her. The next day, Jordan offered her a Chupa Chups lollipop and asked her to be his girlfriend. She said yes but only because she wanted to go to Melanie Kenney's rec room after school on Friday, and only "couples" were allowed. She necked with Jordan at the party and let him feel her up. "What's the point?" he griped, finding nothing much to palpate on her twelve-year-old chest. She burned with shame and avoided Butterfield for the next three years at St. Michael's. There was Adam Azim, whom she met tree planting during the summer when she was seventeen. She was pretty sure he was queer and just wanted a beard for the season, but she was glad of his friendship and relieved to lose her virginity. They had sex five times (four of them doggy style). In the first year of university, she dated a busker named Joe Benitah for seven months before he decided, out of the blue, to become religious and abstain from all premarital sexual relations. A few weeks after they split, he showed up at her twelfth-floor apartment and invited her out for a platonic walk. On the way down in the elevator, he wrestled her to the ground, kneeled on her shoulders and tore her shirt open. While she thrashed and cursed, he pulled down her bra and stared hungrily at her tits. That was the end of Joe Benitah.

She was picking sour cherries in a stranger's backyard when she first spoke to Stephen Dale. She was twenty-three at the time, majoring in sociology at the University of Toronto. He was a year younger—a community-minded IT nerd and self-proclaimed "hacktivist" who had created a database of fruit-bearing trees in the city. He and a friend had organized teams of volunteer pickers to harvest the fruit and donate it to local food banks. Pickers were rewarded with a share of the harvest, and Alana had plans to bake a sour cherry pie after a long, hot day of volunteering. Stephen was the "pick leader" in her group that day. He was an impossibly skinny human who seemed to carry most of his weight in his hair, which was the color of honey and grew in about fourteen different directions. He wanted to know what Alana was listening to on her iPod and was impressed when she pulled out her right earphone and answered: *The Salesman and Bernadette*.

"No way. I frickin' love Vic Chesnutt," he said. "He's like my second-favorite musician of all time."

"Yeah, he's great," said Alana, who realized she had a choice in that moment. She could smile and jam her earbud back in, thus ending any further communication or flirtation. Or she could humor this walking stick figure with the intelligent green eyes and the washed-to-oblivion Guided by Voices T-shirt. She thought about it for a second and then took the bait: "So, who's your favorite then?"

They went for a beer after the pick. Six weeks later, he was asking to move in with her. A year after that, he was imploring her to not abort the child she had become pregnant with (she'd assumed, erroneously, that it would be safe to have condomless sex at the tail end of her period when she was still bleeding a little). Why had she said yes to both these things? Whenever she thought back on it, she concluded that it was probably because Stephen was the first person besides her sister who actually seemed to care for her in any real way. And probably because he was pretty much the antithesis of her father. He was gentle, laid-back, and socially conscious (he confided that he and a cabal of like-minded hackers had been working with contacts in Dharamshala to keep the Dalai Lama safe from Chinese malware attacks); he was a pothead who was perpetually broke and didn't seem to care at all about money. When they met, he was sharing a two-bedroom condo with three buddies. His roommates had dibs on the bedrooms, so Stephen slept in the solarium in the corner of the living room. He'd covered the glass walls with newspaper for privacy. It was just big enough for a twin bed, a small dresser, and a duffel bag full of belongings. Even though Stephen had a highly employable skill set, he chose to remain poor, and could barely afford food (he used to steal salt and pepper pack-

ets from the Wendy's across the street from his apartment).
He was entirely unconcerned with Alana's weight or how
much she exercised or what she consumed, and said he'd
always had a thing for "corn-fed" girls and couldn't stand
"razorbacks." Still, she felt self-conscious beside him—he
was painfully thin and she was more than a little plump;
she thought they looked like Jack Spratt and whatever his
wife was called (did she even have a name?).

But they got along. And laughed a lot. And might have
been fine (for a while anyway) if their daughter hadn't been
diagnosed with Duchenne muscular dystrophy. It was a
blow for both of them but especially complicated for Stephen, who, at the age of sixteen, had watched his much-
loved stepfather succumb to ALS within a year.

Outwardly, Stephen pretended to be all in on their re-
vised family journey. He prided himself on being the good
guy, the responsible guy, the kind of guy who would do
all the research and go to all the doctor's appointments and
use his brilliant computer skills to solve whatever problems
needed to be solved. But it became apparent to Alana that
the moment he heard the news, and processed what it meant
and would entail, he was subconsciously seeking a way out.

Of course, Stephen could never be the guy who disappeared because he found out his daughter had an incurable
disease. No. Cognitively, he would never accept that. But
he *could* be the guy who left because his partner was an unbearable bitch on wheels. That was doable. And so he began
orchestrating that, behaving in ways that were certain to
elicit Alana's exasperation or wrath. Whether it was forgetting to take Lily to her physiatrist appointment or leaving
his unflushed turds in the toilet all the time or inexplica-

bly throwing her good sheepskin slippers in the washer and dryer, effectively turning them into hardtack elf clogs, or leaving the freezer door open and ruining sixty dollars' worth of just-purchased food or forgetting to tell her that her GP called with test results that showed she did indeed have a UTI or blowing their grocery money on a vial of hash oil—it was all designed to elicit negative responses from Alana. Soon after the diagnosis, Stephen abandoned his only paid gig so he could focus more on secretly aiding Chinese dissidents. Alana agreed that it was important work but also thought he should be helping out with rent and bills. "You're always ragging on me about money," he would say. "But you don't pick up the phone to call your father, do you? Literally all you'd have to do is pick up the phone and ask Daddy for some cash, but you refuse to do it. You refuse to help this family." She had been cagey about her background and had never divulged who her father was, but he'd found out anyway.

By the time things were blowing up between them, Alana had postponed her own schooling and taken on two part-time jobs, one of which was a grueling overnight shift as a relief worker in a homeless shelter twice a week. She would roll home at eight in the morning, strip down in the vestibule and bag her clothes and shoes (she was terrified of bringing bedbugs into their apartment), shower, and hit the sack until two. Then she'd get up and take over Lily's care so that Stephen could get some work done. One morning, she came home after a shift, took off her clothes, and walked into the living room, where she was gawked at by a heavily pierced waif who was drinking coffee with Stephen while Lily lay prostrate in her playpen.

"Jesus Christ," said Alana, hurrying down the hall and into the bathroom. She heard a bubble of suppressed laughter in the living room. She put on Stephen's ratty robe and came back out.

"Alana, this is my friend Manon. She's in from Montreal and needs a place to crash for a couple nights."

"Nice to meet you," said Manon with a little wave. "And sorry about..." She gestured to Alana's body. "You know."

"Were you guys smoking in here?" said Alana, scooping Lily out of her playpen. "How you doing, baby?" Alana asked her.

"Good," said Lily.

"Manon had, like, two puffs of a cigarette, but she blew the smoke out the window."

"Well, I can smell it," said Alana.

"Well, her lips were literally against the screen," said Stephen.

"You know that can hurt Lily, right?"

"Wow," said Stephen.

"Yeah, wow," said Alana.

"Sorry, I should go," said Manon, standing and reaching for her backpack.

"No," said Stephen. "Stay, it's fine."

"No, it's OK," said Manon. "I'm going to get breakfast. We can talk later. Nice to meet you," she said with a sweet smile, which made Alana feel like an ogre.

"Hang on, I'm coming," said Stephen, grabbing his wallet from his desk.

"No," said Manon. "You should stay."

"You know, I'm really sick of people telling me what to do," he said, striding past them. "The endless ragging," he shouted before slamming the apartment door on his way out.

Manon stared helplessly at Alana, who was full of rage and fighting tears.

"I'm sorry," she said.

"Me too," said Alana. "I'm just tired. I worked all night."

"Sorry." Manon gave Alana a grim smile and left.

Stephen didn't come home until the following evening. He stayed for a few more tense weeks until Alana finally obliged him by suggesting that they "take a break." He pretended to be hurt and sorrowful, but the relief flooding through his body was apparent. He grew excited and told her that he had an amazing job opportunity in Barbuda and that he would send money. And he did, for a few years, a good amount of money, which enabled Alana to hire caregivers for Lily and find a better job. (Mr. Socially Conscious helped launch an online poker site that made a ton of profit until it suddenly disappeared.) She was grateful for the support but also amazed that he never once got in touch to ask about his daughter. He didn't want to communicate. He didn't want to know. He needed to eradicate the connection and all potential for pain.

When the funds stopped arriving, Alana let it slide. Between her job, various government assistance programs, and the money she had saved from Stephen's contributions over the last few years, she had enough to squeak by on. And she had zero desire to try to chase down her ex.

In the first months after he left, Alana felt lost and sad and also guilty. Had she driven a good man away? Was she an awful, overly exacting person? She often talked about it with Lily's caregivers, who she grew close to, and she was comforted by something Ramona said to her way back when: "My husband says I'm the world's biggest nag, but you know what I tell him when he says it? I say, *That's just you trying to get away with shit, Ronald. You know damn well that a naggy wife is really just a lousy husband.*"

16

It took Alana nearly two weeks before she was able to make contact with Stephen. During that time, she had returned to work and everything was pretty much back to normal, apart from the snazzy black minivan in the drive. She had found one with a remote-controlled wheelchair ramp, air-conditioning and heated seats—not brand-new but only two years old—which made her trip out west seem entirely worthwhile.

Alana received regular reports from Martin about Teddy's status. He remained stable. Nothing had changed. Five days after he was admitted, the doctors had eased up on his sedation to see if he could breathe on his own. He could not. They repeated the experiment five days later. Still no spontaneous breathing. After that, the family had been cornered in the hospital by a transplant team, who tried to gently steer them toward the idea of donating Teddy's organs. Ed raged at the team, bellowing and threatening, until they backed off (huffily and with plenty of stink eye, according to Martin). Martin reported that Kelly seemed quite on board with harvesting Teddy's entrails, but she stopped nudging in that direction after Ed went nutsy. The doctors advised trying to ease Teddy off the drugs again in another five days' time. Martin was charged with keeping an eye on things, while Ed and Kelly jetted off to Parrot Cay for a few days to relax and restore. Kelly felt that Ed was inordinately tense and needed a break for both his mental and physical health. Martin thought that Kelly preferred to sit on a beach than in a hospital. He promised to keep Alana informed of any developments, and since she hadn't heard from him for a few days, she assumed nothing had changed.

Alana was about to pack up and leave work when she received two surprising texts. The first was from Kelly, a double surprise since it wasn't even about Teddy: So beautiful here! Your dad says you never visit! Ed and I would be happy for you and your daughter to make use of the house when we're not using it. P.S. He's obviously still worried but feeling less stressed. I think it was a good idea to get away! She included a picture of Ed in a white suit, sitting at a table in a gazebo, with a pristine white sand beach in the background. The table had been set for lunch, and a waiter was topping up Ed's champagne glass and smiling at the camera as if he'd been directed to do so.

Alana studied the photo then sent back a noncommittal Thanks. Looks great.

The other text was from Stephen Dale: I'm around for the next hour. Call me.

All the old contact info she'd had for Stephen had proved obsolete. She was finally able to track him down by messaging his mom on Facebook and assuring her that she needed help with a computer issue (and not a personal matter). She left her number and asked her to please relay the information to Stephen. And now here he was.

She called the number.

"Hello?"

"Hey, it's Alana."

"Hey, how are you?"

"Pretty well, thanks. How are you?"

"Can't complain," said Stephen. "So, what's up? My mom said you have a tech issue you need help with."

"Yeah, I have a MacBook Pro with a bunch of encrypted files that I need to open. Emails as well."

"Oh, OK. I thought maybe the tech thing was a ruse."

Alana sighed. "Nope. I just want to open these files. They're protected by something called ShielderCrypt."

"OK, no problem. I can likely do it. Who sent the files?"

"Um...that I don't know."

"But they were sent to you?"

Alana hesitated. "No. It's not my computer. It's my f—fiancé's."

Stephen laughed. "Trust issues, huh? All right, I can give it a shot. I'm in Toronto until Sunday. At the Le Germain on Mercer Street. You want to drop it off here?"

"No, I can't just hand it over, and I can't stay today—I have Lily. Is there any way you could come by my office tomorrow and do it there?"

"Um, yeah, I guess. As long as it's after ten."

"How about eleven?" She gave him the address.

"All right. And listen, if you need money or anything—"

"No, I'm fine."

"So…Lily's OK?"

"Yeah. You know. As OK as she can be. She's a great kid."

He was silent for a few seconds. "Listen, I'm really sorry, Alana. You know, I thought I could handle it, but I just—I guess I couldn't."

"I know."

"I was too young, I think."

"Yeah."

"I'm younger than you, right."

"Right."

"I'm OK now. You know. I have a family."

"Oh…nice."

"We have a three-year-old son. He's normal—I mean, healthy."

Alana bit her tongue. *Don't berate the man whose help you require.*

"Happy to hear it," she said.

"OK. I'll see you tomorrow."

"Yup. See you."

Alana wondered how she would feel when she laid eyes on her ex. As it turned out, she felt remarkably little. She was mildly surprised to see that the skinniest human on earth now had a bit of a paunch and that his giant pile of hair had been buzzed off, she was amused to note that he was sporting the exact same Guided by Voices T-shirt he wore on the day she first met him, and perplexed by the notion that she had ever wanted to have sex with this person. Other than that: zero feelings. Except maybe relief that she no longer had to contend with him.

"Love what you've done with the place," he joked, walking into her dilapidated office. "Is that where Jimmy Hoffa's buried?" He gestured to the shifting mounds of paper, files, and office junk that covered the banquet table she used as a desk.

"Ha ha."

"I don't think this carpet is stained enough, Alana." He took a seat on the circa 1972 corduroy couch (missing half its corduroy buttons) and set his Jamba Juice down on one of the six Sealtest milk cartons that served as a kind of modular coffee table.

"What, you're all fancy now? You need polished concrete and floor-to-ceiling windows?"

"Nah, I'm just raggin' you. I know you're doing good work here. Remind me to make a donation before I leave."

"Here." She sat beside him on the sofa and set the laptop on the milk carton in front of him.

He opened it and turned it on.

"How long do you think this will take?" said Alana.

"Well, could be twenty seconds or twenty years. Depends."

"On what?"

"The stupidity of your fiancé, no offence."

"Oh, the password is OPEN," she said when the lock screen appeared.

"Well, that bodes well," said Stephen, typing it in.

"Why?"

"Because the key to opening these files is a weak or predictable password."

"Well, I reset that password. I don't know what it was before."

"Oh," said Stephen, staring at the screen. "That's interesting."

"What?"

"Romanian email addresses. All of them. Including your fiancé's."

"I was wondering about those *.ro* emails. So, what does that mean?"

"Something illegal, probably, since Romania is the only country in the world that won't grant the authorities access to private email accounts."

"Oh. Wow."

"I could be wrong. But let's find out." Stephen pulled a USB drive out of his bag.

"Wait, what's that for?"

"There's software on here that I need to upload. For cracking passwords."

"Can't you just decrypt the files directly on the computer?"

"Nope. Not without constituent keys. The encryption is solid. The passwords, not necessarily. That's what I meant by twenty seconds or twenty years. The software will cycle through all the possibilities. It looks like a pretty big group of people sharing with each other, so hopefully one of them is a fuckup. Unless these are criminal masterminds, a brute force attack will likely find an ABC123 man in the mix."

"You're not downloading anything from the computer *to* your drive?"

"No, why would I?"

"Fine. Go ahead," said Alana.

He inserted the device into the computer. "Still paranoid, huh?"

"Well, who knows what's on there? For all I know these are corporate secrets or something."

"Like how they get the caramel in the Caramilk bar?" he said. "If it's the eleven herbs and spices recipe, I'm stealing it."

"Very funny."

"Relax, OK. I'm just going to use Hashcat to run a brute force attack."

"I have no idea what you're talking about, but I'll leave you to it."

"Yup," said Stephen. He took a sip of smoothie and started typing.

Alana went to her desk. She had time to answer precisely two emails before she heard Stephen laughing.

"Okey-doke," he said. "We're in."

"That was fast," said Alana.

"*DROWSSAP15.* Christ, what a moron. Another guy. Not your fiancé."

Alana returned to the couch as Stephen typed in the password. "Oh," she said. "That's *password* backward. Hmm."

"It's a video," he said. "Do you want to do the honors or shall I?"

"Go ahead," said Alana.

He opened the MP4 file. It was a video of a little girl, sitting on a couch, eating a Pop-Tart, and watching TV—there was ambient audio from a cartoon kids' show that

Alana vaguely recognized. The girl looked to be about three or four years old.

"Uh-oh," said Stephen.

Alana's stomach was already clenched.

A man came into the room, but the framing of the camera cut him off at the shoulders. Based on the way he was dressed and how he moved, Alana guessed he was in his thirties. He handed the girl a small glass of milk and left the frame. She took a sip and set the glass down.

"Drink your milk," said the man from off camera. The audio was pretty bad.

The girl drank some more.

The video image slowly dissolved, but the framing didn't change—the camera was on a tripod or propped up somewhere. The girl was lying down on the couch now, apparently asleep, with audio from a different-sounding kids' show playing in the background. The man came back in. He maneuvered the sleeping girl closer to the back of the sofa and sat down beside her. His head appeared in the frame then. He was wearing a curly red clown wig and a plastic nose and glasses.

"Turn it off," said Alana.

"As soon as we know what we're dealing with here."

The man did something strange then. With his left thumb, he pulled up the girl's left eyelid. Then he used his right pointer finger to touch her eyeball.

"Jesus Christ! Did he kill her?" said Alana.

"I think he drugged her. I think he's checking to see if she's out."

The man let the eyelid fall shut. When he reached under

the girl's dress and started to pull down her underwear, Alana slammed the laptop shut.

"Oh my god," she said, jumping up from the sofa.

"What the fuck, Alana? I was expecting gay porn or some shady-ass business dealings."

"We have to get this to the police," said Alana.

"No shit," said Stephen. "But I would send it straight to the RCMP and the FBI. Your local cop shop can't deal with this."

"OK, so how do I do that? I mean, should I just call?"

"You could just call. But I can help you. I have connections."

"You do? Why?"

"You think a man of my abilities is going to squander all his talent on online gambling?"

"So, what, you're a spy or something?"

"I'm not a spy, Alana. I'm a nerd. I know how to spot vulnerabilities. That's very useful if you want to protect anything important."

"Hmm."

"I know people who can get this to the right people."

"OK, but let me just think about it for a second," said Alana, pacing the office.

"What, you're worried about your fiancé? What's his name anyway?"

Alana didn't respond.

"You're not seriously going to protect him?"

"No, it's not that."

"Speaking of which, should we check the email to see if he's sending shit out as well as receiving?"

"Oh god," said Alana. "Maybe we should just let the police deal with it."

"You don't want to know? Jesus, Alana, does he have access to Lily?"

"No! God, no. Never."

"Because I'll fuckin' kill him, I swear to god."

"No! He has literally never met her. I swear!"

"Your fiancé has never met your daughter?"

Alana didn't respond.

"Whose is this?" said Stephen, gesturing to the computer.

Alana met his eye but didn't answer. As they stared at each other, her face grew hot with fear. Maybe she shouldn't have involved him in this.

Stephen opened the sent file in the email program. "Hmm," he said.

"What?"

"Either he hasn't sent anything or he's smart enough to have deleted it."

"So will the police be able to trace these people and stop them?"

"Yeah, when you tell me who this sick fuck really is."

17

Alana was nine years old when her sister vanished. It was early January. Dank and cheerless. Lillian disappeared halfway through the school day on the first Monday back after the Christmas break. Peers noticed her eating lunch in the cafeteria, but that was the last they saw of her. She didn't show up for afternoon classes, and she didn't come home that evening.

The police were called, and Ed hired two separate private detectives to track her down. The detectives told Ed not to worry—Lillian would be found. She hadn't been abducted; she'd left a note for Alana, written on her Care Bear stationery: *I have to go. Sorry. Pretty sure it's going to be OK.* That was it, except for *I love you*, which she wrote inside a hand-drawn speech bubble coming out of Tender-heart Bear's mouth.

A tip line was set up, offering a handsome reward for information leading to Lillian's recovery. The line was immediately flooded with calls. There were nearly a dozen sightings on Vancouver's East Side. Others claimed to have spotted Lillian as far away as Montreal and Halifax. But all of those clues proved fruitless. None of those girls were Lillian. They were other young girls who had cut and run.

The first time the police searched Alfred Island—two days after Lillian was reported missing—they found no trace of her. But after receiving a tip from a water taxi driver in Sidney (apparently, a young girl had tried to hire a taxi but left after being told that Alfred Island was private property and accessible by invitation only), they searched again. This time they discovered a broken window in cottage 4. Ray Phelps, the groundskeeper at the time, let the police into the cabin. In the living room, they found Lillian's peacoat and a knapsack containing money, a half-eaten bag of Doritos, a notebook and Lillian's favorite stuffed animal, Sally (a tiny lamb with a pink nose and questioning eyes). They found Lillian in the bedroom. She had wrapped one of her mother's Hermès scarves around one of her father's leather belts and hanged herself from a wooden beam in the timber-frame ceiling. A premeditated act. Why else would she have left home with those particular items?

For Alana, the shock was extreme. The grief, cavernous. It was her first loss, and the idea that she would never again see Lillian was unfathomable. The mysterious, beautiful sister who loved and protected her couldn't really be gone.

The first days following the discovery were particularly

awful. Nobody would tell Alana anything about what had happened, only that Lillian had died. Teddy and Martin hinted at some secret knowledge but wouldn't share it with her. They relished the power of withholding "grown-up" information (and didn't seem at all sad that Lillian—the interloper who had attracted so much of their father's attention—was gone. In fact, they were quite chuffed about not having to go to school for two weeks). Alana had nobody but her nanny to talk to about it, and Patsy, though kind, would only mouth platitudes about God's plan and how Lillian was in a better place. Alana didn't dare go to her parents. The erratic emotional fluctuations in the household repelled her from both of them. Hushed voices and tense silences followed by screaming and recriminations followed by tears and lamentations. Doors slammed. Glasses dashed to the floor. When her mother came to her room, always intoxicated and morose, it was to seek comfort not offer it.

At school, Alana's teachers and some of her peers were nicer to her because of what had happened (she enjoyed that part of it, maybe even milked it a little, if she were being honest), while others stayed away, not knowing what to say or how to react. It was at school that she learned that Lillian had taken her own life. "Sorry about your sister," Melanie Kenney said to her. Then, as if she were asking on behalf of the entire student body: "Do you know why she did it?" That was the question in everyone's mind. Why would a beautiful young girl, a talented athlete with good grades, from one of the wealthiest families in the country, cut short her enviable life?

Why?

Alana didn't know why at the time. When she was old

enough to broach the subject with her parents, they always gave the same answer: Lillian was "troubled." She had been "troubled" for years. They said her night terrors and the strange scribblings in her notebooks were proof that she was troubled. In the notebooks, Lillian wrote ambiguously but extensively about a girl named Gloria. Judging by the passages, Lillian and Gloria were confidantes who knew each other intimately. Sometimes Gloria wrote about Lillian in the notebooks (in a different-colored gel pen). But Lillian didn't have any close friends, and didn't know anyone named Gloria. Ed and Kat had determined that Gloria was a made-up person in Lillian's head.

Lillian was troubled.

That's all there was to it.

Alana accepted this narrative for many years. But as she grew older, tiny tendrils began to sprout between snippets of memory. Slowly, slowly, Alana began to pull together *why* Lillian was so troubled. She remembered being in the pool as kids, Martin and Teddy doing dives and cannonballs, literally screaming for their father's attention: "Dad. Dad! *Dad!* Watch this!" They would swim to Ed and tug on his arms or jump on his back, trying to engage him, but he'd shrug them off. He was focused on Lillian. His hands were on Lillian. His eyes, Alana recalled at a certain point, were always on Lillian. And what about all the photos from when Kat and Ed got together, when Kat was pregnant with Alana, and Lillian was four. Why were there so many pictures of Lillian and so few of Martin, Teddy or Kat? And why were there so many videos of Lillian in the bath or being toweled off afterward? When Alana came along, there were barely any photographs of her. But over the years, Ed had taken thousands of pictures of Lillian.

And what about that time when Alana was about five years old, when she was with Patsy in the big playroom on the second floor of the family home in Victoria. Lillian, Martin, and Teddy were at school. Ed was who knows where—at work or out of town. Kat was in the living room on the main floor, talking to someone on the phone. Alana wasn't paying attention and couldn't hear what she was saying, but she could make out the cadences of complaint. Kat was unhappy and must have been drunk or stoned because occasionally she would bellow something that would penetrate upstairs: "You don't understand who I'm dealing with!" The outbursts scared Alana, which Patsy could see. She turned the TV on and cranked the volume. But just as Alana was being soothed by Smurfs, she heard her mother jeer: "He was never interested in *me*!" And what about all those private lessons Ed arranged for Lillian? The ones that took place in cottage 4, ostensibly so that Lillian could have privacy and stay focused? Lillian was doing well at school. Why did she need to have French and math and English tutors coming to Alfred Island all summer? Why were those "tutors" always men Ed seemed to know? And why was he always jetting Kat off to Canyon Ranch or Schloss Elmau or some other spa retreat for extended periods of time? Was that really for Kat's benefit?

Alana remembered a thing that Lillian used to say to her all the time when she was little: "Anything bad happen today?" Alana would say "Nope." Lillian would say "Dope." Back then, Alana thought it was just a little word game, a meaningless ritual between sisters. But at some

point—when all the strange flashes of memory finally co-
alesced in Alana's mind—it took on a darker meaning, and
she knew, she knew for certain why Lillian was asking and
why Lillian was so "troubled."

Lillian had left the family home on January 4 with a plan
to end her life. When she wrote *Pretty sure it's going to be OK*
on Alana's Care Bears stationery, she wasn't talking about
her own future; she was talking about her sister's. Nothing
bad had happened between Ed and Alana while Lillian was
around, and she was pretty sure it was going to be OK for
her sister once she was gone.

Alana was fourteen years old when she finally confronted
her mother. Kat denied any knowledge of abuse and told
Alana she was delusional. But Alana could see she was lying
(the hard dry swallow, the clench of the jaw). When she
pressed the matter further, Kat clutched Alana's forearms
and warned her to never mention such a thing again to
her or anyone else. "I'm serious," she hissed, her eyes wild.
"Never ever even hint of this to your father, do you understand me? Or your brothers. Or anyone. You keep your
mouth shut!" When Alana tried to squirm away, her mother
gripped harder, sinking fingernails into flesh. "Listen to me.
It's too late to help your sister. You have nothing to gain
here and everything to lose. And I mean everything. Do
you understand me? I'm talking about your *life!*" When her
mom released her, Alana's arms were gouged and bleeding.
She took off, sickened by her mother's complicity. She left
the house and walked for more than an hour in the rain,
fueled by rage.

Later that same night, when Teddy came home from a
party, Alana corralled her brothers and confronted them as

well. They didn't deny Ed's focus on Lillian. How could they? They'd felt it keenly, resented it, and commented on it ever since the families merged. But that's as far as they would go. When she asked why they were always stationed outside cottage 4, chasing her away when she got too close, they admitted that Ed had paid them to act as sentinels while Lily was having her lessons.

"But we had no idea what was going on inside," said Martin.

"Yes, we did," said Teddy, kicking Martin's foot and giving him a look. "Lillian was with her tutors, and Dad didn't want her to be disturbed during her lessons."

"Well, yeah, obviously," said Martin. "Duh."

"Really, like that time I heard her screaming, but you wouldn't let me near the cottage? Remember? I kept trying to get to her, and you kept pushing me away. And then you carried me off and dumped me in the woods."

"I don't remember that," said Teddy. "And if anything else was going on, which I seriously doubt, it was beyond *our* control."

"Beyond your control?" she parroted with disdain.

"Yeah, beyond our control," said Martin. "We were kids, for fuck's sake. We didn't do anything to Lillian."

"OK. I guess you guys know which side your bread is buttered on."

"If I were you, I'd be very careful about making accusations," said Teddy, getting up and signaling to Martin to leave with him. "Best to just drop it, Alana. Put it out of your mind."

Over the next few weeks, Alana grew increasingly sullen and withdrawn. She couldn't look at any member of her family without feeling disgusted and alienated. Her brain scrabbled for a solution, but the more she thought about it, the more she understood how powerless she was. Her mother wasn't going to back her up. Her brothers certainly weren't. Nobody in their right mind would challenge the colossus that was Ed Shropshire. Whoever tried would be either bought or destroyed. Alana believed her mother in that regard.

And so there was nothing Alana could do. Not without a shred of evidence.

She tried to get on with her day-to-day life but couldn't. She felt like a busted window with a cold wind howling through.

"What the hell's the matter with her?" Ed asked Kat during dinner one evening, when he'd received a particularly surly scowl from Alana.

"Nothing," said Kat, firing her daughter an intense warning look.

"Doesn't look like nothing," said Ed.

"Guess I'm *troubled*," said Alana, dropping her cutlery with a clatter and leaving the table.

She couldn't look at their faces, couldn't bear to stay in the family home any longer. She decided she wouldn't go back to St. Michael's for grade ten. She emptied nine years of saved allowances from her childhood bank account and fled to Toronto. No detectives were dispatched to bring her back, she noted (and not without a pang). She rented a room in a shared house in the Annex. Her bedroom was in the dining room, which meant she couldn't get to sleep until her genial but noisy housemates vacated the adjacent living room and went to bed. Five of her six roommates were university students; six out of six were slobs. The drafty, underheated house had mice and roaches and abysmal water pressure—you had to flush three times to get anything but piss to go down the toilet—but she felt calm there. After a lifetime of luxury, she felt strangely drawn to deprivation. She signed herself up for grade ten at Harbord Collegiate (the course work proved hilariously easy after the rigors of private school) and got a part-time waitressing job at By The Way Café.

Much to her family's relief, Alana had taken Teddy's advice and "dropped it."

But she never put it out of her mind.

No.

18

The world was a rotten place, full of rotten people, doing rotten things. Alana felt this deep in her bones, deep in her amygdala.

She had almost always known it.

After Stephen left RedTree, she had to process a family who had just arrived, a pregnant woman with two young boys. The woman was nervous and apologetic because she wasn't sure she was "abused enough" to be there. Her husband had never hit her, she confessed. He only shouted at her and the children all the time, called them stupid and useless, called her a whore (she pronounced it "hewer") if he thought her clothes were too provocative. Sometimes he shook her by the shoulders, but he never hit her, so she wasn't sure if she should be there.

She was worried about her children though. Alana noticed that the boys were very still and quiet and unusually closed off. She assured the woman that she was right to come. She had done the right thing. Alana took the children to the playroom, where some volunteers were leading a puppet-making workshop. Then she went back to register the mom, who was now weeping in her office.

By the time Alana got home that evening, she felt simultaneously depleted and agitated. She took a hot bubble bath and then slathered herself with bergamot-scented lotion. She made a cup of tea and worked on a puzzle with Lily, who was feeling better after suffering from leg cramps most of the day. Then they ate delicious veggie burritos for dinner while bingeing several sweet and gentle episodes of *Detectorists*, which they both loved. But all of that felt like a shiny skin on a wormy apple. The rot of the world was festering just under the surface of Alana's evening. She couldn't shake the image of the little girl on the couch. She kept thinking about the man's finger on the girl's eyeball. And kept trying not to think about anything else the man might have done that day or ever.

Alana wondered how long it would take before the cops were at Ed's door and how it would all play out. In the end it didn't matter. All that mattered was finding those people and stopping them as soon as possible. She still felt strangely uneasy about involving Stephen but couldn't figure why it wasn't sitting right. He had connections to higher-ups in law enforcement; it was likely the best way to go. Still, something small and vague was gnawing at her. Maybe she should have just thanked Stephen for his assistance, withheld pertinent info, and taken the laptop to the police herself.

In an ideal world, it all could have been done digitally

and anonymously—she would hang on to the laptop, Stephen would send the files to his contact, and that would be that. But because of the way the perverts had set up their accounts in Romania, it apparently couldn't work that way. Stephen said someone had to hand the laptop to the authorities and let them know who it belonged to. Alana was afraid to be the point person, so when Stephen offered to do it, she assented. People in positions of power knew him, and, more importantly, would believe him and act quickly. It would save time, stop the bad guys faster, and keep her out of it (for now, anyway). It made sense. But she still felt oddly anxious.

After she put Lily to bed, Alana hit the couch with her book, but found herself rereading the same passages over and over again, her mind on another plane. She turned on the news, but it was either tragic or rage inspiring and just made her more jittery. She retrieved her phone from where it was charging in the kitchen and studied the photo Kelly had sent earlier. Her father in his white suit with a white rose on his lapel, in his white gazebo, on his white sand beach. With a great deal of satisfaction, she deleted it.

Alana put her phone back in the kitchen to charge. She brushed her teeth and got into bed. But when she turned off the light, her mind began to twitch with questions. What would happen if the cops showed up at her father's place and he denied everything? Could she prove that the laptop belonged to her father? What if Ed claimed he was being framed by a delusional stepdaughter who inexplicably blamed him for her sister's death? Would Martin back him up? Of course he would. Martin didn't give a toss about

Alana; he just needed her to help him get rid of Kelly. Ed had a laptop in his safe with zero incriminating evidence on it, she suddenly realized. But the authorities would have his actual laptop, with his fingerprints on it (presumably). Unless she and Stephen had wrecked any fingerprint evidence by handling the laptop and typing on it. Even if Ed's fingerprints were there, and they could prove that was his laptop, could Ed say that she planted that material on it? Would the cops believe her over her eminent father? And even if the cops knew Ed was guilty, would he be able to just buy or threaten his way out of it? Didn't everyone have a price? God, what if he succeeded? Powerful people got away with all kinds of things if they had friends in the right places.

Alana sat up and switched on the lamp. There was no way she could sleep; her brain was roiling. She tried her book again, but it was no use. Her mind wouldn't stop churning. If the cops went to Ed and he discovered that all the allegations had started with her, what would he do? Or, more accurately, what wouldn't he do? She remembered the frantic look in her mom's eyes when she tried to warn her: "I'm talking about your *life*." Alana's face grew hot with fear. She had an impulse to contact Stephen and call him off, but then she thought about that little girl on the sofa. And about her sister being dragged into cottage 4 for "lessons" with those strange men. And Ed having zero compunction about creeping into her dead sister's room to blithely and greedily watch other children's lives get destroyed.

God!

Alana's fear turned to fury. The more she thought about her father watching those despicable videos, the more irate she became. She couldn't wait to deprive him of his liberty and his power, and would do whatever it took to have him arrested and tossed into prison for the rest of his miserable life. She started to calm a bit. As she relaxed, she became more rational. Of course the authorities would investigate Ed—they'd probably love to take down a billionaire. And they'd certainly be able to track the laptop to her father if he used a credit card to purchase it. Didn't every computer have a distinct serial number? Alana took a deep breath and began to feel sleepy. As she drifted off, she thought about how relieved she would be when Ed was behind bars. And publicly exposed. No more kowtowing from almost every human he encountered. All those pediatric hospital wings would have to be renamed.

19

"Mom, are you all right?"

Alana opened her eyes and saw Lily in the doorway. She sprang out of bed and went to her daughter. "Are you OK? What's going on?"

"*I'm* fine—I'm worried about you. It's late."

"What time is it?" said Alana, disoriented.

"After eleven."

"Oh my god, are you serious?"

"I thought we were getting camp stuff this morning."

"We are. Sorry, lovey. I didn't fall asleep until around four."

"Oh. I shouldn't have woken you."

"No, I'm glad. Do you need to go to the bathroom?"

"I went. I managed."

"Good. Did you eat?"

"Toast and peanut butter."

"Good girl. Any pain?"

"Mom, *I'm fine.* Can we please just go?"

"Yeah. We'll go in half an hour."

Alana had coffee and a banana, then loaded Lily into the minivan to make their annual pilgrimage to Camp Connection. It was an errand they looked forward to, ever since Lily was seven, and started attending summer camp for kids with muscular dystrophy. It was her favorite week of the year, and the prep was part of the fun. They always went to the same store, which was always hopping with campers and their parents, picking out new shorts, shirts, bathing suits, sun hats, rain gear, pajamas, and sweats. They both loved the vibe of the store, and Alana loved the smell. A happy summer smell, like new garden hose, like fresh skipping rope.

"Do you need a flashlight?" said Alana, picking up a pretty turquoise one.

"I have one, but I don't know where it is."

Alana tossed it in the cart. She was feeling spendy. "Ooh, look at these. Do you like the ladybug or the butterfly?"

"I have a water bottle."

"I know, but these are so cute. And light. Easier for you to hold."

"Ladybug," said Lily.

Alana tossed it in the cart.

While she was paying for their items, her phone pinged, but it was deep in the bowels of her tote, so she ignored it. On the way back to the car, it pinged again. And then again as Alana loaded Lily into the van.

"Someone's texting," said Lily.

"Yup," said Alana, wondering if the cops could have descended on Ed so quickly. It seemed unlikely, but her heart jumped a little. "I'll just get the AC going." She settled into the driver's seat and fished her phone out of the bag. There were three texts from Martin. The first: Teddy checked for breathing this morning. No go. Meeting with doctors now. The next: Docs have declared Teddy brain-dead. Dad freaking. And finally: Hospital said we have to move Teddy to a private facility if Dad wants to keep him on life support. Call me.

Alana texted back: Driving. Will call when I get home.

She slipped her phone back in her bag.

"What's going on?" asked Lily.

Alana looked at her daughter in the rearview mirror. "My brother Teddy died."

"Oh. Wow. Sorry, Mom."

"It's OK."

"Aren't you sad?"

Alana thought it over. "No, not really."

"You didn't like your brother, right?"

"We were never close." Alana buckled her seat belt and backed out of the parking spot.

"That's your stepbrother, not your real brother?"

"Yeah. Both my brothers are stepbrothers."

"But your sister was your real sister?"

"Yup. Well, we had the same mom. Different dads, so I guess, technically, my half sister."

"Your family is confusing."

"That is very true. Hey, since we're up this way, should we go get Dairy Queen?"

"Seriously? I thought that was only for the last day of school or special occasions?"

"I know. But I'm jonesing for something sweet."

"I'm jonesing for a Skor Blizzard," said Lily.

Alana turned the minivan north.

Once Alana was home and Lily was settled, she called Martin. "Hey," she said. "How are you doing?"

"You know…"

"I'm sorry."

"Thanks."

"What's going on?"

"Well, the doctors have declared Teddy brain-dead. So that's it. They want to take him off life support. Actually, they won't even call it that anymore. They're calling it *organ* support now."

"Wow."

"Yeah. They're basically saying he's been dead for a while. One doctor was like, 'I'm sorry, but we can't keep the cadaver in the ICU past Tuesday,' which pissed Dad off, of course. Pissed me off too, to be honest."

"So, is Ed going to move him?"

"I don't know. I mean, nobody thinks he should. What's the point? The doctors all say Teddy has zero chance of recovery. Zero. And even if they're wrong, even if he somehow miraculously regained enough brain activity to take a breath, he still wouldn't have any real cognitive function. He's never going to be Teddy again."

"I don't think he'd want to live like that."

"I know. It's magical thinking on Dad's part at this point. Anyway, Kelly is trying to convince him to donate Teddy's organs, but Teddy never signed his donor card, so who knows what his wishes would be. It's basically up to the family."

"You mean, up to Dad."

"Yeah. Of course, the hospital wants them."

"Why wouldn't he donate them? May as well help someone else."

"I guess. Anyway, I'll keep you informed as things develop."

Three days later, Alana still hadn't received further updates from Martin. It was Monday now, which meant that if Ed was going to keep Teddy on life support, he would have to move him the following day at the latest. Curiosity got the better of her and she texted Martin: What's happening with Teddy? She kept checking her phone all day at work but didn't hear back until she got home. She was making dinner when he finally replied: Still waiting. Frustrating. Ed AWOL.

Ed AWOL? What the hell did that mean? Alana's heart jumped. Had the cops picked him up? Was it all going down right now? She felt excited and distracted, very nearly sliced the top of her finger off while chopping broccoli. Luckily, Lily's friend Zoe was over, so when dinner was ready, Alana let them eat in front of the TV, while she hustled to her room to call Martin.

"Hey."

"Hi, sorry to bug you. I'm just wondering what's going on. What do you mean Dad's AWOL?"

"It's weird. Something's up with the business, but he won't tell me what. I don't know why. A couple days ago, he was super pissed about something, then he fucked off to the island and spent the night there. Then yesterday morning he flew to Zurich. He hasn't given me an answer on Teddy, and I can't reach him. I'm making arrangements to have Teddy moved, just in case, but it would be nice to know."

"Does Dad have a business in Zurich?"

"No. Just accounts. And Fort Knox."

"Fort Knox?"

"He stores most of his gold there."

"Oh. Hmm. Did Kelly go with him to the island?"

"No. He just took off. Said he had to deal with a business thing. I figured he was heading to Vancouver or Toronto, but his pilot told me he took him to the island. And then yesterday morning, he flew to Zurich."

"Strange."

"Very."

"And you're sure he's in Zurich and not somewhere else?"

"Like where? Where else would he be?"

"I don't know," said Alana, flummoxed. Had Ed been contacted by the police? Was he on the lam? If Zurich was where her father stored a mountain of gold, was he in the midst of some kind of escape? Physical gold couldn't be traced.

"Anyway, he knows tomorrow is the cutoff to move Teddy, so I'm assuming I'll hear back from him tomorrow morning at the latest."

"All right, keep me posted," said Alana.

"Will do."

When she hung up with Martin, Alana tried texting Stephen. Hey, any updates? But the message didn't go through. It bounced back with a red exclamation point and a Not Delivered message. She tried calling the number. It was out of service. Alana's heart started to pound. The only way she could reach Stephen now was through his mom. She logged on to Facebook and searched for Sandra Dale. Three profiles came up, none of which belonged to Stephen's mom. Alana searched again. Same result. The account had been deleted.

"Fuck..." Alana's heart was racing now. She felt nauseated and scared. She didn't know what this meant—both Stephen and Ed disappearing—but she had a feeling there was a connection and that something very bad had occurred.

Indeed, later that evening after Lily's friend went home and Alana had put Lily to bed, there came a pounding on her front door, followed by the bell ringing three times in quick succession. Terrified, Alana grabbed a knife from the kitchen before peering through the peephole. She saw a man in a baseball cap, mirrored sunglasses, and hoodie. He was holding a small cardboard box. She opened the door.

"Alana Shropshire?"

"Yes."

The man handed her the box and jogged back to his car, a nondescript gray sedan that was idling at the curb. She waited to watch it pull away so she could make note of the license plate number, but it was covered in mud and impossible to read.

Alana carried the box to the kitchen and set it on the counter. It was around nine inches high and six or seven inches across. It felt like it weighed around three or four pounds. There was no shipping label on the box, not even a handwritten address; it had been sealed shut with packing tape. Alana stared at it for a full minute, her heart hammering. She hadn't ordered anything online. There was no reason for this package to have arrived. It occurred to her that the thing might contain a bomb. Maybe from one of Ed's henchmen who had learned of her treachery. Or maybe from a husband of one of the women she'd helped at the shelter. She had received death threats in the past. Quite a few. But not in the last year or so. Could you even send a bomb in a cardboard box? Maybe it was full of human feces. Or anthrax. No, anthrax came in little envelopes. Alana's mind was flitting. She judged that the package was pretty much the size, shape, and weight of a carton containing cremated remains. Was this what was left of Stephen, her accomplice?

Eventually, Alana steadied her nerves and carried the box and knife outside the front door. If the thing was going to explode or spray chemicals, she didn't want Lily to be affected. She set the package on the ground and gingerly sliced through the packing tape. Then she took a deep breath and opened the box.

20

What Alana wanted was justice. What Alana wanted was reckoning. What Alana did not want was a cardboard box full of pirate treasure.

When she opened the flaps of the carton, she saw the top of a very thick plastic bag folded in on itself. *Cremains*, she thought. But no. Inside the bag were dozens of shiny gold coins. Alana hustled the box back inside and bolted the front door. Then she locked herself in the bathroom, sat on the floor and upended the contents onto the bath mat. The coins were Canadian. From 2006. There was a veiny maple leaf on one side and Queen Elizabeth in pearls on the other. Each was stamped: *Fine Gold 1 OZ Or Pur 9999*. She counted the coins as she dropped them one by one back into the container. There were fifty in total.

Alana went to her computer and Googled *50 ounces of gold value.* "Holy fuck," she said, staring at the result: $88,350 USD. She felt instantly vulnerable. That was an amount of money someone would cheerfully kill for. She grabbed the box and scanned the apartment. Where could she hide it? She'd seen enough movies to know that the freezer and oven were out of the question. She was thinking about sewing the coins into various coat linings when she realized that if anyone were to break in for the loot, she would happily hand it over. She slid the box under her bed, then sat there wondering how the arrival of the coins was connected to her father jetting off to Zurich, where he stored his gold. She was running scenarios in her head when her phone rang, jolting her out of her reverie. She ran to retrieve it, expecting it to be Martin, but the caller was unknown. Typically, she would assume it was spam or telemarketing and let it go to voice mail, but something in her gut told her to answer.

"Hello?"

"I just want you to know that everyone on that email chain is being rounded up," said Stephen.

"Oh. Great! That's great!"

"Except one. I deleted one person from the list. And I'm very sorry about that."

"What? Who?"

"Listen, he wasn't generating anything, OK? I checked. He was just viewing. He's not a threat."

Every muscle in Alana's body clenched and she began to hyperventilate. "Oh my god. What did you do?"

"You have nothing to worry about. I promise. No names. Nothing traceable. He has no clue who shook him down.

And he won't find out. And all those other pervs are going to jail."

"*He* needs to go to jail, Stephen!"

"Trust me, this is better for you in the long run. And I think you know why. I'll be sending more. I just didn't want to overwhelm you."

"Don't you tell me what's better for me! I don't want money, I want him in jail! I want that laptop back!"

"I'm sorry, Alana. I couldn't pass up the opportunity. I just couldn't. And like I said, he's not generating anything. OK? Take care."

Alana heard three little beeps and the line went dead. With shaking fingers she called back the number, but somehow the line was already out of service. Alana hurled her phone across the room and moaned in frustration. That's why her father had flown to Zurich. Instead of giving him up to the police, Stephen had blackmailed him, betraying not only Alana but every past and future victim of her father's.

And now, as always, Ed would go unpunished for his crimes.

Alana put her head in her hands and pulled at her hair. It was her fault. It was her fault for involving Stephen, for trusting him. She should have just taken the laptop to the police! After all these years of knowing that Ed was sick and dangerous, but having no way to prove it, how could she have handed off evidence when she finally had it? What an idiot! And now it was too late. She would never have the chance again. Alana's face grew hot with shame and remorse. She had never felt so stupid or useless. She had never hated herself or the world more. She sank to the floor and stared unseeing into the dusty void under the couch until she heard Lily cry out in pain.

"What is it?" said Alana, switching on the night-light in Lily's room.

"My calves. And my heels," said Lily, pulling her BiPAP mask aside.

"Here…" Alana carefully removed the braces from Lily's legs.

"Ow!"

"Oh god, I'm sorry!" She felt Lily's calves, which were swollen and hard as stone. And her heels had been rubbed raw from the braces. Alana wanted to hurl the cursed devices out the window and run over them with the van. "I'll get the ointment. Do you need an ibuprofen, lovey?"

"I think so."

Alana fetched the pill, some water, and the salve.

"Can I please sleep without them for one night?"

"Yes."

After Lily had taken the ibuprofen and secured her breathing mask, Alana switched off the night-light and sat on the edge of the bed. She faced away from Lily, so her daughter wouldn't see the tears filling her eyes as she smoothed ointment onto the poor red heels.

"It hurts," Lily whimpered.

"I know, baby. I'm sorry." Alana stifled a sob and fought to keep her body from quaking. She massaged her daughter's tender feet and cried silently in the dark, whispering, "I'm sorry… I'm sorry… I'm sorry…"

21

Alana opened her eyes. One moment of calm before memory filled her with thick and heavy regret. She had an impulse to find the chef's knife she'd used to open the box of coins and sink it deep into her wrists. Bleed out and disappear from a terrible world.

She wallowed in this thought. Even teared up at her own demise. But no, such an act wasn't possible. And not just because of Lily.

Alana refused to be another casualty of her father's—another silence, another victory for Ed. He had killed her sister; he wasn't getting her too. Alana thought about a book of poems a client had brought her years ago at the shelter, a gift given in thanks for her help: *There Are Men Too Gentle to Live Among Wolves*. It was still on her office shelf (largely unread), but whenever her eyes grazed the title, she would think of her sister. And though Alana felt despondent and maddened by the events of the previous night, she knew she was made of sturdier stuff. She wasn't a wolf, no. But neither was she a lamb.

Alana got out of bed and opened the blinds. It was early, just after six. Lily was still asleep. She retrieved the chef's knife from the coffee table and washed it. As she soaped the blade, she imagined drawing it smoothly across Ed's jugular. Then she pictured carving out Stephen's heart and stuffing the cavity with gold coins. She dried the knife and put it back in the knife block. Then she made herself a cup of coffee and drank it in the comfy chair, in a ray of morning sunlight.

It wasn't long before she felt revived—not only by caffeine but by the plan that was crystalizing in her brain.

She knew what had to be done.

She just had to figure out the best way to do it.

22

A propitious phone call from Martin. "So, Dad's back. And it looks like Kelly convinced him. They're going to take Teddy off life support tomorrow."

"Oh...wow. Wow. I'm sorry, Martin."

"Thanks. Sorry to you too."

Alana searched for something appropriate to say. "Well, at least someone will benefit from this."

"Yeah, someone who just got away with murder. You know the cops ruled it an accident. Case closed."

"I was talking about the organ donation."

"Yeah, that's not happening. Dad said no."

"*What?* Why?"

"He said he doesn't want a bunch of scavengers dissecting his son."

"Are you serious?"

"I mean, I can sort of see where he's coming from," said Martin. "There's something gross about being stripped for parts."

"There's something grosser about depriving a desperate person of something you don't even need."

"Kelly's pissed too. She said she was going to call you. She wants you to help convince him, so don't be surprised if you hear from her."

"OK," said Alana. "But I doubt my opinion is going to sway him."

"Speaking of you-know-who, we need to talk. I've learned something interesting. You're coming to the funeral, right?"

"It depends. I'm on vacation as of this Thursday, but I have to drive Lily to camp in Illinois. I'll be dropping her off on Friday. Then I was going to stay in Chicago until I have to pick her up."

"I could arrange a flight from O'Hare. I'm guessing the funeral will be Saturday or Sunday."

"Yeah, OK," said Alana. She didn't want to attend Teddy's funeral. She'd much rather have a week to herself in Chicago. But she needed to talk to Martin as much as he needed to talk to her. "Once you know the details, get in touch and we'll make arrangements." Her phone beeped and she saw that Kelly was calling. "Oh, that's Kelly on the other line."

"All right, I'll let you go. But listen, if you end up calling Dad, remember he just lost his son, so be nice."

Alana tensed. Every cell in her body recoiled from that idea. "I have to go," she said, disconnecting from her brother.

23

It was a joy to see Lily reunite with friends and counselors in the camp reception area—a dusty parking lot buzzing with conviviality, love, sunshine, and high spirits. Pretty much the opposite of how Alana felt now, eighteen hours later, in the chapel of the Sequoia Centre, wedged between Gertrud and an overcologned stepcousin she hadn't seen for thirty years. She was wearing her one and only funeral dress, which was uncomfortably tight and too warm for the weather, and she'd been holding in some gas since the ceremony began, causing her stomach to make ungodly noises, always at the quietist, most somber moments of the eulogy.

While the minister driveled on about what a brilliant athlete, businessman, son, and brother Teddy was, Alana stole glances at the small group of family, friends, and business associates who had assembled for the invitation-only service. Was anybody buying it? The gathering was almost entirely made up of white-haired men in finely tailored suits—probably board members or higher-ups from Ed's various companies. There were a few younger men who looked like aging frat boys, their well-dressed, well-groomed wives by their sides. Alana guessed these were friends of Teddy's. Near the back was a beautiful woman in a cleavage-baring black dress who Alana pegged as an ex-girlfriend. And there was a ragtag cluster of people she didn't recognize, likely Ed's nieces and nephews from Boston, along with their spouses and children.

Alana, asphyxiating in a fog of Dior Sauvage, couldn't figure out why one of the cousins, Billy, had chosen to sit in the front row with the immediate family, until the minister ended the service and called upon the pallbearers, at which point Billy lunged forward as if he had been waiting his entire life for this glorious opportunity. She saw her father and Martin exchange a glance so withering she almost guffawed out loud.

Once the pallbearers had carried the casket outside to the hearse, Alana hurried to the bathroom, grateful that Teddy had opted to be cremated—there would be no traveling to a cemetery to endure another service. She just had to get through the reception at the funeral home. Alana adjusted her constricting dress and quickly left the bathroom without making eye contact with anyone. She spent the next hour fielding condolences from people she either didn't know or recognize, while trying to poke a bit of food down her throat. Cousin Billy—"Oh, I'm just *Bill* now"—was almost aggressively sympathetic, swooping her into a too-fierce, too-long hug even though she barely remembered him from a smattering of childhood visits when his mom, Ed's sister, was still alive. Alana watched as he repeatedly tried to get to her father, hovering awkwardly on peripheries while Ed spoke to others. She overheard him trying to wrangle himself an invitation to the house while he was in town, not just with Martin but also Kelly, who was having none of it: "We're all just trying to process right now. Ed's pretty worn out, as I'm sure you can understand. But definitely the next time you're in Victoria."

Billy even tried his hand with Alana. "Listen, I would love to buy you a drink and catch up. I feel like our families have grown so distant."

Alana laid it out plain: "I'm pretty much estranged from my family. I rent an apartment in Toronto and work at a women's shelter. I'm only here for a few days."

"Oh," said Billy, his eyes dimming, and Alana was reminded of those lizards with the translucent membranes that slide up over the orbs.

Later that evening, when Martin met Alana at her hotel for a drink, he told her that Billy had hit up Ed for a number of loans over the years for various businesses and schemes that never succeeded. The most recent was a chain of pop shops, with flavors like watermelon and basil, that went bust within eight months. Ed called him "The Dud."

"That's harsh," said Alana.

Martin shrugged and drained his beer. "Let's take a walk," he said, signaling for the waiter.

They headed outside to the hotel's pool, where a lone swimmer was just toweling off and leaving.

"This is good," said Martin, selecting a lounge chair.

"Phones," said Alana, settling into the chair next to his. She pulled out her iPhone and switched it off, putting it back in her purse.

Martin raised his eyebrows but followed suit.

"So, what's up?" she asked.

"I found out something interesting about Kelly," said Martin.

"And what's that?"

"She's using an alias. Kelly McNutt isn't her real name."

Alana felt a shiver rush up her arms and across her shoulders. "How do you know that?"

"I hired a detective."

"Whoa! If Ed finds out, he's going to shit a brick."

"Is he though? He might be happy to learn that his fiancée isn't who she claims to be."

"So, who is she then?"

"Aisling Hayes."

"Ays-ling?" Alana repeated Martin's faulty pronunciation. "You mean *Ashlin?*"

He spelled it out. "A-I-S-L-I-N-G."

"Yeah, that's pronounced *Ashlin.*"

"Oh," said Martin.

"And what have you learned about her?"

"That she's a nurse from Winnipeg."

"And?"

"Kelly said she was from Brandon, but she's actually from Winnipeg."

"So...the only difference is her name and which town in Manitoba she's from?"

"So far, yeah. I mean, she doesn't have a criminal record, she's never been married before..."

"So, how is this meaningful?"

"It's just dodgy, don't you think? I mean, why would she change her name?"

"Maybe people kept pronouncing it wrong."

"Very funny," said Martin. "Then she would have changed it to Kelly Hayes. *McNutt* is a name you change *from*, not *to*."

"Yeah, maybe. Well, given this new information, my solution is making more sense than ever."

"What solution?"

"I don't think we should be breaking our brains trying to get rid of Kelly. We know she's duplicitous, wily, possibly dangerous—"

"*Possibly?* Ask Teddy about that."

"Fine. She's dangerous. And smart. And wary of us."

"So, what's your solution?"

"A much simpler idea," said Alana, lowering her voice, even though there was no one around. "I think we've been barking up the wrong tree…" She waited in vain for Martin to catch her drift.

"What do you mean?"

"I mean, we should be thinking about Dad, not Kelly."

"*Dad?* What? You're not serious."

"He's old, he's already had a stroke. Who knows how long he's going to live anyway?"

"He's my father," said Martin, looking affronted. "My loyalty is to my father."

"And his loyalty is to Kelly. She just convinced him to unplug his firstborn son—nobody else could have swayed him. If it weren't for her, Teddy would be in a private hospital right now. Probably for the rest of our lives."

"True."

"If she suddenly wanted you out of the business, or out of their lives, you don't think she could make that happen?"

Martin was quiet now. Thinking.

"You just said she was dangerous. Once they're hitched, how long do you think it will be before she puts Ed in her sights? He's an old man with health issues. If he suddenly tumbled down the stairs, you think anyone is going to suspect her of anything?"

"That's true."

"Honestly, there was a point where I thought maybe she really loved him. Or even if she didn't, that she would at least let him live out his time while she enjoyed his money. I don't think that anymore. Not after Teddy. Trust me, Ed will be gone pretty soon after he marries her—you won't be able to protect him. But if what I'm proposing happens *before* Ed and Kelly get married, then you basically take over—get everything, control everything."

"Wow," said Martin. "You're kind of blowing my mind right now."

"I know, I get it. But think about it. Ed's already old and unwell. And Kelly has got it in for him anyway—she was fucking Teddy, which means she was never in love with Dad."

"I never thought she was."

"We have a small window of opportunity right now. They're obviously not going to have a big wedding after a funeral. But when I was leaving the *Andiamo*, I ran into Kelly and she told me she doesn't want a big wedding anymore. So, they're probably just going to sneak off to city hall or something, which means if we're going to do this, we have to act fast."

"Jesus," said Martin, massaging his forehead. "Let me

just think about this for a second." He got up and walked to the pool, stared into the water. "But wait a minute," he said, returning to the lounge chairs. "What's in it for you?"

"I don't want to see her win."

He narrowed his eyes. "And you hate Dad."

Alana shrugged. "Once he's married, he's in danger anyway. It'll happen sooner or later. Plus, the money Dad left for Lily in his will, it's probably good for her to have that, and I don't want it to go away once they're hitched."

Martin nodded.

"So yeah, we could stick with plan A and try to go after Kelly," said Alana. "But she's watching her back, and we don't have much time. Also, if a young, healthy person dies, there will be scrutiny. A lot of scrutiny—Dad will see to that. But if an old man who has already had a stroke has another stroke…"

"And how are we supposed to make that happen?"

Alana opened her purse and angled it so that Martin could see inside. Among the usual contents—wallet, comb, Purell, phone—was a bottle of quercetin supplements.

"That would cause it?" said Martin.

"No," said Alana. "Quercetin is a completely harmless supplement. Totally inert. But remember why Teddy and Kelly had to go back to Alfred Island? She forgot Ed's medication. I did some research on what he takes and it comes in capsules." Alana discreetly fished a quercetin capsule out of the bottle. She pulled it apart, emptied the contents into the palm of her hand, and then put it back together. "If we can get a hold of his prescription, we can replace the contents of the capsules with quercetin. A few days without his blood thinner…"

"It's not exactly foolproof."

"I know. But Kelly's a nurse and she seemed pretty frantic for him to not miss even one dose."

"That's true," said Martin, reaching for the capsule in Alana's hand. He pulled the thing apart and put it back together. Then he did it again.

"This is simpler," said Alana. "It might take a few weeks, but it's far less risky. And just think of the pleasure you'll have escorting Kelly out of Dad's house and out of your life forever."

Martin handed the capsule back to Alana. He ran his fingers through his hair and took a deep breath. "Wow. I don't know… I just lost my brother. I don't know if I'm prepared to lose my father too."

"You'll still have cousin Bill," said Alana.

"Very funny."

"Sorry. Look, I get it. And honestly, the safest thing, and probably the wisest thing to do, is to forget the whole thing. Let them get married, let it play out. Even if she succeeds in cutting you out of the business or the will, you'll be fine, right? You own a nice home in Victoria, a fancy car, probably a bunch of investments. And you have the connections to get a good job, if you want one. I'm sure you can live a very comfortable life even if you do get excised from the business and the will."

Martin nodded and thought it over. But not for very long.

He looked his sister in the eye and said, "If I decide to do this, I'm going to need your help."

"That's why I'm here," said Alana.

24

The following morning, Alana Ubered to Oak Bay for Sunday brunch at Ed's main residence, which was down the street and around the corner from her childhood home (and, she noted, twice the size for no good reason). The family then drove together to pick up Teddy's ashes from the crematorium. His will stated that he wanted his ashes scattered on the twelfth hole of the golf course on Alfred Island, and Alana was invited to attend the family-only ceremony.

It was drizzling when they arrived, and Ed decided that they would wait until the weather cleared before venturing to the golf course. Once everyone was settled, Martin and Ed went up to the home office to deal with a pressing business matter, while Kelly, Alana, and Gertrud had drinks on the covered terrace. They talked about the funeral, Lily's camp, and Teddy's choice of the twelfth hole versus the others for his ashes. Gertrud said that while the twelfth hole was one of the shorter ones on the course, it was also the most scenic and the most challenging, at least that's what Martin had told her.

Mrs. Keith came out to see if any of the women wanted a refill. Gertrud and Alana were still working on their first round. Kelly, who had drained her glass, uncharacteristically declined.

She got up and stretched. "I feel like I've been sitting for a week. Does anyone want to go for a walk or a dip in the pool?"

"I thought you didn't swim," said Gertrud.

"I don't," said Kelly. "But I can move around in the shallow end."

"But it's raining," said Gertrud.

"Barely. And there's no thunder. We can hop in the sauna if we get cold."

"Um, OK," said Gertrud. "Alana?"

"Sure."

"All right. Let's do it," said Kelly.

Alana went to her cottage to change. When she was on her way back to the pool, she ran into Martin, who had been looking for her. He was hyperventilating over a blowout he'd just had with Ed about an employee Martin let go while Ed was in Parrot Cay—a woman who was now suing for wrongful dismissal. Alana stood in the drizzle while Martin fumed about the employee's incompetence and how Ed had taken her side, even though he had no idea about the day-to-day minutiae in the hotel division. He complained about how Ed didn't trust his judgment or even believe him when he stated facts about the employee in question. When he was done ranting, Alana waited a beat and asked coolly, "So…are we doing this?"

Martin took a deep breath and let it out. "Yeah," he said, finally looking her in the eye. "We're doing it."

The swim in the rain was perfect. Alana roasted in the sauna until she couldn't take one more second of heat, then plunged into the gloriously cool pool. She swam lengths or just floated on her back, letting the rain hit her face. When she started to feel chilled, she headed back to the dimly lit cedar womb to warm up. It was wonderful. Invigorating. Kelly joined her a couple times in the sauna but didn't last long. Within minutes, she would turn almost comically red and have to flee. Gertrud only came in once.

After the swim, Alana showered and dressed. She had an hour before dinner, and she took the opportunity to get the quercetin ready for when Martin brought Ed's prescription to her cottage. They agreed that it made sense for Martin to nab the bottle, since it was natural for him to be upstairs in the home office, which was right next to Ed's bedroom. Martin would bring it to Alana and they would quickly empty and refill the capsules before he returned the prescription to Ed and Kelly's bedroom. Alana emptied thirty quercetin capsules into a large baggie so that they wouldn't waste any time making up the new doses. She swallowed the empty gelatin capsules, just to be safe, and tossed the bottle with the few remaining quercetin supplements into her toiletries bag alongside her vitamin B_{12}.

Alana still had a bit of time, so she flopped on the couch and checked Facebook. Lily's camp made the kids surrender their phones for the week, but they posted pics daily on their Facebook page, and Alana found Lily in a couple of snaps. One was a panorama of an Olympic-sized pool filled with kids and counselors. Lily and her camp bestie, Sarah, were together in a giant flamingo floaty. The other was a slightly blurry shot of Lily and Sarah, laughing and eating marshmallows beside a campfire. Alana smiled, pocketed her phone, and headed up to the house for dinner.

Martin and Gertrud were already at the table when she arrived. Alana greeted them and took a seat just as Ed and Kelly entered.

"I hope everyone is doing as well as can be expected this evening," said Mrs. Keith, breezing in and taking two bottles of wine from the buffet.

"We're hanging in there," said Kelly. "How are you?"

"Very well, thank you," said Mrs. Keith. "White or red?" she asked Gertrud, then proceeded to pour the wine of choice for everyone but Ed, who opted for water.

Alana noted that Kelly handed Ed his medicine to take as soon as Mrs. Keith had filled his glass. She seemed to have only brought the one capsule, which meant the prescription bottle remained upstairs in their bedroom. Alana looked at Martin, who seemed to have also been watching, and they locked eyes for a moment, both realizing that the prescription would remain untouched until the following morning.

"I have an idea," said Martin, as Mrs. Keith served the salad course. "After dinner, maybe we should all watch Teddy's favorite movie."

"Oh, that's a nice idea," said Gertrud.

"I love it," said Kelly. "I'll make popcorn." She turned to Ed. "I'll put olive oil and rosemary on it, like you like."

Ed, who had just forked a large kale leaf into his mouth, vaguely grunted his OK.

"What was his favorite movie?" said Alana.

"Moneyball," said Martin.

"I've never seen it," said Gertrud.

"And *Bad Santa*," said Martin. "But I don't think we should watch a Christmas movie in July."

"What's *your* favorite?" said Gertrud to Martin.

"*Top Gun*, baby. I think I saw it about ten times when it came out."

"Oh yeah, I think I knew that."

"What's yours, Gertrud?" asked Kelly when nobody else bothered to inquire.

Gertrud said she couldn't possibly pick because she loved so many so much. Ed said his was *Spartacus*. Then Mrs. Keith brought in the main course, and the conversation drifted back to Teddy.

After dinner, everyone except Alana settled in the family room to watch *Moneyball*. She begged off, feigning a migraine. She was hoping that Martin would pick up on the ruse, and she hovered at the front window of her cottage, scanning for him.

Martin watched twenty minutes of the movie before excusing himself to go to the bathroom. Instead of heading into the main floor washroom, he dashed upstairs, found the prescription bottle—there were several on the bedside table but only one that contained capsules instead of tablets—then bolted down the stairs and out the back door. He sprinted all the way to Alana's cottage.

Alana opened the door before he even got up the front steps.

"Come back when you're done," he said, panting. "Say you're feeling better."

Alana watched him tear back toward the house. Her

hands were shaking as she tried to quickly empty and refill the capsules. They were slightly smaller than the quercetin capsules and far more difficult to open—for a moment she thought she wasn't going to be able to do it and accidentally cracked one by squeezing and twisting the end too hard. But she soon got the hang of it and was able to refill the eighteen capsules in short order, carefully cleaning the quercetin dust—and her fingerprints—off each one. Using a tissue, she slipped the bottle into the pocket of her dress. An internet meme on the utility of dress pockets popped into her head as she hurried back to the house, looking as if she were carrying nothing at all.

Martin, meanwhile, had returned to the living room and taken his seat next to Gertrud on the end of the distressed leather sofa.

"Are you OK?" she whispered. "You're sweating."

Martin put his hand on his belly and grimaced. "I think I ate something that didn't agree with me."

"Oh no."

"I'll be OK," he whispered, squeezing Gertrud's leg and turning his attention to the screen.

"Do you want some ginger tea?" said Kelly, who was curled up at the other end of the large sofa. "It'll settle your stomach."

"Um, maybe later," said Martin. "Thanks."

Not long after, Alana returned, saying she had taken an Advil and was feeling better.

"Great," said Kelly. "You missed half the movie though."

"That's OK. I've seen it," said Alana, taking a seat in a club chair. When Martin looked at her questioningly, she slipped a hand into her dress pocket to indicate that the prescription bottle was there.

He seemed to get it. He waited about two minutes and then stood and patted his stomach. "Maybe I should have that tea. Anyone else want anything?"

"I'll have an Aberlour if you're going," said Kelly, holding out her glass.

"I'll have tea if it's being made," said Alana.

"You want tea?" Kelly asked Ed.

"I want Scotch," he said.

"I know, I'm sorry." She gave him a sympathetic pout.

"You need help?" Gertrud asked Martin.

"I'll go," said Alana, standing. "I've already seen the movie." She followed Martin to the kitchen. On the way, she discreetly passed him the tissue-wrapped bottle, and he slid it into his pants pocket.

They found Mrs. Keith at the kitchen island playing solitaire on her laptop.

"What can I get you?" she said, smiling.

"Just a pot of ginger tea," said Martin.

"All-righty-do," she said, heading for the kettle. "I'll bring it in."

On the way back, Martin handed Kelly's glass to Alana. "Get the Scotch. I'll meet you back there."

Martin ducked up the stairs and quickly replaced the bottle on the bedside table. But when he got to the bottom of the stairs, he ran into Kelly on her way up.

"Oh," she said, surprised to see him.

He froze for a second, then said, "Stomach issues. Didn't want to use the bathroom downstairs."

"Ah." She smiled. "Very considerate." She breezed past him and continued upstairs.

Martin hurried back to the family room, where the movie was on pause.

Alana returned with the Scotch and placed it on the coffee table in front of Kelly's empty space, noting her absence. She shot Martin a slightly alarmed look. "You OK?" she said.

"Yup. I'm good. My stomach's just a bit wonky."

"If you're getting stomach flu, go lie down," said Ed. "Nobody needs that right now."

"Fine," said Martin, who seemed relieved but also irked to have been dismissed. "I'll see you guys in the morning."

"Want me to come?" said Gertrud.

"No. Finish the movie."

Kelly walked in with a cardigan for Ed, just as Mrs. Keith brought the tea tray. Martin poured himself a cup and bid everyone good-night. Then he made a quick detour to the games room bar, where he dumped the steaming yellow liquid down the drain and replaced it to the brim with Colonel E.H. Taylor straight Kentucky bourbon.

25

The following morning was overcast and damp, but by noon it started to clear. And at four, when Ed directed everyone to meet at the house, it was sunny and warm—all blue sky and poofy white clouds. They drove golf carts to the course: Ed and Kelly in one, Martin, Gertrud, and Alana in the other (Alana in the back on a bench seat that faced to the rear).

The twelfth hole *was* very pretty. A dogleg with gently undulating hillocks, banks of mature willows, and two organically shaped sand traps that seemed to be cradling and lifting the green in smooth white fingers. The grass was immaculately tended and felt soft and pliant under Alana's feet.

Kelly had brought a portable chair for Ed to sit in while he read his tribute to Teddy—a heartfelt memorial, marred only by an expletive-filled outburst when Ed spotted a deer moving in the distance among the willows. Next up was Martin, who talked about how his big brother had always been his best friend and, because Teddy could reliably beat him in any sport or physical contest, his athletic role model too. Alana and Gertrud politely demurred when given the chance to say a few words. Kelly, though, accepted the offer, and said that while she hadn't known Teddy for very long, she would always be grateful for how generously he welcomed her into the family. Alana glanced at Martin when she said that, but Martin was staring at the ground. Next, Kelly unfolded a sheet of paper and read a short poem, while Ed and Martin used a small scoop to distribute some of Teddy's ashes onto the green.

"Warm summer sun, shine kindly here. Warm southern wind, blow softly here. Green sod above, lie light, lie light. Good night, dear heart, good night, good night."

When Martin and Ed were done, everyone just stood there, gazing solemnly at the ashes, which were thicker and much coarser than Alana expected. They didn't blow away or even move in the breeze; they just sat heavy and gray on the green.

After about a minute, Ed, who had tears in his eyes, said, "OK. That's it."

On the way back to the golf carts, Gertrud touched Kelly's elbow. "That poem was beautiful. Did you write it?"

Martin snorted.

"No," said Kelly. "It's by Mark Twain."

"Oh." Gertrud looked confused. "Wait, I thought *Mark Twain* was a book."

"Wow," said Martin under his breath, but everybody heard it.

"You're thinking of *Huckleberry Finn* or *Tom Sawyer*, which are *by* Mark Twain," said Kelly.

"Oh yeah," said Gertrud. "I must be tired."

Martin grimaced at Alana, but she didn't return his judgmental smirk. Gertrud looked like she was going to cry.

"Nobody's thinking straight today," said Kelly, kindly. "I think we could all use a drink." She patted Ed on the back. "Including you, sir."

"That's the best news I've heard all day," said Ed.

A thick silence on the drive back in the golf cart, punctuated by only one low-volume exchange. Gertrud said: "Embarrassing." Martin said: "Very." When they got to the house, Gertrud jumped out of the cart and started walking quickly toward the cottages. Martin rolled his eyes but went after her.

Later, when the family reconvened on the terrace for drinks, Martin showed up alone.

"Where's Gertrud?" asked Kelly.

"She had to head home. I'm supposed to relay her regrets and goodbyes."

"Oh, that's too bad," said Kelly.

"I sent her in the jet," Martin said to Ed. "I hope that's OK."

"That's fine," said Ed, who was enjoying his first Manhattan in a very long time and seemed quite tranquil.

"Maybe if you hadn't shamed her," said Kelly under her breath.

"Seriously?" said Martin. He laughed but looked profoundly pissed off. Alana could sense the angry explosions going off in his head as he stifled a response and turned a deep shade of crimson.

"Do me a favor," said Ed. "Text Darla and tell her to get that deer on the golf course."

"Yup," said Martin, pulling out his phone, his mouth pinched tight.

"I asked her to deal with this. How hard is it to shoot a few deer?"

Martin wasn't listening. He sent the message and slid his phone back in his pocket. Then he looked squarely at Kelly. "Let me ask you something, *Aisling*," he said.

Oh shit, thought Alana, tensing.

"That's your real name, right? *Aisling Hayes*."

Ed looked at Kelly, whose expression had morphed from snide and confrontational to full-on terrified.

"Your name's not Kelly McNutt, right? It's Aisling Hayes."

"How do you know that?" said Kelly, breathing hard.

Martin shrugged. "A little birdie told me. Dad, you knew that, right? That she's been using an alias the whole time she's known you. I wonder why."

"What the hell is he talking about?" Ed asked Kelly.

"I have no idea why you've been snooping around in my past, Martin," said Kelly. "But I seriously hope you haven't just endangered me or your father."

Martin blinked.

"What the hell is going on?" said Ed.

Kelly took Ed's hand and held it on her lap. "I didn't want to get into this, but remember I told you about that relationship I was in?"

"The bad one?"

"Yeah," said Kelly. "But I never told you how bad it really was." Tears were forming in her eyes now. She swallowed hard. "He wasn't just a jerk...he was weird and violent. Very violent. He especially liked to choke me until I passed out. That was his thing, if you know what I mean."

"Jesus," said Alana.

"He cracked my ribs twice. But usually he was smarter about it—he'd hit me on the head so the hair would cover the wounds."

"I hope you're kidding me," said Ed.

"No," said Kelly, tears spilling down her cheeks. "Of course, he'd apologize, swear up and down he was never going to do it again..." Kelly laughed bitterly. "Obviously, I tried to leave. Many times. But he would stalk me. No matter where I went, he would find me. I mean, I'm a nurse. It's not hard to ask around at the local hospitals. That's why I took a private nursing job. And why I don't do social media."

"What's his name?" said Ed, glowering.

"No," said Kelly. "I want to leave all that behind. I just want my new life with my new name. He would never think to look for me here. Unless Martin messed things up by digging around."

"What the hell have you done?" said Ed to Martin.

"I'm sorry, I was just— I just wanted to make sure everything was on the up-and-up. I was trying to protect you," said Martin.

"From what? From the sweetest woman on God's green earth? How is it your business anyway?"

"Because he thinks there's no way I could actually care about you. He thinks I'm some kind of gold digger. He's always thought it and that's how he treats me!" cried Kelly, jumping up and storming out.

"You're a stupid ass, you know that!" said Ed, struggling to his feet.

"Well, I'm sorry if we happen to have your best interests at heart," said Martin.

"*We?*" said Ed, swiveling to glare at Alana. "Were you part of this little investigation?"

"I was not," said Alana.

"Was she?" Ed asked Martin.

"No," Martin admitted.

"I want you to listen to me and listen good," said Ed. "You don't know anything about my interests, best or otherwise. And you know why? Because you're a fucking numbskull!" As he left the room, he snarled, "You'd better hope you didn't bring any trouble that girl's way."

Martin, looking scared and chastened, glanced at Alana.

"Whoops," she said.

"Yeah, more than fucking whoops," said Martin. "Thanks for backing me up, by the way."

"Hey, I told you not to hire a detective, and I told you not to say anything to Dad about it. Why should I take the heat?"

Martin sighed. "You think all that shit about her ex is true?"

"If it isn't, give the woman an Academy Award," said Alana.

"Yeah. Even I believed her," said Martin. "Buddy sounds like a piece of work."

"She sure knows how to pick 'em," said Alana.

Martin cradled his head in his hands and groaned. "Fuck. That's it. Dad is never going to forgive me."

"I wouldn't worry about it," said Alana. She sat down beside her brother, patted him on the back, and whispered, "It's maybe not a bad thing that he's so upset. Get that heart rate and blood pressure up."

Martin lifted his head and stared at his sister, who was waggling her eyebrows and very nearly grinning.

★ ★ ★

Kelly strode across the lawn toward the back garden and slipped into the rose bower. From the outside, this was a circle of tall, sharply trimmed hedges, but inside the enclosure were dozens of meandering rosebushes and, at the very center, a pretty wrought iron bench. It was one of her favorite places at the summerhouse, usually for reading, but today for consoling and composing herself.

Darla, who happened to be weeding on the other side of the hedge, heard someone crying and went around to the bower's entrance to see who was there.

"Oh," said Darla. It was Miss McNutt, looking like a sweet dryad surrounded by flowers. "Sorry to disturb. Are you OK?"

"Yeah. Sorry," said Kelly, drying her eyes and forcing a smile. "I'm fine. Just needed a good cry." She sighed.

"Is there anything I can do?" said Darla, moved by the tiny creature.

Kelly considered the question carefully. "Not unless you can convince Martin that I have love in my heart and I'm not some evil gold digger."

"Oh," said Darla, her expression darkening. "Well, not that it helps, but I think you're one of the most down-to-earth folks I've ever met, and one of the kindest, which is more than I can say about everyone around here."

"That does help," said Kelly, laughing and getting up. "Thank you, Darla." She moved to the woman and hugged her warmly. "You're a peach."

Darla's heart fluttered a little in the embrace. Kelly's hair smelled like fresh green apples.

"I probably shouldn't say this," said Kelly, stepping back. "But that man scares me sometimes."

"Oh, I don't think you have to worry about Martin. He may not always be the nicest dude, but I don't think there's any harm in him."

"I'm not so sure." She stared up at Darla with wide blue eyes. "But I hope you're right." Kelly mustered a smile. "I should get back. I have to give Ed his pill and get some healthy food in him. You're doing a brilliant job on the garden, by the way."

"Thanks," said Darla, watching Kelly move across the lawn. Such a tiny thing. So delicate. So sweet.

When Alana arrived for dinner, she found the table set for one. Mrs. Keith told her that Ed wasn't feeling well, so Kelly had taken a tray up to their room. Martin had opted to make pizza by the pool. Perhaps Alana wanted to join her brother? No, Alana did not. She ate her surprisingly delicious vegan meat loaf alone at the long table while surfing on her phone. When she was done, Mrs. Keith prepared a selection of desserts to take back to her cottage along with a chardonnay traveler.

Alana got into bed with the wine, the treats, and her book and made a night of it. She went to sleep at ten thirty with the intention of getting up early to meet Kelly for yoga on the beach.

Martin, still stinging from his rebuke from Ed, also spent the night alone in his cottage. He was agitated and had no one to talk to. Gertrud wasn't returning his texts, and he was peeved at Alana for not backing him up with Ed. He knew that to make it right with his father, he would have to apologize to Kelly, and the thought of ingratiating himself made him sick. He wondered how long it would take for the quercetin to work its magic. Probably not fast enough. He was going to have to suck it up and apologize.

A knock on the door pulled Martin out of his reverie. He assumed it would be Alana, but when he opened up, he found Kelly on the front porch.

"Hey there, can I come in for a sec?"

"I don't think so," said Martin. She had killed his brother. Had she come to do the same to him?

"Fine. Whatever. We can talk here," she said in a low voice.

"What can I do for you?"

"Well, for starters, you can fuck off out of here in the morning," said Kelly. She smiled.

"Excuse me?"

"Then you can resign your position in the company and go start a new life somewhere far away from me and Ed. I'm thinking East Coast. Maybe New York or Boston."

Martin laughed, but his anger was rising. "You're pretty funny, you know that."

"I don't know about funny, but I am pretty benevolent, which is why I'm prepared to offer you the same deal you offered me. Twenty million dollars. A million when you quit your job and tell Ed to rot in hell, and the balance once you've stayed away for three months."

"And why in God's name would I do that?"

Kelly smirked. "I hope you're enjoying that watch," she said.

"What? What watch?" said Martin.

"You know, the Montblanc, the one with the snake coiled around the dial."

"That's Ed's."

"Yes, I know," said Kelly. "At least it was. Until someone stole it from his closet."

Martin scoffed. "Seriously? You think I'd steal a watch from my father? Are you daft? I could buy ten of those tomorrow if I felt like it."

"No, I'm not *daft*," said Kelly. "And maybe you didn't pinch it. It's really beside the point."

"So, what is the point?" said Martin.

"Well, after it went missing, I wondered if whoever took it might try it again, since we never mentioned it to anyone. So, I set up a few nanny cams in the bedroom."

Martin felt a wave of heat flood over his face.

"And when I bumped into you coming down the stairs last night, looking all skulky and nervous, I decided to have a look at the recording."

"And?" said Martin, struggling to stay composed.

"And…no watches were harmed in the video. But I *did* see you scurry away with Ed's Pradaxa and then return it later. Odd," said Kelly. "I wonder what would happen if I gave the video and the medicine to the cops. What might they find in those capsules?"

Martin didn't respond. He resisted an impulse to grab her by the throat and bash her head against the doorframe. Did anyone know she had come here to talk to him?

"I assume Alana was helping you," said Kelly. "I noticed she magically recovered from her headache a few minutes before you went upstairs to replace the medicine."

Martin said nothing.

"Well, I hope she was involved. It would be great to kill two birds with one stone. Alas, I can only prove that *you're* guilty. So, I guess we'll have to let the cops sort it out. Unless of course you choose to bugger off, in which case no one will ever know and it's all moot."

Martin couldn't think straight.

"What's the matter?" she taunted. "Cat got your tongue? It's not exactly Sophie's choice—Ed's wrath and a possible prison sentence or twenty million and a shiny new life."

Martin finally managed to croak out a response. "All right."

"Great," said Kelly. "I figured you'd like the offer since you basically dreamed it up."

"Did you murder my brother?" he said.

"Wow. What a question."

"I know you did, so why not just give me closure before I leave?"

"Of course I didn't. But if I *were* going to kill someone, I wouldn't do it on video like some kind of dum-dum. Some *daft* dum-dum." She smiled. "All right, off to bed. See you in the morning—well, actually I won't. Yay."

No, you won't see me, thought Martin, watching her flit down the path through the woods. *But I'll see you.*

Martin awoke at five. He downed a coffee, then dressed and made his way to the groundskeeper's quarters. Behind the modest clapboard residences was an enormous greenhouse and a long brick garage that contained riding mowers, spare lumber, and other gardening and maintenance equipment. Martin ducked into the side door of the garage and fished his key to the firearms cabinet out from under the first layer of tools in the red metal toolbox. He unlocked the case and selected the AR-15 with the Steiner scope. He loaded the magazine with fresh rounds and seated it on the rifle.

He knew what he was about to do was dangerous, but the timing was excellent. Only yesterday, Ed had been griping about deer on the golf course. Martin was just trying to help out with the cull. Sure, there would be repercussions; he would be interrogated by police and probably face some kind of reckless manslaughter charge, but given his standing in the community, and a cadre of top-notch lawyers, that charge would likely be dropped—he certainly wouldn't serve any time. Who could prove it wasn't an accident?

Ed would be furious, of course. But at the end of the day, blood is thicker than water. How could he not forgive his only remaining son, who was full of remorse and willing to do anything to make it up to him? It would take time, sure, but Ed would come around. And even if he didn't, it would still be worth it to rid the earth of that red menace and the overhanging threat of exposure. As long as she had power over him, he would never be free. She would show that video to Ed at some point, if only to get him cut out of the will. And he suspected that even if she transferred the first million to his account, she would undoubtedly renege on the balance. She wasn't exactly trustworthy. And there was no reason for her to actually pay up. She held all the cards. It would be her final fuck-you. He could envision her cackling about it, savoring it.

A million bucks then. For a lifetime of service. What a joke. Even if he were extremely careful, he would burn through that in a few years. He couldn't live on it. And Gertrud would be long gone. Maybe if Kelly had been more generous, he could've spared her—maybe if she hadn't killed Teddy. But that smug, conniving bitch deserved to die.

Martin exited the garage and pulled the door firmly shut behind him. It was time to go hunting.

Kelly, an early riser, was invariably up before Mrs. Keith. Luckily, the housekeeper had taught her how to use the fancy espresso machine, so she was good to go. She downed two perfect shots and then headed to the beach to do yoga. It was a fresh and temperate morning and she was feeling spry. Things hadn't gone at all like she had planned, but they were working out beautifully nonetheless. Soon Martin would be out of her hair, and all for the low, low price of twenty million dollars. She laughed, thinking about how that had come to feel like a trifling sum.

Kelly breathed in the sweet morning air and exhaled slowly. It had been a fraught six months. She wasn't used to this level of tension and was frankly exhausted by all the plotting and machinations, all the calculating and recalculating. When this was over, she was going to take a long vacation. Somewhere tropical and relaxing. No thinking. Just chilling for at least a couple weeks. Kelly placed her thermos and phone on a log near the tree line. She moved closer to the water, turned her face to the rising sun, and took a slow, deep breath.

Only a couple more hurdles and it would all be over.

Alana woke up a few minutes before her alarm was set to go off. She took a piss and brushed her teeth. Then she put on her sweats and brewed a Keurig. The last time she'd stayed in the cottage, there'd been a stainless-steel thermos in the kitchen, but she couldn't find it, so she decided to have her coffee in the living room. She would be a bit late for yoga, but it didn't matter. Alana was scrolling the MDA camp's Facebook page for pictures of Lily when the calm of the morning was ripped apart.

She heard a woman scream *"No!"* followed by two gun-shot blasts and the most hideous wail of pain.

26

Alana's hands were shaking so hard, she had trouble pulling her shoes on. She heard Martin screaming *Oh my god oh my god* and what sounded like Darla shouting *Call 911! Hurry!*

She jumped down the porch steps and ran to the back of the cottage, where the cries were coming from. In the distance, through the foliage, she saw Darla take off her shirt and kneel over someone Alana couldn't see. Through the trees now, a flash of color—Kelly running toward the scene from the beach.

"They're on their way," Kelly shouted to Darla. "*My god!* What happened?"

As Alana got closer, she saw Martin stretched out on the ground, his upper body slick with blood. Darla was holding her balled-up flannel shirt to his neck, trying to stop the blood that was pulsing out in spurts.

Alana grew dizzy and her vision began to blur into shimmery pins and needles.

"Keep the pressure on," said Kelly, sinking to her knees.

"He shot at you," said Darla. "He aimed and shot!"

A long squirt of blood as Darla moved aside for Kelly to take her place. That was the last thing Alana saw before she slumped to the ground. When she came to, Darla was kneeling beside her. "Are you OK?"

"I think I blacked out," said Alana.

"Sit up slowly and hang your head between your knees," shouted Kelly, who was pressing the shirt against Martin's neck.

Alana felt like she was going to puke. She kept her head down and took deep breaths.

"Will they come by air or boat?" said Kelly.

"I don't know," said Darla. She looked dazed. "Should I go to the dock to meet them?"

"No, I think you're in shock. Here's what you do—call your staff or the golf course staff and tell them we need at least two carts waiting at both the dock *and* the airstrip. Tell them we're in the woods behind cottage 4."

"OK," said Darla, grateful for direction.

Alana didn't dare look up. She listened to Darla make the calls and heard Kelly murmuring words of comfort and encouragement to Martin.

They waited.

"Oh god, what's taking so long?" said Darla, pacing back and forth. "Where are they already!"

Alana lifted her head and risked a look. Martin wasn't

moving. The flannel shirt and Kelly's hands were completely soaked in blood.

"What did I do?" Darla wailed, hitting her own forehead repeatedly with a clenched fist. "What the hell did I do?"

"You saved my life," said Kelly. "That's what you did!"

27

What seemed like an hour but was, in fact, only seventeen minutes later, police and EMTs arrived on the scene. Two officers moved in first to secure the firearms and make sure there was no imminent danger. Then the medics got to work on Martin, radioing for an air ambulance when they saw his condition. They transported him via stretcher to the beach, where the helicopter would have enough space to land.

Corporal Forgie and Constable Hammell gathered initial statements to determine what had transpired, then, calmly and over the protestations of Kelly and Alana, read Darla her rights and arrested her for attempted murder. When Darla again explained that she was only trying to protect Kelly, and had been aiming at Martin's rifle, not Martin, Corporal Forgie—a big man with a shaved head—reminded her that anything she said could be used in court.

"I told you I don't need a lawyer," said Darla. "He shot at her. He was going to shoot again! I had to do something!"

"She saved my life," said Kelly.

"I understand," said Corporal Forgie. "But this is the way we have to proceed." He called the Major Crimes Unit for assistance. Then Constable Hammell, a tall woman with small watchful eyes, stayed with Darla, Kelly, and Alana while Corporal Forgie went up to the house to speak with Ed.

As he made his way across the vast expanse of lawn, Corporal Forgie received a text informing him that Martin had died en route to hospital. This was now a murder investigation. And he had the unhappy task of delivering the worst news any parent could receive.

It was midmorning when the Major Crimes team arrived on the island. Several officers taped off the scene and began taking photographs, measuring trajectories and collecting physical evidence, while the primary investigator, Sergeant Maxwell, reviewed the information that had been gathered thus far.

Corporal Forgie and Constable Hammell took Darla back to the detachment in Sidney, where she declined to contact a lawyer and insisted on proceeding with her videotaped statement.

"I got up at five thirty to go hunting. Mr. Shropshire does not like fallow deer on his island," she said. "He spotted one on the golf course yesterday, and I got a text from Martin asking me to take care of it."

"OK," said Corporal Forgie.

"I can show you the text, if you like," said Darla.

"Sure." Corporal Forgie handed Darla her phone. She typed in the passcode and found Martin's text from the previous afternoon: Deer on the golf course. Mr. Shropshire not happy. Please do your job.

"Kind of nasty," said Constable Hammell.

"Not really," said Darla. "That's just his way."

"So, you got up early to go deer hunting on the golf course," said Corporal Forgie.

"Yup. But when I unlocked the gun cabinet, I saw one of the AR-15s was missing."

"Are you aware that's a restricted firearm?"

"I know. I never use them. But Martin likes them, and it's not my place to get rid of them. All the firearms were bought legal. We have all the paperwork. The ARs were bought in 2018, I think."

"OK. So, Martin's a hunter?"

"No. He shoots now and again—maybe two or three times a summer—but it's always target practice. He doesn't hunt, although he did go out once not too long ago. Bagged a deer."

"So, until recently, he never hunted?"

"Right. At least, not while I've been on the island. Which is why I had a funny feeling about that gun being out so early. Especially since Miss McNutt was saying yesterday that Martin scares her. And she does yoga on the beach every morning."

"Miss McNutt told you yesterday that Martin scares her?" said Constable Hammell.

"Yeah. I found her crying in the garden. I think Martin

upset her. She said he thinks she's a gold digger and that he scares her sometimes."

The officers exchanged a glance.

"Miss McNutt is Martin's wife or girlfriend?" said Corporal Forgie.

"Neither," said Darla, surprised by the very idea. "She's his father's fiancée."

"Edward Shropshire's fiancée?" said Corporal Forgie, his eyebrows raised.

"Yep. There's an age gap for sure."

"OK."

"But she isn't a gold digger. She's salt of the earth. And anyone can see she cares for Mr. Shropshire. She was his nurse to begin with."

"I see."

"So, anyway, I just had a weird feeling about the AR being gone, so I figured I'd go check on her. And thank goodness I did, 'cause when I got out that way, I spotted Martin. He was facing the beach, taking aim. I tried to be quiet as I got closer, 'cause I didn't want to scare off a deer."

"OK."

"But when I came up the little ridge, I saw he was aiming right at Miss McNutt."

"How could you tell he was aiming at her and not a deer?"

"'Cause I have eyes!" said Darla. "Here was Martin." She pointed to a spot on her upturned palm. "And right here, straight ahead, was Miss McNutt on the beach. Clear as day he was gunning for her. I was here," she said, marking the third point of a triangle. "I could see there weren't any deer between the two. And you couldn't miss her in that orange-and-blue leotard. So, I yelled *No!* But he shot! And took aim again! So, I fired at his rifle. I wasn't trying to shoot him."

"Then what happened?"

"When he dropped, I yelled at Miss McNutt to call 911. And then I went and tried to stop the bleeding. I used my shirt. Then she took over until you all got there. She's a nurse."

"And what's your relationship with Miss McNutt?"

"She's my boss's fiancée, so I guess she's kind of my boss."

"Do you have a lot of dealings with her?"

"Not really. I mean, she had us change to nontoxic pesticides and fungicides, so we talked about that a fair bit a few months ago."

"You like her?"

"Yeah. She's super nice. Down-to-earth."

"And what's your relationship with Martin like?"

"Well, he's kind of my boss too, since he's Mr. Shropshire's son."

"You like him?"

Darla shrugged. "He's all right. At least I thought he was, until this morning. He's not an overly friendly type—he's pretty much all business—but I didn't think there was any harm in him."

"Ever have any altercations or disagreements with him?"

"Nope. Never."

"Ever hear him talk about Miss McNutt?" asked Constable Hammell.

"No."

"OK. Thanks, Darla," said Corporal Forgie. "I think that's all for the time being."

"So now what happens?"

"You'll have a bail hearing this afternoon. I expect you'll be released until all the evidence is gathered and the Crown decides whether or not to bring charges."

"I wasn't trying to hurt him," said Darla. "I was just trying to stop him."

"OK," said Corporal Forgie.

Sergeant Maxwell interviewed Kelly at the house. Normally, she would have been brought to the detachment, but Ed had requested that she be allowed to stay put, and for compassionate reasons, Sergeant Maxwell agreed to it. The poor man had lost two sons in the space of a few weeks. All the money in the world couldn't make up for that.

"Ready?" asked Sergeant Maxwell.

"Yes," said Kelly, settling herself on the living room sofa.

"Please tell me what happened this morning."

"I went to the beach around six to do yoga, like I always do. I guess I was about ten minutes into it when I heard Darla yell 'No!' And then two gunshots. Then Darla was screaming at me to call 911, which I did. You know, I told all this to the other officers."

"I know. And what was your relationship like with Martin Shropshire?"

Kelly sighed. "Not good," she said. "I mean, it was fine when I was his father's nurse. But when Ed and I got together, that was it. He hated me."

"You told Darla yesterday that Martin scared you sometimes. Is that correct?"

"Yes," said Kelly. "And it's true."

"Why would you divulge something so personal to a member of the staff?"

"Well, I shouldn't have—but she caught me at a vulnerable moment. I was in the rose bower having a cry. It's a secluded spot, but I guess Darla was out there doing something and heard me. She asked if I was OK and I guess I overshared because I was upset. I'd literally just found out that Martin hired a private detective to dig up dirt on me."

"I see."

"Of course, there was nothing to dig up, but I knew what it meant."

"What did it mean?"

"That Martin didn't trust me. That he thought I must be some black widow with a dark past." Kelly laughed bitterly. "The fact is, Martin has hated me from the moment his father and I got together. He thought I was after Ed's money."

"Why would he think that?"

"Because I'm a lot younger than Ed. And because he has no idea how a human heart really works."

"Had Martin ever threatened you?"

"Threatened? Hmm…not exactly. But he wanted me gone. He tried to bribe me to disappear. I guess when that didn't work, he decided to kill me."

"When did he try to bribe you?"

"Not that long ago. I can give you the date because he wired a million dollars into my bank account, and told me that if I stayed away without any contact, he would give me more. I have proof of that, if you want it."

"So, you refused to go and returned the money?"

"No," said Kelly. "I was offended. So I donated his money to charity. I have proof of that too. Ed's daughter works at a shelter in Toronto. So I donated it to that shelter. He was pissed off, of course. Not only did he not get rid of me, it cost him a million bucks."

"So you think Martin was angry about that. What did he say?"

"Nothing. He didn't want Ed to find out that he'd tried to get rid of me, so he said nothing. But I could feel his rage in every look and snide comment."

"Did you tell Mr. Shropshire about it?"

"No."

"Why not?"

"Because it would hurt him to know that his son is a manipulative person who's more interested in his money than his well-being."

"And how did you come to be dating Mr. Shropshire?"

"I'm a nurse. I was hired by the family to care for Ed after he had a stroke." Kelly paused to reflect. "At first, I just saw him as a patient, although I always thought he was handsome. Even at his age, he's an extremely good-looking man. I'm sure you've seen pictures."

Sergeant Maxwell didn't respond; he waited for her to continue.

"Anyway, things developed. The relationship between nurse and patient is very…intimate," she said. "Not just physically but emotionally. I feel, and so does Ed, that I was a big part of his recovery. I put him on a plant-based diet, which has improved his cholesterol and blood pressure—before me he was eating meat every day, sometimes at every meal. He feels good now. Even his complexion has improved." Kelly could see the sergeant's focus start to drift. "Anyway, as he got better, we discovered that there was a mutual attraction. Well, more than that…we'd fallen in love. But Martin couldn't understand that. He just wanted me gone."

"So, you think Martin was trying to shoot you this morning?"

"I'm sure of it. And thank goodness I have a witness. Darla saved my life, which I still can't quite wrap my head around. I could have died this morning," said Kelly with a shudder. "I guess he was going to kill me and pretend it was some kind of hunting accident."

Sergeant Maxwell didn't respond.

"The sad truth is that Martin didn't care about his father's happiness. He didn't care if his father would be lonely without me. All he cared about was making sure he inherited every cent of Ed's money. But here's the ironic part: I told him flat out that I didn't give a hoot about Ed's money. He could have it. I made no claim to it. I've honestly never cared about money in my life. As long as I have my health and a roof over my head, I'm happy as a clam. But Martin couldn't believe that. He couldn't conceive of anyone not being as greedy as he was." Kelly paused as tears welled in her eyes. "I tried," she said. "I tried really hard to show him that I'm a good person with a good heart, but he just— He just wouldn't let me in."

Sergeant Maxwell pushed a Kleenex box across the table.

"Thanks," said Kelly, drying the tears that were rolling down her cheeks. She blew her nose, took a moment to collect herself, and then gazed sincerely at the sergeant. "I'm very sorry that Martin died, especially for Ed's sake—but I'm not sorry it worked out the way it did. If he had killed me this morning, how long do you think it would be before he set his sights on his father? I'm pretty sure Darla saved two lives this morning."

★ ★ ★

Sergeant Maxwell steeled himself for the next interview.

"I'm very sorry for your loss," he said. "Especially given... recent events with your family. If you'd prefer to do this later—"

"Let's wrap it up," said Ed. "I'm not feeling well."

"Yes, of course. Just a few questions. I understand you have a problem with fallow deer on your property. Was Martin in the habit of hunting them?"

"No. That's Darla's responsibility. And her crew."

"And what was the relationship like between Martin and Darla?"

"There wasn't one. She's an employee."

"Would you say the same about Kelly and Darla?"

"Yes. But Kelly's friendly. She takes the time to chat with the staff. They all like her. Everyone likes her."

"Did Martin like her?"

Ed paused. "I don't believe he did, no."

"And why is that?"

"He mistrusted her motives. Frankly, he stuck his nose where he had no business sticking it."

"He hired a detective to check up on her."

"And found nothing. Kelly's a good girl. I love my son, but he was very misguided when it came to Kelly," said Ed. He cleared his throat hard. "And for the record, she offered to sign a prenup. She told me to leave everything to my children."

"Did Martin know that?"

"Yes. But he also knew I would never agree to it."

"So, he didn't want you two to marry?"

"I assume so."

"And do you think Martin was deliberately trying to shoot Kelly?"

Ed mulled it over for a good ten seconds. "I'd like to think not. But I wouldn't put it past him."

Sergeant Maxwell nodded. "Just one more question. How long have you and Miss McNutt been engaged?"

"We're not engaged," said Ed. "We were married a couple weeks ago in Parrot Cay."

Alana was the last to be interrogated. She should have been nervous, but she felt strangely composed. Maybe it was because Martin was gone and couldn't contradict her. Maybe it was because she was being questioned in the living room, where she had a direct view of a large framed photo of her and her siblings as children. It was a picture taken down at the swimming pool. Teddy and Martin, all sun-kissed and skinny, in matching Speedos, flexing their muscles. Chunky Alana, in a frilly one-piece, smiling shyly at someone off to the side, probably Kat. Lillian, who couldn't have been more than six or seven, in a bikini, one arm stretched across her chest, holding the other arm, which hung over her crotch, shielding herself. She was obviously uncomfortable, scowling at the camera (at Ed behind the camera).

Alana focused on her sister's troubled expression, then looked at Martin and Teddy beaming smugly at the lens. She could see them so clearly, standing guard outside cottage 4, chasing her away or literally carrying her off when she tried to get to her sister, when she heard Lillian's cries of distress. The photo made her steady and resolute.

"So, you heard Darla yell 'No' followed by two gunshots?"

"Yeah, and when I got outside, I saw Kelly running from the beach to where Darla was with Martin."

"Do you think your brother was trying to shoot Kelly?" asked Sergeant Maxwell.

"I hate to say it, but yes, I think he was."

"Why do you think that?"

"Because there was no way he could have mistaken her for a deer from that angle. But also, because he didn't trust her and didn't want her to have any claim on my father's money."

"How do you know that?"

"He started emailing me about it as soon as my father started seeing her."

"You still have those emails?"

"Yeah. I mean, I didn't delete them. I assume they're still there."

"What did he say in the emails?"

"He always called her 'the skank.' Said we had to close ranks to protect my father. He wanted to get rid of her."

"Did he ever talk about harming Kelly?"

"Um…not in a serious way. But he joked about it."

"What kind of jokes?"

"He joked about cutting the brake line on her car—my father bought her some stupidly expensive sports car, which pissed him off. When we were having dinner on the yacht, he joked about tossing her over the side." Alana paused, then seemed to remember something. "Oh shit," she said, putting her hand to her mouth. "I think he did joke about putting a bullet in her head. But he said it so flippantly, you know. Just like people casually say things about people they hate. Obviously, if I thought he was serious, I would have told somebody."

"And what's your relationship like with Kelly?"

"I mean, I don't really know her—I live in Toronto—but she's been friendly with me. Do I think it's weird that she's with my father? Yes. But he obviously adores her. And it looks like she's taking good care of him. Is she doing it for the money? Who knows. It makes zero difference to me."

"Your brother was unhappy about the marriage but you're fine with it?"

"Honestly, I couldn't care less. My father and I have never been close. I'm only here for my brother's funeral. He could marry an orangutan for all I care."

"Thank you for saying orangu*tan*. I hate it when people call them *orangutangs*," said Sergeant Maxwell.

Alana blinked. "I hate when people say based *off* instead of based *on*."

"Agreed," said the sergeant.

"So…are you going to need me for anything else? I'm supposed to fly to Chicago tomorrow, but I could postpone by a day if necessary."

"No, that's fine. I'd like to get those emails, but you're free to go."

Alana stood. "Please tell me Darla's not going to be charged with anything."

"That's up to the Crown. But assuming the physical evidence aligns with the evidence I've gathered, I can't see them bringing charges."

"That's good," said Alana.

"Just one more question," said Sergeant Maxwell. "Both your brothers recently died in accidents. As the last remaining child of Edward Shropshire, are you at all concerned about your safety?"

Alana was taken aback. "No. I don't see why I would be. But I haven't really thought about it."

As Alana made her way back to her cottage, she started to think about it.

28

Alana spent the remainder of the day on her own. Kelly and Ed were lying low and keeping to themselves while the Major Crimes Unit did their work in the woods. It was unusually hot and Alana was longing for a swim, but she didn't want to appear frivolous or callous lounging by the pool on the same day her brother was shot dead. She mostly stayed in her cottage with Sergeant Maxwell's question playing in her mind. Did she have reason to fear Kelly McNutt? She didn't think so. On the other hand, she hadn't thought Teddy and Martin were in any danger. Was Alana a loose end that needed to be tied up? If not now, then eventually? No, she told herself, don't be absurd.

She had dinner alone on the patio—an Instagram-worthy salad crowned with Marcona almonds and a generous sprinkling of spicy edible flowers—then went to her cottage to pack up. She couldn't wait to get back to Lily but kind of wished she could take the food and Mrs. Keith home with her.

By ten o'clock, the police had left the island, and it was dark and quiet enough for her to sneak in a swim before bed. She turned on the sauna before shedding her cover-up and slipping into the pool. God, it was nice. Better than nice. The water was the perfect temperature and glowed deep purple at night with the lights. There was nothing quite like the feeling of having a private pool all to yourself. It was the thing she missed most when she left her family's wealth behind all those years ago. Now, she and Lily swam at the community pool, which was always crowded, too warm, and probably full of piss, and if there wasn't a brat cannon-balling onto your head or screaming in your ear, there were annoying seniors plowing into you as they selfishly tried to do laps, or people with horrifying open sores, or babies with gross, soggy diapers.

Alana wanted Lily to experience this other kind of swim-ming. Lily was magic in water. She could move freely and without pain. Alana imagined presenting Lily with a pool of her own and the vision brought tears to her eyes.

When she grew chilly, Alana ducked into the sauna. She spread out her towel, lay flat on her back, and took a deep breath. The hot air burned her nostrils, but the smell of the cedar was wonderful, a balm. She'd had a couple glasses of wine earlier in the evening and now felt pleasantly drowsy. She closed her eyes and was just about to drift off when she heard the heavy door open with a dull sucking sound. It was Kelly.

"Woo, that's hot," she said, pulling the door shut behind her.

"Hey," said Alana, sitting up.

"I saw you out here swimming."

"Oh."

"Are you almost done? There's something I want to show you."

"What is it?"

"Come, I'll show you. You don't have to get dressed." Alana hesitated.

"Come on, it's fine," said Kelly. "I promise."

Alana wrapped a towel around herself and followed Kelly out of the sauna.

"This way..." She left the pool enclosure and moved along an unlit flagstone path.

"Where are we going?" said Alana, fully alert now.

"Just over there." She pointed to a distant spot in the garden. "But I want to avoid Mrs. Keith's cottage. Don't want to wake her," explained Kelly.

They went the long way around, through a stand of trees, and stopped in front of a large scalloped flower bed. Kelly spoke in a low voice. "You see those flowers?" She pointed to a cluster of tall green stalks covered in dozens of tubular bell-shaped blossoms.

"Yeah."

"That's foxglove," said Kelly. "Very pretty. Also, very poisonous."

A blast of fear set Alana's heart spasming. Had she been poisoned? Had Kelly added those flowers to her salad?

"The whole plant is toxic," said Kelly. "But the leaves can easily kill someone, especially if they've been dried."

"What are you saying?" Alana felt dizzy, couldn't quite focus or breathe.

"I'm saying that it's much more effective than whatever you and Martin put in Ed's Pradaxa. So...I figured, since I have video of Martin fiddling with Ed's prescription, there's really no reason not to speed up the process." She smiled. "Everyone will assume Ed died of a heart attack—he's been under so much stress, poor thing—but even if they end up doing an autopsy, we have Martin to blame."

"Oh..." said Alana, starting to process the information. She recalled now that the flowers on her salad had been yellow and orange and looked nothing like the pink foxglove blossoms. "That's amazingly diabolical," said Alana. "Speaking of which, what happened to Teddy?"

"Didn't I tell you the last time we were in the sauna?"

"You were about to, but Gertrud came in."

"Oh yeah. Well, I obviously wasn't planning that, but when we were on the boat, he did something that was very triggering for me. I got pissed off and pushed him in the water. I guess I could have fished him out, but I suddenly realized I had the perfect chance to get rid of him. And since he was my route to Ed and knew a little too much, I figured it wasn't a horrible idea."

"Well, I was your initial route to Ed," said Alana. "Are you going to get rid of me too?"

"You're joking, I hope," said Kelly, looking wounded. "You know I would never do anything to hurt you. You know that, right?"

"Yeah."

She grabbed Alana's hand and squeezed it. "I would *never* hurt you. You saved me from a monster, and I'll be grateful to you forever."

"I didn't save you—I just did my job," said Alana.

"No, you went way beyond. You gave me cash for a hotel when the shelter was too full to take me. You helped me change my name. You got me into affordable housing when I was looking for work. You were my friend. You gave me my life back."

"I think you've more than evened the score," said Alana. "You've invested almost a year of your life in this little escapade. And almost got yourself killed in the process."

Kelly shrugged. "A lot of it's been fun. Getting shot at, not so much."

"I can imagine."

"Are you pissed about Teddy?"

"No. I was just worried because it postponed the wedding, which was dangerous. Ed's not exactly the healthiest person in the world."

"Yeah. But I knew I could convince him to do it with just the two of us. That's why I suggested we go to Parrot Cay. We'd talked about getting married there before we decided on the *Andiamo*. I sent you that picture of Ed to let you know. I figured the white suit and champagne would be a tip-off."

"I think it was the baby's breath and white rose on his lapel that clued me in."

"God, we have so much to catch up on," said Kelly.

"I know. I have so much to tell you. But we have to stay incommunicado for a bit longer. I think there are only two texts between us, right? And they're both completely innocuous."

"Yeah," said Kelly.

"We're so close," said Alana.

"Closer than you think," said Kelly.

★ ★ ★

Ed, totally ashen and slick with sweat, lay tangled in the bedsheets, breathing fast and shallow. The room was dark, illuminated only by the glow of a night-light spilling from the en suite bathroom. "I gave him the capsule with dinner," whispered Kelly. "He'll be gone before morning."

"The police will be back in the morning," said Alana, alarmed.

"I know. It's perfect. Who in their right mind would kill someone with all those cops around?"

"Um, the most brazen person in the world…maybe."

"Well, you're leaving tomorrow," said Kelly. "I wanted you to see this." She went to the bedside and joggled Ed's shoulder.

He groaned. "I don't feel well."

"I know," said Kelly.

"My stomach is killing me."

"Yes, that's right."

"What?" said Ed. He opened his eyes and squinted at Alana, who was standing at the end of the bed. "What's she doing here?"

"She's here to watch you die," said Kelly.

Ed tried to sit up, but a stab of pain forced him back down. "She knows what you did to her sister, Ed. And I know too."

Ed moaned. "What are you talking about?"

"Oh, I think you know, *Daddy*. You like it when I call you that, don't you? And when I wear her clothes."

"Jesus Christ," said Alana, shuddering.

"I don't know what you're talking about."

"Really? I'm talking about me in the baby doll pajamas, pretending to be asleep, and then you come in… You always liked it more when I cried, didn't you, Daddy? Why is that, do you think?"

He gawped at Kelly and gasped for breath.

"Well, guess what? Martin was right. I don't love you. In fact, I'm sick to death of you. You're a monster. And you turned your sons into monsters. Did you know Teddy was fucking me? And that Martin wanted you dead?" She turned to Alana. "Should I show him the video of Martin messing with his prescription?"

Ed struggled to get up, but Kelly held him in place until he tired and slumped back onto the pillow. He grabbed his shoulder and cried out in pain.

"Uh-oh," said Kelly to Alana. "If you have something to say, you'd better say it soon."

Alana moved closer to her dying father. "I was the one who sent Kelly your way. And it was me who found the videos in your safe. I know all about you. I've always known. And when you're dead, I'm going to make sure everyone else knows too."

"Tell him what we're going to do with Alfred Island," said Kelly.

Ed's mouth opened and closed like a fish gulping for oxygen.

"First, we're going to bulldoze the cottage where you and your friends tortured my sister," said Alana. "Then we're going to give your precious island back to its rightful owners."

"Oh, you'd hate that, wouldn't you, Ed?" said Kelly. "You'd always say 'Over my dead body' whenever the lawsuit came up."

"Well, there you go," said Alana. "Prophetic."

Kelly smiled. "You want to tell him what we're going to do with all his money?"

"I do, but I think it might be too late," said Alana.

Ed's eyes were open, but he had gone limp. A trickle of saliva slid down his chin.

Kelly felt for a pulse. "Yup," she said. "Are you OK?"

"I think so," said Alana, sitting on the bed. "I think I am."

"It feels weird to be almost done," said Kelly. She sat next to Alana and sighed. "Do you feel a bit...flat?"

"No," said Alana. "I feel free."

Kelly smiled. "And you're sure you want to give it all away?"

"Almost all of it. No one needs billions. And it'll shut up anyone who tries to say you were with him for his dough."

"True," said Kelly.

"I want to give a ton to the Muscular Dystrophy Association. And obviously any organization that protects kids from abuse."

"Definitely. We're going to have fun spreading it around."

"Speaking of fun, I also want to take Lily to Greece. And anywhere else she wants to go."

"Of course. I can't wait to meet her."

"I want her to see the world while she still can."

"Hey, why don't we run the foundation from the boat for the first six months? We can cruise around Europe. Work, play, travel."

"But Lily has school," said Alana.

"Hire a tutor. Hire ten tutors."

"Not a bad idea."

"And we should hire Darla for something."

"Or just give her money to retire. She saved your life, after all."

"True," said Kelly. "And let's do something nice for Gertrud."

"Good idea. Of course, Darla already has."

Kelly laughed. "That's dark."

"Sorry," said Alana. She stood. "I'd better get going before anyone sees me."

"OK. Love you."

"Love you too."

The women embraced.

"If I don't see you in the morning, safe flight home."

"Thanks."

As Alana was slipping out of the room, she heard Kelly whisper *Wait*. She stopped and poked her head back into the bedroom. "What?"

"I just wanted to say that your sister would be proud of you."

Alana's eyes filled with tears. "Thanks."

"Good night."

"Night." Alana closed the door quietly. She was halfway down the stairs when she heard the bedroom door open and fast footsteps behind her. She turned around.

"Just one more thing," said Kelly from the top of the staircase. She had one hand behind her back.

"What's that?" Alana wiped away the tears that were streaming down her face.

Kelly held up a yellow key chain with a prancing horse on it. "I'm keeping the Ferrari."

"You're damned right," said Alana.

★ ★ ★ ★ ★

ACKNOWLEDGMENTS

Many thanks to Patrick Crean, Jackie Kaiser, Nicole Brebner (and the team at Mira), Jennifer Lambert, Iris Tupholme, Noelle Zitzer, Canaan Chu, Zeena Baybayan, Karen Becker, Sean Kapitain, everyone at HarperCollins Canada, John Sweet, Mary Ann Blair, Bridgette Kam, Gil Adamson, Andrew Adamson, Kevin Connolly, Peter Ormshaw, Marina Endicott, Stuart Ross, Feriel Chebba, Randall Cole, Alan Zunder, Corporal Carrie Harding, Mangesh Inamdar, Natalie Hoban, Carol Kitai, Susan Scinocca, Colin Tobias, Kyle Buckley, Ron Barry, Jill Margo, Ted Dick, Aaron Fogorasi, Jerry Pietrzyk, Greg Rhyno, Mark Rhyno, Michael Sawyer/Infinity Yacht Charters, Barbara Gowdy, David Johnston, Tina Cooper, John Critchley, Lee Hoverd,

Robyn Friedman, Danny Friedman, Otto Friedman, and Max Friedman-Cole.

I am truly grateful for the support of the Toronto Arts Council, the Ontario Arts Council, and the Canada Council for the Arts.